"Is there something about me in particular you distrust, Susannah, or are you just paranoid?"

Paranoid? How many judgments did Alex Blake intend to throw around? "It's something about you."

"I see. I can take a certain amount of unpleasantness but you're part of a team. This kind of behavior could sabotage the museum's work if it goes on too long. Care to have it out?"

That would be some conversation...make that some outburst. "There's nothing to have out."

"Then I suggest you hold your bitterness toward me in check. I wouldn't want it to be a barrier to the way the museum functions."

It was a threat. How on earth had she gone from being Bruce's anointed successor to being seen as an expendable liability?

She stood as straight as she could on her sprained ankle. "I'm not confident that you have this museum's best interests at heart, Dr. Blake. If you don't, you can expect a lot more than a few hostile words from me. So it's really up to you how well the museum functions." She wished she could stalk out of his office, but lopsided hopping was the best she could do....

Dear Reader,

I've gone three times to the Royal Tyrrell Museum of Palaeontology in Drumheller, Alberta, and although I just got back from the third trip, I already want to go again. The place fascinates me. From small pieces of smooth shale bearing detailed imprints of tiny organisms that lived more than five million years ago to huge-jawed carnivores that make you gulp even now, the museum explores the variety and complexity of living things. There's a time line in the layered hills and hoodoos nearby. You can see dark shale deposits where the skeletons of marine reptiles might be found, lighter shale where tyrannosaurs might lie and the thick K-T boundary containing iridium from a meteor that may have contributed to the dinosaurs' extinction.

During the drive home after my second visit, I began planning *Into the Badlands*. The museum in the story is a fictional place, and some details of the surrounding area have been changed to suit the story's needs, but the qualities I find so intriguing—the exotic terrain, the anticipation of discovery and the dedication of the people who search for clues to our planet's distant past—are part of the daily lives of paleontologists Susannah Robb and Alexander Blake.

I'd be glad to hear from you. You can reach me at P.O. Box 20045, Brandon, Manitoba R7A 6Y8 Canada.

Sincerely,

Caron Todd

Into the Badlands
Caron Todd

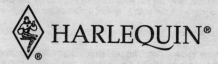

HARLEQUIN®

TORONTO • NEW YORK • LONDON
AMSTERDAM • PARIS • SYDNEY • HAMBURG
STOCKHOLM • ATHENS • TOKYO • MILAN • MADRID
PRAGUE • WARSAW • BUDAPEST • AUCKLAND

ISBN 0-373-71053-4

INTO THE BADLANDS

Into the Badlands

CHAPTER ONE

THE BONEBED LAY in a narrow, winding gully in the Alberta badlands, edged by layered hills and eroded hoodoos. Susannah Robb worked in the shade of an orange tarpaulin surrounded by members of her team and a dozen children—dinosaur enthusiasts who had signed up for two weeks at the museum's science camp, eager for a chance to dig at a real paleontology quarry.

She had found the fossil site that spring, after hiking along the same dry riverbed where she'd walked many times before. Nearly at the point of returning to the museum for the day, she'd sat on a boulder to rest, and looked down to see part of a hadrosaur skull protruding from the wind-worn rock at her feet. Now there were bones everywhere, nearly spilling out of the ground, helped by each gust of wind and every rainfall.

With an ungloved hand, she brushed debris from a tibia that peeked through the crumbling sandstone. "This is a beauty."

Her assistant didn't look up from the trench he was digging on the other side of the fossil. "It's in great shape," he agreed. James had been working for Susannah off and on for five years, as his studies allowed. This summer he was running the science camp, as well.

She let one fingertip drift over the huge specimen, tracing its curving line, feeling gravelly rock matrix, fine dust and solid fossil. Like a psychic trying to sense someone's whereabouts or history from an article of clothing, she rested her hand on the sun-heated leg bone. She imagined the powerful muscles that had driven it, contracting and expanding with leisurely heaviness during the animal's constant foraging, then letting it explode into desperate flight when a predator appeared at the edge of the herd.

Cretaceous herbivores were Susannah's specialty. The contradiction of their power and vulnerability had drawn her to them. They could have easily crushed a human, if a human had existed to get in their way, but their only real defense was that they traveled in herds. Good for the species; not so good for the individuals whose capture and demise allowed the others to escape.

"I think we're going to find a complete skeleton here, James."

"Are you backing that opinion with anything more than wishful thinking?"

She reached for the clipboard that held the project's grid maps. "Look what we have so far. There's the skull, the spinal column—"

"A few sections of it, anyway."

"We haven't dug far enough to find the rest, but it'll be there."

"No ribs, yet."

"But the legs have begun to appear. Look at the way the bones are lying. There's form to it—they're not just scrambled like most of the others."

James nodded slowly as he studied the drawing. "That would be great…exciting for the kids, too."

With a soft groan, Susannah straightened her back. "I'm getting old." Her age was usually the last thing on her mind, but her most recent birthday had startled her. Thirty-three little flames gave off a surprising amount of heat.

James grinned. "That's okay. I like older women."

"Too bad for you. I'm no cradle robber."

"You wouldn't be stealing."

Susannah smiled tolerantly and stepped out from under the tarp, stretching to loosen stiff muscles. James followed, brushing sand from his bare knees.

"It must be forty degrees out here today." She threaded her fingers through French-braided hair, lifting the dark strands to cool the skin underneath. In seconds, that slight relief was erased by the burning sun. Despite the August heat, she wore khaki slacks and a long-sleeved loose white shirt to protect her skin. "The kids are wilting."

"I'll take them for a swim soon," James promised. Not far from the camp there was a swimming hole, a loop in the Red Deer River shaded by wolf willows. The children spent most afternoons there, and returned to the quarry in the cooler evening.

Susannah pulled a watch out of her shirt pocket and checked the time. "Could you sketch in that tibia for me, and paint on the preservative? I need to get back to the museum. I told Bruce I'd be in by one o'clock."

"Did he say he'd have news for you by then?"

"He hasn't said a word. I promised to help him get some paperwork done."

"We're all rooting for you, if that makes you feel any better, Susannah."

"It does. Thanks." Watching her friends waiting to hear if she was the new head of dinosaur research was even harder than waiting herself. It couldn't be much longer before they all heard. Bruce was leaving Friday, just four days away.

SUSANNAH SWUNG OPEN her office door, rippling papers on her bulletin board. As she went by, she straightened one, a crayon drawing of a tall, thin stick lady with a long black braid, wide gray eyes and a big smile. It was labeled Auntie Sue and signed "XXX OOO Tim," in spidery letters that careened across the page. Tim was her best friend's five-year-old. Diane's office was just across the hall.

While she waited for her computer to boot up, Susannah started a pot of coffee dripping and checked her answering machine for the morning's messages. There was just one, from a Calgary television producer named Sylvia Hall. The message didn't give any details. Curious, Susannah sat at her desk to return the call.

Ms. Hall's voice was calm and confident. "I saw a piece in the *Herald* about your hadrosaur quarry. It sounds fascinating. I'm not exactly sure where it is, though. The article was a bit mysterious about that."

"We don't publicize the locations of our quarries," Susannah explained. "Fossils can be surprisingly fragile, so we like to restrict traffic, even foot traffic. Unfortunately, sight-seers have been known to make off with whatever they can carry."

"I understand. Could we bring a camera out there in a week or two? Of course, we'd be careful to keep the location secret."

"I'd be glad to show you around." Susannah began to jot notes on a pad of paper beside the telephone. "We've barely started, though. By next year we'll have more concrete information—"

"My viewers are fascinated by the process. They don't need to wait for the results. *You're* part of the story. Picture this—one of those gigantic old bones upright against the sky. A petite paleontologist standing beside it proudly—"

Susannah put down her pen. "I'm not all that petite."

"You get the idea. We want to capture that *eureka!* feeling when you find something wonderful, the adventure of the experience—"

"Adventure?" Susannah repeated mildly. "The most exciting thing I've done out there lately is try escarole on my tomato sandwich. It was kind of bitter."

There was a pause. "I sense you have a problem with the concept, Dr. Robb."

"What you're describing is entertainment, not science. That's not my style."

The producer's cool voice encouraged Susannah to be reasonable. "Why shouldn't my audience be entertained by your science? You'll catch their interest, they'll want to visit your museum—"

It was exactly the kind of thinking that got under Susannah's skin. "When we've had a chance to assess the significance of what we've found, I'll be glad to do a program."

Crisply Ms. Hall said, "That's science, dusty chalk on a blackboard science. I'm afraid that's not my style. Give me a call if you change your mind." There was a click as the phone disconnected.

Susannah sat back in her chair, fuming. Was there any chance she was wrong to resist pop paleontology? Maybe inaccurate publicity was better than none...she knew her cautious style didn't attract a large audience.

Pushing the conversation from her mind, she clicked on the computer screen to open one of the files Bruce had asked her to handle. He wanted to drum up funding for a closed-circuit television system in the lab that would give museum visitors a technician's-eye view of fossil preparation. Funding was only part of the problem. Charlie Morgan, the museum's head conservator, opposed the idea. Of course, Charlie was chronically opposed to new ideas. She could almost see his point on this one. The system would be great for visitors, but you'd hesitate to blow your nose or scratch an itch with the world looking on.

"Susannah? Got a minute?"

Kim Johnson, a student who was getting field experience at the Bearpaw Formation quarry, stood hesitantly at the door. Her slight build and willowy arms suggested she should be waving a fan, not swinging a geologist's hammer, but sharp eyes and a delicate touch with fragile specimens made up for her lack of muscular strength. For one distracting moment, Susannah imagined her on a television screen dwarfed by a King Kong bone. *I know somebody who can make you a star...*

"Come on in. Taking a break?"

Kim sat on the edge of a chair across from Susannah's desk. She glanced at the open door and lowered her voice. "I wanted to talk to you about Bruce's party."

"How are the plans coming?"

"We've got a couple of problems. The baker's having trouble with the cake, for one thing. He says the tyrannosaurus either falls on its snout, or its head falls off. He wants to do a centrosaurus."

"Bruce is a carnivore specialist. It's got to be a tyrannosaur."

Kim nodded. "I know, but he says a centrosaur stands on four short legs. It's got a good base."

"What if the T-Rex attacked a centrosaurus?"

"And it could hold the T-Rex up," Kim said quickly. "That should work."

"If it doesn't, we'll just say the centrosaurus won."

Kim laughed. "Okay, could happen. I'll suggest it." Her smile faded. "The other problem is with the decorations. Paul's insisting on an idea that probably goes too far.''

''Again?'' Paul was the field technician who helped run the Bearpaw Formation quarry, but he didn't let his responsibilities interfere with having a good time.

''He wants to lie down in the tyrannosaur exhibit, splashed with ketchup, with a spotlight on the whole tableau. I thought you might not want him to do it, in case the T-Rex got damaged.''

''Bruce would love it. As long as Paul doesn't try to climb into the skeleton's jaws, it's all right with me. You don't look happy with the idea, though.''

Kim hesitated. ''It's not that.''

''Is something else worrying you?''

''I'd like your opinion...'' Kim's voice trailed off.

Susannah waited.

''I don't want to make trouble for anyone.''

''No, of course not.'' What could be wrong? A dry bank account? Unsatisfactory field experience? Gossip at the quarry? The Bearpaw team was having an unproductive summer; tempers might be fraying. Even small problems could become irritating when a team worked for a long time under a hot sun.

After another moment of uncertainty, Kim seemed to make a decision. ''You know, I think I should try to handle it myself first. It's kind of embarrassing to come here and make a fuss, and then duck out.''

''Don't worry about it. We can talk later if you change your mind. In the meantime, tell Paul he can go ahead with his bloodthirsty scenario.''

Kim dredged up a smile. ''He'll be so pleased. And I'll stop at the bakery on my way to the quarry. Thanks, Susannah.'' She left the office, still radiating worry.

Moments later, footsteps sounded in the hall, and Bruce

appeared in the doorway, bearded and shaggy haired. When Susannah saw his face, her stomach began a free fall.

He got right to the point. "The board has gone with someone else, Susannah. Alexander Blake. Heard of him?"

She nodded. Alexander Blake was a high-profile kind of a guy. Anyone who dug up bones for a living had heard of him. Although she hadn't seen him in more than ten years, the man had got in her way a few times.

"He's a little older than you are," Bruce said, "a little more experienced. Well traveled, good contacts. I made it clear what I wanted, but they had their own ideas. I don't know—maybe it's for the best. You came awfully close."

Close? Susannah looked away from Bruce's sympathetic eyes. "We'll be lucky to have someone of Blake's caliber here."

IT WAS NEARLY NINE o'clock when Susannah finally let herself into her small cedar house. She had showered and eaten dinner at the museum, then poured her frustration into Bruce's paperwork and got it done.

She moved quickly past the unconcerned eyes of relatives who stared from a family tree of photographs on one wall of the living room, then the unperturbed residents of a large aquarium that separated the galley kitchen from the dining area. She filled a glass with filtered water from the fridge, and drank thirstily before turning to the aquarium. She hardly noticed the fish pounce when she sprinkled flakes of food and some freeze-dried shrimp onto the water's surface.

In what way was she inadequate? Knowing she was Bruce's choice, the board had looked past her to a stranger. *Timid.* That's what Blake had thought of her. Did the board agree? Was she too mild, too immersed in her own work, too female, too tall, too short, too young? Bruce had said it might be for the best. Did he doubt her ability to do the job?

Tired, but too tense to sleep, she went out onto the screened porch and sank into a wicker chair big enough to curl up in. She looked past the river that meandered behind the house, and watched as the setting sun turned the sandstone and ironstone of distant hoodoos gold and pink. Glossy blue-black swallows swooped to and from nests in the river's bank, chestnut breasts and forked tails flashing.

There was a photograph she couldn't get out of her mind, a picture illustrating one of Blake's magazine articles. It showed a tall, sandy-haired man standing perfectly at ease in the hot sun and red sand of the Gobi Desert. He had a geologist's hammer in one hand, and an open, boyish grin on his face. Huge white ribs curved out of the sand behind him. Susannah kept trying to file the photo away, under something harmless and dull like "miscellaneous." Tuck it into the folder, close the drawer and forget about it. But the damn thing wouldn't stay filed.

Staring into the gathering dark, she thought of the confusing summer she'd worked with Alexander Blake at an Australian quarry thirteen years before. He'd been a graduate student from the University of British Columbia then, assisting the leader of a joint Canada-Australia dig, but no one would have known it wasn't his quarry. He was the kind of person who always seemed to be in charge. He'd probably advised his kindergarten teacher on the finer points of printing.

It had been her first quarry, her first trip outside Canada, the first time—the only time—she'd met a man like him.

With the overbrimming confidence of someone who apparently had never done anything awkwardly and for the first time, he had noticed her just long enough to issue a damaging assessment of her performance.

She could take the disappointment about the job. She knew she was still young to head a research department. In a way, it was better not to have administrative distractions just when the hadrosaur quarry was looking so promising. It might even be interesting to work with Blake again. He might have changed. Maybe that photo was an old one, and really he had a potbelly and a mellow disposition and five kids.

Her smile faded. It was more likely that he hadn't changed at all.

CHAPTER TWO

SUSANNAH WAS ALONE in the museum. Except for Charlie, of course, down in the preparation lab, always up to his elbows in work when most people were just pressing the snooze button. She'd come in earlier than usual, anxious to finish her report on the hadrosaur quarry. Almost the minute he'd got the job, Alexander Blake had sent a fax saying he wanted summaries of all the museum's current projects on his desk when he arrived. There was less than an hour to go, and her report wasn't anywhere near ready.

She swiveled her chair toward the window, turning her back on the computer screen and its constantly flashing cursor. Outside, the grassy hills edging the badlands rolled on for miles. Cars were beginning to arrive, almost as steadily as if there was going to be a wedding, or a funeral. She could see gradually smaller clouds of dust all along the road from town.

She missed Bruce already. After the farewell party on Friday, complete with Paul in his role as a dinosaur's meal and a chocolate T-Rex that leaned heavily on a helpful vanilla centrosaur, he'd left with hardly more than a wave, suitcases visible in the back seat of his car. He'd seemed glad to go.

Now everything would change. Blake would take Bruce's chair at the conference room table, armed with plans she knew wouldn't be good for the museum. How could she go to his meeting this morning, listening meekly, when everyone knew she'd expected to get the job?

Abruptly Susannah turned off the computer, without bothering to save the changes she'd made. She wouldn't sit *timidly* waiting for Blake's arrival. There was plenty of work to be done at the quarry. Why should it stop just because a new staff member was coming to town?

She hurried to the closet for her backpack, always filled with water bottles, sunscreen, insect repellent, a hammer, chisel and brush. Halfway to the door, she stopped. The way was blocked by her closest friend, Diane McKay.

"Hey, Sue." Diane sipped coffee from a mug that had World's Greatest Mom emblazoned on its side. Dark smudges underlined her bleary eyes. "Ready for today?"

"Nope."

"Me neither. I keep wondering if I've turned in all my samples to the lab, if Tim, when I let him play computer games, deleted all my notes...you know how it is."

"Like Cinderella waiting to meet her stepmother for the first time."

Diane smiled. "Will he be mean? Will he make us work too hard? I'm hoping he'll be like Bruce was, and just leave us to get on with our work, but what are the chances of having two decent bosses in a row?" She started across the room. "Can I take the comfortable chair?"

"Help yourself." Susannah didn't move from her spot near the door. "You look as if you've been up for days."

"Just about. I drove all night from Mount Field, got home in time to have breakfast with Richard and Tim, then felt my way here." Yawning, she sank into the upholstered chair behind Susannah's desk. "I still can't believe you didn't get the job. We all thought you were a shoo-in. Nobody knows this area better than you.'' She took a long, restorative gulp of coffee.

Susannah smiled fondly at Diane. They both knew Blake was more qualified. ''Dr. Blake has a few things going for him. He's worked at all the major quarries…he's been published in all the major journals…he's been on the Discovery Channel and The Learning Channel and a couple of major networks. The board probably thought he'd do a better PR job. I'm terrible at hooking people's interest. Look at our articles. Mine are as dry as sandpaper, his are pure entertainment.''

Diane nodded. ''Tim loved the one about Blake and his team stumbling across Paleolithic cave paintings by accident while they were looking for fossils.''

''Exactly. Wherever he goes, he and his sidekicks always have adventures.'' Susannah heard a trace of resentment in her voice and tried to cover it with humor. ''Just call him Indiana Blake.''

''He won't stay long, Sue. He'll get bored in no time. Then our employers will wonder what on earth they were thinking and do what they should have done in the first place.'' Diane noticed Susannah's backpack. ''Are you going somewhere?''

''To the quarry. James has his hands full out there.''

''Are you sure that's a good idea?''

''Blake won't care where I am.'' Susannah lifted her hand in a quick wave. ''Good luck today.''

She hurried downstairs and out the back door to the staff parking lot. She chose her usual field vehicle, a faded blue pickup truck that tended to be temperamental. The engine's irregular rasping didn't start a moment too soon—as she steered out of the parking lot, a black Dodge Stealth glided past her. Susannah caught a glimpse of the man inside. She got an impression of height and strength.

Sending up clouds of dust that obscured the Stealth's reflection in her rearview mirror, she accelerated. The old Ford rattled over the narrow access road, turned onto a gravel road and continued through a treeless landscape, past arid fields dotted with rhythmically dipping oil pumps.

When she was out of sight of the museum, she drove more slowly, unhappy eyes on the lookout for potholes and prairie dogs. She was already having second thoughts about playing hooky. Provoking her new boss might not be a wise strategy.

After a long ten miles, Susannah turned onto an uneven rock-strewn track leading into a gully. She stopped beside the science camp's school bus and sat for a moment, fascinated as always by the extraterrestrial appearance of the deeply rilled hills and time-carved hoodoos.

He can't change this.

She grabbed her backpack and slid from the truck to the rocky ground. A fifteen-minute walk would take her the rest of the way to the quarry.

ALEXANDER BLAKE TURNED into the museum parking lot just as a battered pickup truck clattered out. He got a quick look at the tense-faced woman at the steering wheel. Dark hair pulled back from a pale, oval face. Slender. Whoever she was, she was in a hurry.

He parked in a reserved spot, then stood beside his car surveying the place that had lured him away from the field. The museum was long and low and the color of sandstone. It fit right in with the sedimentary hills and dry, rolling prairie. To the east, there was a wide, winding river. Far to the west, the Rocky Mountains' faded blue foothills merged with the horizon. Not a bad place to spend a couple of months.

He swung open the staff door and stepped inside. To his left was the preparation lab. Through the small window that let visitors watch technicians free bone from rock, he saw that someone was already at work.

The galleries, off to the right, were still quiet. They'd be humming with voices soon, when visitors crowded in to see the displays: the primordial invertebrates, the fish that had dragged themselves from the sea onto the land, and the dinosaurs, frozen in flight and ravenous frenzy.

There was an elevator, but Alex took the stairs two at a time and arrived at the top breathing easily. The nameplate on the first door to his right caught his eye—S. Robb. Hadrosaur nesting habits, he remembered. She'd been short-listed for the job he was about to start.

An auburn-haired woman was in the room, reading at the desk...the World's Greatest something or other, according to her mug. Her desk was free of clutter, free, even, of dust. Neat rows of journals, textbooks and color-coded file folders lined a ceiling-to-floor bookcase along one wall. On another, six identically framed photos of quarries formed a perfect rectangle. A collection of rocks stood in orderly rows on shelves under the window, as straight as soldiers on parade. World's Greatest Organizer?

The woman noticed him and said warmly, "You must be Dr. Blake."

"That's right. Dr. Robb?"

She looked surprised. "Oh! I forgot where I was. No. Diane McKay." She went around the desk to meet him, hand outstretched. "My perfectly usable office is across the hall. I just couldn't overcome my inertia once I'd sat in Susannah's chair."

"McKay," he repeated. "Burgess Shale?"

Diane nodded. "My team has been up there for most

of the summer, but I've been going back and forth. I want to spend as much of August as I can with my son.''

"You must have a reliable team.''

"Don't tell my boss, but they hardly need me. The same group has been with me for years.''

Alex could hear morning clatter coming from the other offices. "I'd like to hear more about your quarry, but I don't want to be late for my own meeting.''

"You'll have to come up to Mount Field with me. There's no place like it anywhere in the world.'' The soft-bodied creatures from the Burgess Shale site often seemed like reckless experiments of nature. One, the Opabinia, had five eyes and claws on its nose.

The suggestion fell in nicely with Alex's plans. "Are you going back soon?''

"In a couple of weeks, just for a few days.''

"Sounds perfect. I'll be able to take some time away from the museum by then.''

Diane walked with Alex to the conference room. He sat at the head of the long table and waited for the staff to get settled. He didn't recognize most of them. Field and lab technicians, probably, or the teachers and artists who helped prepare exhibits. A few paleontologists working at faraway quarries, like those in South America or on Ellesmere Island, near the Arctic Circle, hadn't made it back to the museum to meet him.

He could only identify four people at the table. George Connery, a rumpled, dark-haired man fidgeting with his pen and looking as if ten weeks of sleep would do him good. He headed the Bearpaw Formation quarry, studying marine reptiles. Diane McKay, still grasping the mug he now saw praised her parenting skills. Lynn Seton, a dignified older woman…where had he met her? A conference at UBC, he thought. She'd lectured on fossil pollens. She leaned away from a young man sitting beside her…Jeff Somebody, studying links between dinosaurs and modern birds. Had a few too many last night, from the look of it. Alex wondered if it was habitual. Guilty conscience? Stress? Maybe just a special occasion, somebody's birthday. Across the table was a man of medium height and early middle-age, white coated and frowning, with faint chemical smells clinging to him—probably Charlie Morgan, the head conservator. Susannah Robb seemed to be absent. That was odd. Her quarry was just half an hour away.

Alex sat forward, a small movement that signaled the meeting was about to start. Shuffling and talking stopped. Twenty faces looked back at him. A lot of people to get to know before he could prove that at least one of them was a thief.

AT FIRST NO ONE NOTICED Susannah had arrived. She stood on the periphery of the site, watching James work with the new group of children from the science camp, the last group of the summer. Some of the campers used chisels and toothbrushes to chip and brush soft rock away from the specimens. Others painted exposed fossils with preservative, or wrapped them in plaster, to protect them during their trip to the museum.

"Dr. Robb!"

Susannah was already familiar with that excited voice. Matt was the busiest, most talkative ten-year-old she'd ever met. He ran toward her, clutching something to his chest. Sand sprayed against her leg when he skidded to a halt at her side.

"Look what I found!" He was so bursting with eagerness he seemed to take up several feet of space in every direction. He handed her a saucer-size fossil. "It's a back-bone, right?"

Susannah used her cuff to rub dirt from the specimen. "It's part of a backbone," she agreed. "How did you know?"

Crowding next to her, he traced the fossil's shape with his finger. "It's like the backbones on my models at home. It's a circle, and it's got these two points."

"Those are the pedicles. They formed part of the neural arch, where the spinal cord went through. Any idea how old it is?"

Matt hesitated. "Seventy-five million years?" James and Susannah had explained how old the site was, and had tried to help the kids make sense of that amount of time. He added, "Before pyramids. Even before people."

"That's right. It's from the Late Cretaceous period. Where did you find it?"

"Over there." He pointed vaguely along the dry river-bed.

"Exactly where over there? We need to know, because we might find more vertebrae in the same place."

Matt's small body expressed the beginnings of agitation. "Um…"

"Retrace your steps in your mind," she suggested quietly. "You left the site and walked…where?"

"Up the hill."

"Up the hill!" Susannah reminded herself the problem at the moment was the exact location of the fossil, not the fact that Matt had ignored warnings about disturbing delicate ecosystems, damaging specimens or falling down sinkholes. Time enough for that later. "Okay. Up the hill and then?"

"Then I slid down it." Matt darted an exploratory glance in Susannah's direction. When she didn't comment, he continued more confidently. "Then I followed the riverbed, and I saw the backbone just lying there on the ground."

"Where those new hoodoos are forming?"

He nodded.

"Okay. Ask one of the counselors to help you map it, and add it to the collection."

Matt didn't move. "Dr. Robb? How did you find the bonebed?"

"I just went for a walk, and there it was."

"Really?"

"Almost. Really, I went for lots of long walks, looking at the ground, and looking at the ground—like you did this morning when you found the vertebra—and then one day, I saw part of a skull, just barely nudging up out of the rock."

"And that's how you find dinosaur bones?"

"Absolutely."

"Like me this morning," he repeated. Matt's eyes wandered past Susannah, to the badlands stretching beyond the quarry. He had the bug: he was clearly imagining the dinosaur he would find one day. The biggest, the best, the first of its kind.

"What are you going to do now, Matt?" Susannah prompted.

His eyes met hers, questioning. "Oh! Map the vertebra."

"Good. And, Matt, don't wander away from the group again. You have to stay with the other kids. It's important." She watched him hurry off without giving any sign that he'd listened to her warning.

A young woman stepped carefully around a chiseling camper to join Susannah. With sun-streaked blond hair scraped back into a ponytail, and a bright yellow T-shirt and denim shorts that revealed long, tanned arms and legs, Amy looked more like a teenage baby-sitter than a fourth-year geology student. "I didn't expect to see you here today, Susannah."

"It was a sudden decision. How are the kids doing?"

"Settling in. They're already finding out how boring paleontology can be." Amy gestured toward a small girl with short, curly hair and pink-framed glasses. Her head was bent low, her chin tucked into her chest. "Julia had a tough night. Homesick. Think you can do anything to help?"

"I can try. I'll put these water bottles in a cooler first."

"I'll do that for you." A little more insistently than Susannah liked, Amy put a hand out for her backpack. "Julia's going to burst into tears any minute. She'll get all the younger ones started."

Susannah quickly relinquished her pack. She'd been at the campsite on Saturday afternoon to welcome the children, and had spent that evening getting to know them. Julia had seemed upset right from the start, as if she really didn't want to be there. She looked and acted younger than ten—she probably wasn't ready to spend two weeks away from home.

Hoping she wouldn't say or do anything to release pent-up tears, Susannah knelt on the ground near Julia. "Finding anything?"

The small, curly head shook from side to side.

"I get days like that, too. I had about five years like that when I was just a bit older than you. I grew up on a farm in Manitoba. Not prime dinosaur country."

"Wheat," Julia muttered, still looking at the ground.

"Lots of wheat," Susannah agreed. "But I was interested in paleontology, so I'd go out into a pasture, rope off an area and start digging."

Julia glanced up. "But you didn't find anything?"

"Not much. Rusted metal that broke off a plough about a hundred years ago. Bone from a bison. One summer I lucked out—found a pioneer garbage dump."

Julia had stopped her halfhearted digging and was giving Susannah her full attention. She wrinkled her nose. "Yuck."

"It wasn't yucky. There were old medicine bottles and broken dishes and a pretty chamber pot with hand-painted flowers on it. Do you know what a chamber pot is?"

Julia shook her head.

"Maybe I shouldn't tell you."

The girl's gaze intensified. "You can tell me."

Susannah whispered in her ear. Julia drew back, her face twisted in pleased disgust. "Eew! With flowers on it?"

Susannah nodded. "Those pioneers must have had a sense of humor. The thing is, where I turned up bottles and dishes and chamber pots, you'll turn up a hadrosaur bone."

Using her geologist's hammer and a chisel, she began to chip at the ground. Julia watched Susannah's even motion and began to copy it. It wasn't long before they uncovered the tip of a bone.

"Finally. A rib. We found this animal's skull, its spinal column, and its tibia, but we couldn't find its ribs. Good for you!"

Julia smiled up at Susannah, her glasses glinting in the sun. Smiling back, Susannah realized she had passed thirty minutes without a single thought about Alexander Blake.

THE SUN, STILL HOT, was in the west. A few plaster-coated specimens lay drying on the ground. Some of the children worked slowly, obviously tired; others sat together, resting and talking.

"James?" Susannah said. "I don't see Matt."

"Again? He'll be around somewhere."

"I told him not to go too far."

"Your definition of too far and Matt's are probably very different." James raised his voice. "Matt!" He listened for an answer, then called again. "Matt, if you know what's good for you, you'll get back here pronto!" But no apologetic Matt, full of explanations, trotted back to the bonebed.

"I saw him near the dining shelter," one boy said. "Maybe fifteen minutes ago."

"He was just here, wasn't he?" asked another camper. "Wasn't he talking to Julia?"

Julia, her eyes huge, shook her head. She looked from James to Susannah, ready to panic.

One of the older girls said, "I was digging with him about an hour ago. He left to get some preservative, but he didn't come back, so I just got it myself and kept working." Uncertainly she added, "I guess I should have looked for him."

"He'll be somewhere nearby, Melissa." Susannah spoke quietly to James. "Let's take a quick look around. He could be behind any of these hills or walking along the riverbed—he found a vertebra there this morning. Maybe he went bone hunting again."

When they didn't find Matt near the quarry, in the dining shelter, supply tent, or back at the school bus, Susannah and James organized a more thorough search. Four pairs of one counselor and one camper fanned out from the quarry, carrying whistles as a simple form of communication. Hoping useful action would help ease the girl's worry, Susannah asked Melissa to be her partner.

As she walked, Susannah thought about how often Matt had been told not to wander off. She hadn't paid close enough attention to him. For most of the day, she'd been preoccupied with work and angry feelings about Alexander Blake, sometimes almost forgetting the children were there. In all the years the museum had run a science camp, no one had ever got lost.

Self-recrimination at this point was counterproductive. Nothing bad would happen to Matt. He was lost. They would find him. Later—alone and awake at night, or assessing the summer camp at the end-of-season board meeting—there would be lots of time for guilt.

They were nearly a mile from the quarry when Susannah noticed a pile of shale at the foot of a hill. Scraped ground leading to the top suggested someone had climbed up recently.

"Look at that, Melissa. I'll bet Matt slid down the other side. He's probably sitting happily in the shade, making sand castles." She called Matt's name, waited, then called again, louder.

"I think I heard something," Melissa said eagerly. "It sounded really far away, though."

"I'll go up for a look. Wait here."

Carefully Susannah edged up the side of the hill. At its crest she saw what she had been afraid of seeing: a hole about two feet across, with an uneven edge. She wriggled closer on her stomach and looked down into the stale darkness. "Matt?"

A faint voice reached her. "I'm down here!"

Susannah fumbled in her backpack for her flashlight and shone it down. There: a ghostly reflection. She called to Melissa, waiting at the base of the hill. "Have you got the whistle? Try to get someone's attention—three blows means help." She wished she could see Matt better. The flashlight's beam barely reached him. "Are you hurt, Matt?"

"Get me outta here, Dr. Robb!" His voice quavered.

Get him out. Good idea. But how? From the sound of him, Matt couldn't wait for the others to arrive, if they ever did arrive. There was no guarantee anyone would hear the whistle.

She could hear and see Matt, so the sinkhole wasn't all that deep. She tried to estimate the distance to the pale face illuminated by her flashlight—thirteen feet, maybe more. Not a long enough drop to kill you, but long enough to hurt you, long enough to keep you stranded. She had to make sure Matt wasn't hurt, reassure him, get him out.

His voice wafted up to her. "Dr. Robb? Are you there?"

"Of course I'm here. I won't leave you."

She couldn't get him out. She could throw the flashlight down so he'd have light. She could send Melissa back to the quarry for help, and lie there with her head down the hole carrying on a long-distance conversation to keep Matt calm.

Bad idea. She didn't want another child wandering alone in the badlands, and she wanted to have a good look at Matt, as soon as possible. He was talking, but that didn't mean he wasn't hurt.

She'd have to go in after him.

Her body tensed at the thought. She didn't like heights or the dark or jumping. She didn't like fast sports or danger. But here she was, proposing to plunge into a dark void. Without a net. Well, she wasn't exactly a couch potato. She did a lot of on-the-job hiking and climbing. She was fit.

Again she shone the flashlight into the hole. About a yard from the top, she noticed a small outcropping. Here and there along the sides were uneven areas that might provide hand- and toeholds.

"Melissa, I need you up here." She waited until the girl joined her at the top of the hill. "Lie on your stomach so your weight is spread out—the ground could cave in again. I'm going down to see if Matt's okay, and I'll try to help him out." She spoke calmly, as if she were just going to walk down some stairs to check on him. "Be ready to give him a hand." She tucked the flashlight into the backpack.

"Matt? Is the ground clear? I don't want to land on rocks."

Several seconds passed while she waited for his answer.

"It's clear!"

"Move out of the way—I'm coming down."

Susannah sat on the crumbling edge of the hole, feet dangling. *I can't do it.* She willed her muscles to relax. *Do it.* She let go and felt herself falling. She hit the ground and rolled, and pain shot through her left ankle and shoulder. Seemingly very far above her, she saw a small circle of evening light, and Melissa's anxious face. Two small hands clutched her.

"Are you okay, Dr. Robb?"

"I'm fine." Cautiously she flexed her arms and legs. It didn't take much movement to convince her she'd injured her shoulder and ankle. Not seriously, though. Grimacing, she sat up. "Throw down the backpack, Melissa!"

The pack landed with a thump near her feet. She retrieved the flashlight and shone it on Matt. Apart from a few blood- and sand-encrusted scrapes, he seemed to be in good shape.

"Are you mad at me, Dr. Robb?" One hand still clung to her shirtsleeve.

"Definitely. But it's nothing you can't survive."

"I was hiking, like you did. I wanted to find another bonebed. Then I fell in and I thought, wow, there really are sinkholes."

Susannah's eyebrows rose in surprise. What did he think, sinkholes were the bogeymen of the badlands? She had a strong urge to give him a good, long lecture, even though she knew it wouldn't do any good. Instead, she said, "I've got a plan. Are you any good at math?"

"Yeah." Matt sounded puzzled.

"If there are enough stones down here to make a big pile to stand on, you plus me plus the stones should just about equal the height of that ledge near the mouth of the hole. See it?" She shone the flashlight upward.

Matt peered up into the faint light. "I think so."

"If you can reach that ledge, Melissa will grab your hands. The sides of the sinkhole are closer together there. You can plant your feet against them and climb out."

"I dunno…I'll try."

"That's the spirit!"

Susannah shone the flashlight around the floor of the sinkhole. There were plenty of stones, large and small, scattered here and there. She didn't want to think about what would have happened if she or Matt had hit a knee or head on one of them. "I'll need your help to move some of these rocks, Matt."

He sprang to her side and helped her roll and push some rocks into place. He seemed glad of a chance to demonstrate his strength. With some difficulty, Susannah climbed onto the pile. "Can you jump up on me, piggyback?"

"Sure." Matt's confidence was streaming back.

Susannah put one hand against the cold wall of the sinkhole, but she still swayed under Matt's weight. She tried to ignore the stabbing pains that accompanied his climb. A pointed elbow, then a bony knee, dug into her. Fingers grasped her forehead. Their bodies swayed.

"I can't reach," he gasped, fear returning to his voice.

"You're nearly there, Matt," Melissa called. "A couple more inches. Stretch!"

Finally he was on the ledge. She waited, ready to break his fall if he couldn't hold on. She heard scraping sounds and the children panting, then Melissa called, "I've got him!" Loosened sand rained down on Susannah's head.

Two faces appeared at the mouth of the hole. "How are you getting out, Dr. Robb?"

She hadn't planned that far. "I'll just hang around here for a while. I've always wanted to study the ecosystem inside a sinkhole." The children didn't laugh. "So I'll get started on that. Any sign of the others?"

"I don't see anyone coming," Melissa answered. "And I didn't hear a whistle."

"Then you two trot back to the quarry. Ask someone to look after Matt's knee, and to come back for me. Tell them if they bring a couple of tent poles and a rope, I should be able to climb out."

Matt seemed unwilling to go. "Maybe I should stay and keep you company."

"I want the two of you to stick together."

As soon as the children left, there was total silence. Susannah stood in an eerie puddle of light thrown by her flashlight. "At least I hope I'll be able to climb the rope. I was never much good at it in gym class."

She picked up her backpack, wincing when she put weight on her ankle. It was beginning to swell over the top of her shoe. Bending down, she loosened the lace but left the shoe on for support.

She shone the flashlight around the ground and the walls. "The bad news is, I'm all alone down here. And the *good* news is I'm all alone down here.'' Black widow spiders and rattlesnakes liked the damp coolness of sink-holes.

It was a narrow hole, irregularly carved by rainwater that had soaked in from the top and chiseled through the rock until it forced its way out somewhere along the hill's sides. The inner walls were layered in the same distinctive way as the outside: there were beige and ocher seams of sandstone, gray mudstone, black coal and whitish-gray volcanic ash. She could even see the reddish K-T Bound-ary, the layer of sediment that was like a lid closed on the dinosaur world. No dinosaur fossils were found above it.

''This is creepy. That's my scientific conclusion. I've observed, I've gathered data, and I've concluded that sink-holes are creepy.''

She decided to check the floor to make sure there were no soft spots that might cave in to a deeper hole. Some-times seeping rain carved out a series of openings until the water reached an underground stream. She had almost finished her inspection when her injured foot twisted on a damp rock, sending waves of pain up her leg. She gasped and dropped the flashlight. It went out.

''Oh, no.'' Susannah eased down onto her knees and felt the ground for the flashlight. She found it and flicked the switch. Nothing. She twisted its head to be sure it was tight. She shook it. It shone faintly for a moment, then went out. And stayed out.

She sat still, her breathing audible, her senses instantly alert. The sudden darkness seemed endless and full of threat. Sitting in the middle of the sinkhole floor, she felt like a target. Slowly she crept along the uneven ground until the rock wall was at her back.

It was so dark. There was nothing like the darkness of

a hole in the ground. It was different from the darkness of night. Blackness thick enough to pick up by the handful. She turned her face to the opening far above her. She would keep her eyes on the small circle of light.

"It's just the same place it was a second ago," she whispered. "No more holes, no snakes, no tyrannosaurs. Darkness is a good thing. Nature's protection. Of course there are predators, like owls, that hunt very successfully in the dark. Not that there are any owls here. And not that I'm a rodent."

Alex Blake would understand…she never would have thought that could happen. In one of his articles—the one about finding a Paleolithic cave by accident, while hunting for fossils—he'd mentioned the dank darkness only found underground. The words flowed back to her…*blackness before and behind us, pressing against our eyes, creeping into our lungs, cocooning us, or entombing us…the monsters that politely stay under the beds and in the closets of modern children knew no rules here.*

He'd had company, though, and he and his friends hadn't been trapped. Curious and hopeful, with a sense of adventure rather than fear, they had climbed through a winding passage until they were delivered into a large, high-ceilinged cave. Red and yellow ocher and black charcoal figures had flickered in the beams of their flashlights, appearing to move as the light played over them.

Even though she disliked Blake's pop paleontology approach, the story had excited her. She had seen the glowing pictures in her mind's eye. She had wanted to be the one who first held up the flickering light to see a painted aurochs galloping toward her. Was is possible she was a little jealous of the man? It was an unpleasant idea. She wasn't used to feeling petty.

It seemed like a very long time since Matt and Melissa

had left for the quarry. "With his sore knee, Matt might be slow," Susannah said. "They'd have to explain, and James would have to take down a tent to get the poles, then find his way here. It could take an hour and a half, maybe more. They won't be much longer, though, and when they get here, I'll scurry up the rope like a chimpanzee and that will be that. Teatime."

She tried not to think about the other possibility—that James might not find her before nightfall. If that happened, he'd have to put off the search until morning.

CHAPTER THREE

THE LIGHT AT THE MOUTH of the sinkhole was fading. Susannah shivered. A chill had crept into her bones. She wished she were at home, in her bed, with soft blankets around her. Books and sweet-smelling flowers on the bedside table. Music—something slow and tragic? Billie Holiday? Something calm and balanced? Bach, Pachelbel? Chocolate bars...

She went still. There were scraping, dragging sounds overhead. Bobcat? She sprang to her feet, setting off a new wave of pain. "James?"

A head blotted out the light, and a familiar, teasing voice drifted down to her. "Whatcha doin', angel?"

"Oh, bit of this, bit of that." Her voice shook. "What about you?"

"Nothing much. I've been out walking."

"The flashlight died, James. I've been here in the dark."

His tone changed. "We've brought the tent poles. We'll get the rope secured right away. It has knots every couple of feet...can you climb a rope, Sue?"

"Sure." It had sounded like a good idea a while ago, when she was still awash with adrenaline from jumping in after Matt. Now it seemed ridiculous.

"It's all yours."

Susannah felt for the rope and reached above her head for a knot. Stifling a groan, she pulled herself up until her feet clasped a knot, too. She waited for protesting nerves to stop yelling, then, trying to keep most of her weight on her good arm and leg, she felt for the next knot and pulled with her arms and pushed with her feet again.

Getting out of the hole was worse than staying in it. The rope dug into her hands, scraping her skin. Sharp pains stabbed through her ankle and shoulder with each push and pull of the climb.

Her face drew closer to the light. She could feel fresh air tantalizingly close. *One more knot, then the poles. All I have to do is grab them and swing. Up and out.* She knew she couldn't do it. If she let go of the rope to reach for the metal tent poles, she would fall.

"James?" Her voice wavered. "I can't—"

A pair of strong arms reached toward her and grasped her securely. Her right arm hooked around his shoulder, but the left, weakened by the climb, dangled. She felt his muscles flexing under the soft cloth of his shirt as he pulled her over the edge. They both fell to the ground, and she half lay on a pair of denim-clad legs. She kept still for a moment, feeling the burning of her muscles and the firmness of the ground beneath her. As she rested, she realized this couldn't be James, unless a massive dose of steroids had transformed his build in the past few hours.

She looked up, knowing whose face she'd see, but needing proof. The eyes were the clincher, intensely blue—too blue to be real, she'd always thought. His arm was firmly around her. When she drew away, he let go.

Cobalt-blue? She didn't really know what shade cobalt was, but that was the color that occurred to her. Those eyes had emptied her mind thirteen years ago. She'd seen them while she carefully chiseled and brushed. She'd seen them while she waited to fall asleep in her tent at night. Then the field assignment had ended and she had forgotten all about them. Not true. She'd seen them in the pages of her textbooks that first term back at the university. *Eventually,* she had forgotten all about them.

He hadn't changed…hardly at all. Sandy hair, traces of red highlighted by the evening sun…she had always wanted to touch it, slide her fingers through it. An outdoor face, tanned, with laugh lines in the corners of the eyes…the lines were new. She had forgotten what it was like to be near him. Magazine photographs, showing him three inches tall and frozen in two dimensions, only hinted at his energy and strength.

She realized she was staring. Aware of his hard, warm body half under hers, she moved sharply, grimacing when pain shot through her shoulder.

"Hang on. I've got you." His voice was kind. That was new. He'd sounded different in Australia—edgy, intense. He untangled his legs from hers and his arms came around her again as he helped her sit up. "You're chilled through." He pulled a blanket from his backpack and wrapped it around her shoulders. Her skin tingled where he touched her.

She heard James's anxious voice behind her. "Are you okay, Sue?"

"I'm fine." She hadn't expected to feel like this. It was as if no time had elapsed since the Australian quarry ended. She felt twenty again, bowled over by the most charismatic man she'd ever met, and too inexperienced to figure out how to handle it.

"I'm sorry we were so long getting to you," James said.

"That's okay." An odd cloud around her muffled everything. She closed her eyes, willing it away. If it were just the two of them, just herself and James, she'd be all right.

"It took a while to organize the kids and get the tent poles," he continued. "It's amazing how similar all these hills look when there's a person you want to find in one of them. We climbed several—didn't we, Alex?—till we found the right one."

Alex. So he and James were already friends. Bonding quickly in a crisis. She didn't want James to like this man. "Are Matt and Melissa all right?"

"Safe and sound. Everybody's back at the camp, except Matt. Diane took him to town so the doctor could have a quick look at him."

"Diane was here?"

"She showed me the way to the bonebed," Alex explained. "We got there at the same time as the kids. She was alarmed when they told us you were down a sinkhole. She said you're afraid of the dark."

It was true, but an embarrassing thing to hear said aloud.

"I should introduce myself—I'm Alexander Blake."

"Yes."

Her vague answer provoked an exchange of worried glances between the two men. Susannah wondered why Blake had come to the quarry and why Diane had agreed to bring him. She edged closer to James. "Trust Matt to find a sinkhole."

James grinned. "I'll bet he could find one anywhere. Like those pigs that nose out truffles."

Susannah meant to smile. Instead, she started to cry. She stopped right away, but a few tears were there for Blake to see. He sat back on one heel, leaning an elbow on one bent knee, looking at her assessingly. What was he thinking? That she was a lot of trouble? That she was a mess? That she'd really screwed up the day, running off in a snit and needing to be helped out of a sinkhole?

"I don't like the look of this," he said to James. "She seems dazed and emotional. That could indicate a head injury."

"I didn't hit my head."

"Are you sure?" His voice was gentle, warmer than the blanket. "Sometimes when things happen quickly, dangerous things, the mind can't handle all the information at once. You could hit your head and not be aware of it at first."

"I'm sure I didn't." Was her behavior so odd that only a head injury could explain it? Susannah tried to pull herself together. She'd wanted to meet Blake while she was at work over a prize hadrosaur skeleton or busy at her desk, on her territory, on her terms. Not like this.

"I suppose it's shock, then," he said. "It's no wonder, after the evening you've had. I'd like to check you over before you move around too much, just to be on the safe side."

He reached into his backpack again and brought out a first-aid kit, then scanned her body from head to toe. He'd never really seen her before, not even when she'd put on blush and lipstick before heading to the quarry each day all those years ago, but he was taking a good look now. Now, when dust and sand clung to her, and her ankle was puffed up like a huge white slug. He didn't seem to recognize her. Not so great for the ego, on the one hand, a relief that her fiasco of a summer had slipped his mind, on the other.

His long, tanned fingers curved around her hands, turning them over to expose abrasions inflicted by the rope. "It's probably best to leave those alone for now. There's not much bleeding. Let's have a look at your arm."

Alex unfastened the top two buttons of her blouse and eased the cloth away from her shoulder. "Ouch," he said quietly, when he saw the bruises that reached toward her neck. "I doubt anything's broken, or you wouldn't have been able to climb the rope as far as you did. I'll fasten a sling to take the pressure off your shoulder. James, would you wrap a tensor bandage around her ankle? Figure eight. Right over the shoe for now."

He was taking charge, just as expected. James ran the science camp; James knew the canyon. If anyone was going to get bossy, it should be James.

"It's a long walk out of here," Alex said. "Good thing we brought the truck."

"You brought the truck?" That news jolted Susannah out of her daze. For years she'd protected the delicate fossils that might lie just under the surface. Now Blake had threatened them his first day on the job. "Think of the damage you've done!"

He seemed surprised by her outburst. "We thought you might be hurt."

"And you are," James pointed out.

Susannah looked past the two men and saw the roof of the pickup's cab at the base of the hill. If it had been just one path, two tire tracks from the bonebed to the hill, at least the damage would have been limited, but James had said they'd taken a few wrong turns looking for her. Who knew what specimens they'd crushed under those tires...a juvenile hadrosaur, a nesting site, a clue to the dinosaurs' extinction...

Still, they had a point. She couldn't have walked all the way back to the parking area.

Leaning on James, she pushed herself up, putting her weight on her uninjured foot. Alex rose, too, keeping a steadying hand under her elbow. Susannah was tall, accustomed to being as tall as many of the men she met, but when she turned to thank him, she found she was looking directly at his stubble-covered chin. She had to tilt her head to look into those steady blue eyes. Steel-blue?

Almost as a reflex, she felt for her backpack. When she realized she didn't have it, she glanced toward the sink-hole.

"Did you leave something down there?"

"My backpack…"

Before she could add that she didn't really need it, Alex had pulled on a pair of leather work gloves and eased himself down between the tent poles. Dangling from one hand, he gripped the rope with the other and disappeared. Moments later, she saw his hands on the poles again. He easily swung himself up onto the ground, her backpack hanging from one shoulder. "Cold and nasty down there."

"It could have been worse."

He nodded. "You could have had some dangerous company. Now we'll get you to the doctor and then home. A couple of pain pills and bed sound good?"

"I'd just as soon skip the doctor."

"You could wait and see how you feel tomorrow, but I think it's safer to go tonight."

She knew he was right. What if something were broken, rather than sprained? The main thing was getting some distance from Blake. Once they got to the road, he and James could go their own ways, and she could get to the hospital by herself. Then, after a good night's sleep, she would turn back into a thirty-three-year-old scientist who was perfectly capable of handling anything life threw at her.

"HAD A RUN-IN with a tyrannosaurus, did you?" Bob Smythe made a variation of the same joke every time someone from the museum came in with injuries.

"If you think I look bad, you should see the T-Rex."

The doctor shone a flashlight in Susannah's eyes. "Headache? Nausea? Faintness?"

"No, nothing like that." She was beginning to feel normal again. Stiff and aching everywhere, but herself. "Bob, did you see Matt, the boy from the camp? Is he all right?"

"He'll be fine. From what I could tell, he couldn't wait to get back and entertain the other kids around the campfire." Bob turned his attention to her ankle. "Who was that who brought you in? He looked familiar."

"That's my new boss. Alexander Blake."

"Of course. I saw him on TV a while ago, on a program about a carnivore that was bigger than the T-Rex. Hard to imagine."

Bob picked up a chart and began writing. "You were lucky this time, Susannah. I wouldn't recommend that you try a jump like that again. A nurse will bandage your hands, and I'll order a strong painkiller for tonight. We'll get you a crutch, although with two sprains on the same side of your body, walking will still be difficult. Get in touch with Outpatients if you decide you need a wheelchair. You'll have to take it easy for a while—keep your foot elevated, your shoulder immobilized, your hands clean and dry."

Take it easy? The consequences of her injuries hadn't occurred to Susannah yet. "No digging?"

"You're joking, right? Absolutely no digging."

SUSANNAH WATCHED DROWSILY as the headlights swept past the town, the stands of cottonwood, clusters of rounded hills and the occasional hoodoo. Soon she would be home, and Blake would disappear. He hadn't disappeared when they'd got to the parking area outside the gully, but he would disappear after he took her home. She would crawl into bed and stay there till Christmas.

"Friendly emergency room." His voice sounded soft in the darkness of the leather-upholstered car. No edge at all.

Susannah closed her eyes, too tired to talk. If she had gone to his meeting, she would be at home sleeping by now. She wouldn't have told Matt about taking lots of long walks to find fossils, and he might not have wandered so far from the bonebed. The worst part of her day would have been listening to Blake's plans for the museum. The next time she had an impulse, she would make a point of ignoring it.

"Everyone I've run into in town seems interested in the work we do," Alex went on. "On Saturday, I was in that little grocery store on Main. The lady who runs it—Dorothy—packed my groceries, told me the history of paleontology in the area, and brought me up-to-date on world events, all at no extra charge. Several other people, who didn't seem to be there to shop, wanted to know what's going on at every quarry."

Reluctantly Susannah opened her eyes and tried to do her part for the conversation. "It's a small town. Everybody knows one another."

"And one another's business, I suppose."

"I'm not sure about that. People probably manage to keep a few secrets."

"Where do I turn?"

"At the next road. Left." Five minutes, tops, and he'd be gone. It would be a relief to let her guard down. "Here we are."

Susannah hadn't expected to be out after dark, so she'd

left the yard light off. It was difficult to see where the road ended and the ditch began. Alex nosed onto the driveway and drove slowly to the front of the house. "I'll leave the headlights on so you can see to get in."

Susannah swung the passenger door open as soon as they stopped. "Thanks for everything, Dr. Blake." She tried to maneuver her way out of the car, but the left half of her body was no help at all. Alex was at her side before her good foot hit the ground. He helped her to stand, and waited while she struggled with the crutch. She leaned her whole weight on it, hopped a few inches forward, then rested.

"Can you manage?"

"I think so." Inch by inch, she made her way to the house. She stopped when she reached the porch steps. They looked impassable. They *were* impassable.

"Need a lift?"

She tried to smile. "I'm being punished."

"For what?"

"For skipping your meeting."

After a brief silence, he said calmly, "You must have really wanted to avoid me."

"I really did."

"So...if that had worked better today, what were you going to do about tomorrow?"

"I didn't think that far ahead." She took a deep breath. "It was a mistake. A very childish mistake. I apologize."

"It's probably not as bad as all that. Shall we just get this transportation business over with, then?"

Susannah nodded. Alex lifted her easily. He carried her up the few steps and through the screened porch to the front door. He set her down, holding her until she regained her balance.

"I don't have my keys. They're in my desk." She always locked her valuables in her office when she went to the quarry, just taking the truck's keys and her driver's license with her. She kept an extra house key hidden, but she didn't like to broadcast where.

Alex looked around the darkened porch. Two wicker chairs sat at the far end, separated by a round wicker table. "I'll pull a chair over so you can get off that foot while I look for a way in."

Susannah hesitated, then pointed toward the wall of the house. "There's a spare key behind one of those boards."

"One of these?" Alex touched several of the wide cedar planks. One responded, just barely moving inward. He hooked his fingers underneath and pulled. It came away in his hand revealing a small cavity, and a key. He unlocked the front door, felt for a switch and flicked it on. Soft light filled the living room.

Most of the house—the living room, the shadowed kitchen and dining area beyond and the bedroom loft above—could be seen at a glance. Light sandy walls, hardwood floors and a few patterned rugs in shades of burnt sienna and ocher repeated the colors found in the layered stone of the badlands. Through the living room's large window, distant pillars and giant toadstools of rock glowed in the moonlight. The house's interior had a soothing effect, but the view outside was eerie and unsettling.

"Thank you for all your help, Dr. Blake. Again, I'm sorry about the meeting."

"Will you be all right now?"

"I'll flake out on the sofa. Anything more complicated can wait till tomorrow." He was standing just inside the house, and she couldn't shut the door. Shutting it would be tricky, anyway—her one good hand was clutching the crutch and her one good foot was keeping her upright.

"I think I should stay until you're settled. You could fall—"

"Dr. Blake," she began, making an effort to keep her voice civil, "I appreciate your help. But I managed to deal with life before you arrived today, and I can continue to do so." Her voice started to rise. There didn't seem to be anything she could do about it. "James could have helped me out of the sinkhole and taken me to the hospital and brought me home, and when I said good-night, he would have known that meant he should leave—"

She stopped abruptly. Part of her wanted to keep going; part of her wished she hadn't said a thing. She sank onto the sofa's soft cushions.

"I'm not sure what's going on here," Alex said slowly. "Is this about the job? I heard you were short-listed—"

"I was more than short-listed."

He nodded as if he understood. "It was down to the two of us, was it? Well, that would be a disappointment." He stared at her, frowning. "I can see I should have let James take care of things tonight. I tend to jump in head-first, and find out later whether or not it's a good idea. Like you, I suppose."

Susannah's sudden anger faded, leaving her more tired than before. She didn't bother explaining that she almost never jumped headfirst into anything. This had been the least typical day of her life. "We're letting bugs in."

Alex shut the door, leaving himself on the wrong side of it. "Look, Dr. Robb, it's clear you're going to need help. Why don't you just give me directions? After you're settled in, I'll get out of your hair."

It was past midnight. She couldn't call anyone else to help her. If she only needed to sleep, she could manage, but she was filthy and hungry, too. "I'd like to wash.

While I do that, would you mind finding something for me to eat?''

"No problem. Can you walk to the bathroom by yourself?''

"I think so.''

She struggled to her feet and made her way to the kitchen, pausing by the aquarium to feed the fish. Their dinner had never come so late. She watched the surface feeders leaping at the flakes and wondered where she would find the energy to walk the rest of the way to the bathroom.

"Alex?''

He had started rummaging in the fridge. He straightened, a bag of oranges in hand. Without a word, he picked her up, crutch and all, and headed to the bathroom. He set her down carefully, then leaned over to put in the plug and turn on the taps. An assortment of bottles crowded a shelf over the tub. "Do you want bubbles?''

She nodded. Without the use of her hands, bubble bath was as close as she'd get to soap. He chose the bottle closest to him and poured a generous amount of liquid into the water gushing from the faucet. Soft bubbles started to form, and a lavender scent filled the room.

He gestured toward the window, almost level with the side of the tub. "That's unusual. Don't you feel like you're onstage when you bathe?''

"It's the back of the house. No one ever goes by. I can close the blind if I want more privacy.''

He stared outside. "You can see hoodoos from here.''

"And stars.''

When the tub was three-quarters full, with bubbles reaching to the rim, Alex turned off the taps. "I guess you can...look after the rest of the procedure?''

Susannah blushed. "I'll be fine.''

As soon as the door closed, she struggled out of the shoulder sling, the tensor bandage and her sand-encrusted clothes. Balancing on one foot, and holding her left arm across her chest, she sank thankfully into the soothing water. Dust and dirt from the quarry and the sinkhole had settled into her skin, glued to her by the sunscreen she had applied so liberally. She could only hope the grime would dissolve on its own.

She gazed tiredly at the view framed by the window. The whitish wash of the Milky Way, made pale by the moon, curved through the sky. Absentmindedly, she found the Big Dipper and used it to trace an imaginary line toward the huge, far-distant star, Deneb, and the two other stars of the Summer Triangle, Vega and Altair. She tried to visualize the different constellations to which the three stars belonged: Cygnus the swan, Lyra the harp and Delphinus the dolphin, but, as usual, the fanciful shapes eluded her imagination.

Blake hadn't just taken the job she wanted—he had rescued her. She didn't know which was worse. He didn't stay in his own space like most people, at his own desk and his own quarry, quiet and focused. When he was on the scene, he was everywhere. And there was a complication. He was kind.

WHY HAD HE THOUGHT he was the obvious person to help a strange woman get ready for bed? He hadn't thought about it, that was the problem. He'd just swooped in on his jungle vine. That was Heather's phrase, from the early days, when she'd still liked his tendency to do that.

At least he knew why Dr. Robb hadn't made it to his meeting, or prepared a project report. In a way, her obvious resentment was refreshing. Some people would have hidden their anger behind cold eyes and a tight smile, and waited for a good chance to trip him.

The confusing thing was, when they'd talked on the phone last week, Bruce Simpson had told him Susannah was reliable, the person Alex could count on most for any help he needed. How could he count on someone who was so mad she couldn't stand to be anywhere near him?

He knocked on the bathroom door and heard a startled splash. "Dr. Robb? I've pulled out the sofa bed. Can you tell me where to find sheets?"

"In the cupboard upstairs." Her voice sounded strained. "Fourth shelf."

He found the cupboard easily, tucked between the sleeping area and a computer nook. His hand hovered over a plain white sheet set, then moved to a pair with pink rosebuds. His mother liked flowery things. Maybe they'd cheer up Dr. Robb.

Now for a blanket—the sinkhole had chilled her, and the nights could get surprisingly cool. There were two deep drawers under the shelves. One was full of scarves, mitts and hats; the other held blankets. He felt his way through the pile and chose one that was relatively light-weight. As he pushed the drawer shut, something not quite covered by the blankets caught his eye. He crouched to look closer.

Reaching into the drawer, he picked up a stonelike object. It was a coiled ammonite, about twelve inches in diameter, a common fossil whose presence in a rock sample could help date it. Other fossils sat at the bottom of the drawer: a trilobite, a cluster of clam shells imprinted in limestone, a fern leaf in a flat slab of coal, another piece of limestone bearing a rough pattern that looked like fish scales.

An odd collection for a Cretaceous herbivore specialist,

and an odd place to keep it. One by one, Alex lifted the pieces to get a better look. They were real, not copies. Not rare, not particularly valuable. He pushed the drawer shut and stood frowning at it. Most paleontologists kept a few fossils around. They probably weren't important.

Grabbing a couple of pillows from the bed, he returned to the living room. He could hear the bathtub water draining, so he made the sofa bed quickly, leaving the top sheet and blanket untucked so they wouldn't be tight against her injured ankle. He was fluffing the pillows when Susannah hobbled into the living room.

The sight of a blanket that had shared space with hidden fossils didn't seem to worry her. She looked vulnerable—exhausted, struggling to keep her composure, her hair still full of sand and a soft, blue nightgown draping her body. She brought a faint scent of bubble bath into the room with her. Alex felt an unexpected surge of desire, complicated by an even less expected tug of tenderness. Surprised at himself, he shut the feeling down.

Avoiding his eyes, she eased herself onto the bed and leaned back against the raised pillows. She'd slipped the sling back on, but she hadn't been able to manage the bandage around her ankle. Alex found it in a pile of sandy clothes on the bathroom counter. He shook most of the sand into the sink, then returned to the living room.

"That's really not necessary," she said, as he approached the bed. "I'll have to shower in the morning to get the sand out of my hair, and I'll just have to take it off again."

She seemed flustered, and she was blushing again. There was something familiar about her, but Alex was sure they hadn't met before. "Your ankle will swell more overnight without support. If that happens, you'll have to wait even longer before you can get back to the quarry."

"I suppose you're right."

"It won't hurt to put it on, you know. It'll feel better." He lifted the covers away from her ankle and began rolling the bandage around her foot. When his hand brushed her toes, she shivered.

"Cold? I'm almost done." He kept his eyes on her ankle, away from the curve of her leg above her knee, and the flimsy nightgown that didn't cover her all that well. Halfway up her calf, he fastened the end of the bandage with two thin metal clips, then pulled the covers back in place. "Comfortable?"

"Yes. Thanks." She lifted a bandaged hand to cover a yawn.

"Think you can stay awake to eat your dinner, such as it is?"

"I'm starving."

"It'll just be a minute."

A peeled and sectioned orange, and a raisin scone cut in half and spread with butter and strawberry jam already waited on a tray in the kitchen. Alex poured simmering soup into a mug and carried the tray to the living room.

"I strained the noodles out of the soup, so you could drink it. A spoon seemed a bit much for you right now."

"Thank you." Holding the mug awkwardly, she sipped the warm broth. "You've been very nice, Dr. Blake." She sounded grateful, but surprised, as if the big bad wolf had declined to gobble her up on the way to her grandmother's.

"I'm glad to help." Alex relaxed in an armchair near the sofa bed. He was tempted to mention the fossils in her cupboard drawer. Almost certainly, she'd have an innocent explanation and he could forget about them. The trouble was, her explanation could be a lie, and then he'd have warned her of his suspicions.

"Why did you go out to my quarry this evening?" she asked. "Were you looking for me because of the meeting?"

"Someone from your team called the museum for help. Amy, I think? When you didn't get back to the bonebed after looking for Matt, she went out to the road, away from the gully, where her cell phone would work."

"I guess we should have done that earlier."

"You rescued Matt. That's the main thing. I just wish it hadn't taken us so long to find you."

Susannah yawned and the mug tilted. Alex jumped up and caught it, then lifted the tray to the end table. She slid down in the bed and curled up on her uninjured side.

"I can't stay awake anymore," she muttered. "Could you bring my alarm clock down, and set it? For seven?" Her eyes closed. In seconds, she was asleep.

Quickly Alex did a few chores. He shook her clothes out the back door to get rid of the worst of the sand, then put them in the laundry room. He swept the bathroom floor and rinsed away the sand he'd left in the sink. She hadn't managed to eat much of her meal. He put the leftover food in the fridge and washed the dishes.

Was there anything else she needed? Painkillers. He found a bottle of acetaminophen and set it on the table beside the sofa bed, along with a glass of water. Remembering how weak her left arm was, he removed the bottle's childproof lid. There was a pen and some paper by the phone. He scribbled a quick note and propped it against the water glass. Gently, careful not to wake her, he pulled the blanket around her shoulders.

The blanket rose and fell slightly as she breathed. She looked soft and unprotected, as if she didn't have an angry or defensive bone in her body. Tangled, sand-filled hair had escaped here and there from her braid. Alex was surprised by an almost overwhelming urge to trace the pattern of freckles over her nose.

There was no way she was a fossil poacher.

CHAPTER FOUR

ALEX ROLLED OUT OF BED and tugged the top sheet more or less straight before heading to the kitchen. The one-bedroom suite, with its discolored linoleum and chipped porcelain kitchen sink, had been the only place he could find to rent on short notice. It was luxurious compared to his last home. During the months he spent at a quarry in Mongolia, he'd cooked over a camp stove, washed from a metal basin and shared a tent with a variety of six-legged roommates. Sometimes, especially after a few months in the city, he thought that was the best way to live.

He shook some Cheerios into a bowl and sloshed in some milk. The kitchen window faced north, so rather than enjoying a view of the foothills or the badlands while he ate, Alex looked out at a line of beige brick buildings. In the distance, he could see deciduous woods and rolling meadows. A herd of Charolais cattle, as small as plastic toys, grazed in one of the fields, white splotches against the green.

It was nothing like Susannah Robb's view. Her place was small and comfortable, but sprouting on the edge of the badlands the way it did, it had a feeling of wildness, too. Maybe he could stay put and work in one place for as long as Bruce Simpson had if he lived in a house that didn't crush him. Or maybe not.

The sun was still low when Alex headed to the museum, fifteen minutes from town. It had been a short night, but he had too much adrenaline in his bloodstream to feel tired. He was glad to see that the staff parking lot was empty. Aware that he might not be alone for long, Alex quickly let himself into the museum, then into the prep lab.

Labeled cupboards ringed the main room, and heavy metal shelves holding bones and rock stood in rows at one end. Most of the space was filled by wide worktables with overhead lamps the technicians could raise and lower as needed. A second room, where skeletons were put together, branched off from the first.

Surprised that more advanced technology hadn't found its way onto such an important door, Alex sorted through a ring of jangling keys to find the one that would unlock the fossil storage room. This room was larger than the other two. It had to be, when a single bone could be as large as an average human. On the other hand, some of the fossils could fit in his pocket.

Security cameras recorded traffic in and out. The door was kept locked at all times. Individual drawers inside the room were locked and a locked mesh protected specimens stored on shelves. Stealing from this room wouldn't be a casual affair, but Bruce Simpson thought someone had managed it. The board was clinging to a hope that the discrepancies in the collection were due to honest mistakes.

Alex decided to double-check Bruce's findings first. He opened one of the drawers of Diane McKay's samples. They came from a black shale deposit in the Rockies, an area that had been under water millions of years ago, before the earth's plates had crunched together, forcing it into the sky. Boneless organisms weren't usually preserved. These gave a rare glimpse into ancient invertebrate life.

The label on the outside said the drawer contained pieces of shale with thirty-five one-inch-long Marella imprints. The drawer looked full. Handling the specimens carefully, Alex counted. Just as Bruce had said, there were only thirty-one. He checked the next drawer, which was supposed to hold eleven Hallucigenia, a cylindrical creature with seven pairs of tentacles.

There were nine.

The Opabinia was the rarest of the Burgess Shale fossils. Seven specimens should be here. Aware of tension he hadn't noticed earlier, Alex unlocked the drawer and pulled it open.

Six.

It was the same in several drawers that held groups of small fossils. Instead of ten oyster-laden pieces of shale, there were eight. Instead of thirty small brachiopods, there were twenty-five. Someone had been confident that a casual glimpse in the drawers wouldn't reveal the loss of a few specimens. The brachiopods wouldn't fill anybody's bank account, but the Burgess Shale fossils were well worth the risk.

Alex paced away, too angry to continue counting. He'd spent his adult life finding and studying fossils, trying to build an image of a very different world through keyhole glimpses and guesses. Most of the people he knew did the same thing. He couldn't imagine the greed that let someone destroy that work. Not just anyone. Someone on staff, who understood the harm he or she was doing.

He flipped through the circulation log, checking who had signed specimens in and out of the storage room. He went back days, then weeks. There was no record of the brachiopods or oysters being borrowed, but three people had recently taken out Burgess Shale specimens. Diane, of course, someone called C.W. Adams from the University of Alberta, and one of the lab technicians, who had only signed her first name—Marie. Diane and Marie had signed the fossils back in the same day they looked at them. C.W. Adams, whoever he or she was, had taken several specimens to the university. Would it help to watch security tapes from the days in question? If the images were clear enough to show the actual number of specimens being removed from, and returned to, the drawers—

"What in the hell are you doing?" The voice was loud and angry.

Alex looked calmly toward the open door. "Morning, Charlie."

"What are you doing, skulking in here—"

"Skulking?"

"The lights are off, there's nobody here to see what you're up to—"

"The cameras can see."

Charlie stopped quivering at the door and stalked into the room. "There's a system here, Dr. Blake, a rather intricate cataloguing system. Until you understand it, you shouldn't be here alone. It's very easy to mess things up and then the whole thing falls apart—"

Surprised by the conservator's rudeness, Alex said mildly, "I've put everything back the way I found it."

"As far as you know." Charlie started pulling drawer handles. "Have you locked up after yourself? We have a security system in place—"

"I'm acquainted with the security system."

Something in Alex's voice caught Charlie's attention. He took a deep breath, then spoke more calmly. "Everything seems to be locked."

"I made sure of it. The board has asked me to do an inventory—"

That set Charlie off again. "Why didn't they ask me? It's my system. I don't want people in the lab when it's not open. That's asking for trouble." He tilted his head toward the door. "Ready to go?"

Bruce had warned Alex that Charlie tended to be territorial. He'd been running the lab for so long he seemed to forget it wasn't his personal property. For now, Alex was willing to keep the peace. "I'll have to continue the inventory, though, so prepare yourself for regular company."

As he stepped out of the storage room, Alex nearly bumped into a woman just outside the door. His hands reached out to steady her. He took in, at a glance, blond hair twisted into a chignon, smooth, tanned skin and curves apparent even under a lab coat.

"My fault," she said, a little breathlessly. "I was eavesdropping. What a horrible job they've given you. Can I help?"

"I appreciate the offer, but I don't want to take you from your work." Alex realized he was still steadying the woman, even though it was no longer necessary. He dropped his hands and took a step back. "I saw you at the staff meeting yesterday. I'm afraid I don't remember your name."

She held out a slender hand. "Carol Hughes. I'm a technician here in the lab."

"Would you have time for coffee this afternoon?"

She smiled. "I've got lots of time. For coffee, for a sandwich, for a few days in Bermuda."

SUSANNAH'S EYES JERKED OPEN. Bright hot midmorning sunlight filled the house. She wasn't in the loft—she was on the living room sofa bed. She lay still and sifted through jumbled impressions, trying to sort out what had happened.

Blake. Alexander Blake had happened. He'd pulled her out of the sinkhole, he'd brought her home, and he'd tucked her in. She groaned softly at the memory. Never let the competition tuck you in.

While she'd slept, Susannah's bruised shoulder had set like cement. Painfully she pulled herself up in the bed. Sand sprinkled from her hair onto the sheet when she moved. Under the bandages, scabs had formed on her palms, stiffening her hands. She edged her legs over the side of the bed and flicked off the metal clips fastening the tensor. Her ankle was vividly colored. Shades of purple, blue and red spread out like a sunrise.

"I made a mess of yesterday," she muttered to her toes. "Why did I let him get to me?" She knew how to get along with colleagues and employers, even if they were difficult. She never acted on impulse. Maybe *never* was pushing it. She rarely acted on impulse, precisely because she messed things up when she did.

Her clock radio sat on the end table, calmly beaming the time—ten-fifteen. The alarm hadn't gone off. She was more than two hours late for work, she could hardly move, and she had enough sand in her hair to bury a brontosaurus.

She saw the note first, then the water and the open bottle of pills. Thankfully, she shook two tablets into her hand and transferred them to her mouth, lips against gauze. She needed both hands to manage the glass. Even then, she nearly dropped it.

The note was next. Large sprawling letters covered the page.

Dr. Robb,

You were sound asleep before I put away your dinner tray. I took the liberty of leaving the alarm off in the belief that sleep is in your best interests. Please take some time off—let those injuries heal. I'll tell James you won't be at the quarry for a while.

Alex Blake

Susannah let the paper drop onto the bed. She would have to disappoint him. Taking time off was out of the question. She wanted to check on Matt, and she had a quarry to run. More importantly, she had to behave noticeably like a grown-up in Blake's presence.

It was nearly noon by the time she was able to get to the museum. When she stepped off the elevator on the second floor, she heard animated voices coming from Diane's office. Grasping her crutch, she made her way toward the sound.

"How about *Coprolites Incorporated?*" she heard Diane suggest. "It has an almost poetic ring."

"Nah, nobody'll know what we're about. We need something catchy and to the point, like *We Do Dinosaur Doo-Doo.*"

"That's awful, James. I want something with a little dignity."

"Who needs dignity? We're going to make our fortunes here." James broke off, looking toward the door. "Sue!" He reached her side in one giant step. "What are you doing out of bed? Look at you!"

"I'd rather you didn't. Not today."

"You look better wearing bruises and bandages than most women look wearing silk," James assured her. He kicked a basket of toys out of the way and guided her to a chair. "How'd you get here without your car? Don't tell me you hopped."

"Taxi. The driver acted like it was an international trip—all the way from town to my place, then here. I'll have to make the payments in installments. A year should do it."

Diane scooped a pile of textbooks from an extra chair and eased Susannah's foot onto it. "Shouldn't your ankle be bandaged?"

"Could you help me with it, Di? I couldn't get the tensor back on after I showered, if you can call it showering. I stood there with my hands outside the curtain like a zombie, hoping the force of the water would be enough to get the grit out of my hair. What's all this about coprolites?"

Diane took the bandage and started a couple of turns around the instep of Susannah's foot. "Sophisticated collectors are paying big bucks for the stuff."

"Really? What do people want them for? Bookends?"

"Or paperweights, maybe. Organic decor is in." The tensor, just wound, was already coming undone. Diane sighed and started over.

"So we've decided the amateur bone hunters have the right idea," James said earnestly. "Why spend all those years in university so we can make a living working with fossils when we can do better selling dung?"

"Can I join? I'd love to get rid of the last of my student loans."

"You know I'd do anything for you, Sue, but this is my pet project and my loans come first." James looked at his watch and jumped up. "Gotta go. I have a meeting with Alex."

"Is it about Matt? Wait, I'll come with you."

"Thanks, Sue, but he asked for me. If I'm not back in half an hour, come looking for me." James hurried out the door.

Susannah looked after him worriedly. "Poor James. It's not the way you hope to start out with a new boss...in the middle of your biggest screwup."

"Sounds like the voice of experience." Finally Diane fastened the end of the tensor. "There!" She sat back to admire her handiwork. "Don't ever take it off, Sue. I worked too hard to see it thrown away, as if it were nothing but a disgusting bandage."

"Agreed. It feels great." Susannah looked at Diane more closely. "You still look tired. What's up?"

"I just didn't get enough sleep last night. There's too much going on around here."

"I guess I didn't help, dragging you out to the quarry."

"You didn't drag me."

Cradling her arm, Susannah said, "I can't believe I stalked off like that. Blake must think I'm a complete idiot."

Diane shook her head. "He wasn't even annoyed when he found out you'd gone to the quarry instead of the meeting. He just accepted that you were busy. Maybe you don't have anything to worry about with him, after all." She hesitated, then added, "Actually, I thought he was a sweetheart yesterday."

"I wouldn't go that far. He seems to have mellowed, though. So I'm going to apologize, and thank him, and be my usual professional self. The next thing you know we'll be working together just like any two sensible people."

SUSANNAH KNOCKED on Alex's office door. After a moment it swung open, and he stood before her, only inches away.

"Dr. Robb," he said lightly. "You're never where I expect you to be."

Her good intentions evaporated. She forgot she'd ever had any. "Don't you mean I'm never where you've told me to be?"

He looked surprised, then cautious. "I suppose you could put it like that."

"Wouldn't it make your life easier if you just stopped telling me?"

"You might be right." His voice had cooled. "In any case, I'm glad you're feeling well enough to come to work. Would you like to sit down? It's just a suggestion. You're free to do whatever you like. I have a guest who's been worried about you."

Susannah craned her neck to look past him. Sitting on a hard chair in front of Alex's desk was Matt, happily examining a plastic triceratops model. He didn't look like someone who'd been called on the carpet, but Susannah's protective instincts flooded through her anyway. "You have a list of people to deal with today, I see. I know James was here earlier. Flexing your authoritarian muscle?"

"I was going to leave you until you were feeling better."

He was close enough that Susannah could feel his breath on her ear when he spoke. Eager to put some distance between them, she made her way to his desk and sank thankfully into a chair near Matt's.

"Have you seen this, Dr. Robb?" Matt held up the triceratops model.

"Not that particular model, but in my office I have a wooden hadrosaur skeleton that I made myself."

He nodded without much interest. "Look at this one. It's really cool. You can take the skin off to see the bones. And Dr. Blake's got a sand table where you can see how dead dinosaurs got covered up, and you can practice digging them up. Dr. Blake says the current in the river washes them downstream, and then they get caught where the river turns a corner, so that's a good place to dig.''

Dr. Blake says...? She and James had said the same thing on the first day of science camp. She looked from the sand table to Alex, lounging against his desk. Her eyes followed the long line of his body, from the sandy hair and broad shoulders to the firm stomach and casually crossed legs. Strong, tanned arms were folded across his chest, seeming to cuddle a bloodthirsty tyrannosaur that glared out of a silk-screened subtropical forest. The shirt was more appropriate for a kid like Matt than a man in his late thirties. It suited him, though.

Alex's attention was on the boy. ''Where were we?''

Matt shifted uncomfortably. ''You were talking about a...contract.'' He clearly didn't like the word. ''For me to remember the rules.''

''How far did we get?''

''I'm supposed to stay off the hills and stay with the other kids.''

''Two things to remember,'' Alex agreed. ''Tough things, but I think you can do it. Now, my part of the contract is the consequences.''

His expression mutinous, Matt stared at the floor.

''Here's the hard part. If you break the rules, I'll send you home.'' Alex waited for that to sink in. ''But the flip side is that if you follow the rules, you can earn a reward. Would you be interested in spending an afternoon in the prep lab putting together a dinosaur skeleton?''

Matt looked up. ''A real one?''

''As real as it usually gets. The technicians have been working on a triceratops—just like that model. They've made fiberglass replicas of the fossil bones. Would you like to help put them together?''

Face glowing, Matt nodded.

"Then it's a deal. We both sign the contract, and we shake on it." Together, they walked to the door. "Amy's just down the hall. She'll take you back to camp. Good luck, Matt."

Alex closed the door and turned to face Susannah.

"A contract?" she said. "Isn't that a bit cold?"

He didn't answer until he returned to his desk and sat down. "I suppose it could sound cold. My sister's a teacher and she swears by contracts. She says they help kids stay focused and grown-ups stay consistent. The stakes are too high at the quarry. Matt won't be safe there unless he remembers the rules."

Susannah nodded, thinking of the rocks on the sinkhole floor. "I'm concerned about your offer to take him into the lab."

"Oh?"

"We've all learned what he's like. There are tools and chemicals he could get into, and specimens he could break."

"I'll keep an eye on him."

Alex's attitude was frustrating but not unexpected. "Despite that disagreement, I appreciate the way you handled Matt. It's easy to get mad at him. Your approach gives him a chance to learn."

"I know the type—from experience."

"Do you have kids?" She hadn't noticed any family pictures around the office, but that didn't mean there wasn't a family.

He shook his head. "I was a lot like Matt—full of energy and enthusiasm. Rules were mere speed bumps. They just slowed me down a little as I ran over them."

Susannah didn't have any trouble believing that. "You probably climbed a few hoodoos in your time, too."

"I couldn't find any in North Vancouver, or I would have. There were other things to do, though, like jump into rivers from canyon walls."

She stared at him. "Lynn Canyon, you mean? But people die doing that."

He nodded. "That's what my parents kept saying."

"But it's illegal, isn't it?"

"They said that, too."

She tried not to smile. "You're telling me you were bad."

"I was never bad. I just liked having fun."

The conversation had strayed far from the direction Susannah had intended to take it. "I came here to apologize—"

"For the meeting? You already have. And I've accepted."

"All right." He was making it too easy. "I wanted to thank you again for helping me yesterday. Taking me to the hospital and home, fixing dinner. The pills, too, and leaving the bottle open…" She paused, then continued with a trace of embarrassment. "And I saw this morning that you cleaned up after me…the sand, and the clothes. I'm really very grateful."

"But?"

"But…I'd prefer a more professional relationship. I'd like you to stop deciding what I need when I haven't asked for help. I didn't want to sleep in today, and I don't need to take time off."

Alex gave a brisk nod. "You're right. We met in a strange way. I guess the sense of emergency blurred the usual boundaries."

"The situation with Matt…"

"Yes?"

"Nothing like that has ever happened before. I take full responsibility."

"So did James."

"I knew what Matt was like. I should have arranged to have him partnered with an adult."

"That's a good idea. You don't have to rake yourself over the coals about this, Dr. Robb. Accidents happen. James will step up supervision at the quarry, and the contract should help."

"Good. That's settled, then." She smiled uneasily. It was hard to reestablish control when he was so reasonable.

"There's one other thing," Alex said. "The next time you go out to the quarry—I understand it'll be a while before you're up to the rigors of that kind of day—I want to go along. Since you weren't able to meet with me yesterday, and I don't have your report, I'm not familiar with your project. You can walk me through it."

Susannah's neck stiffened. It was a reasonable request from the head of dinosaur research, but she'd seen his sense of ownership in Australia. "Do you plan to visit all the current projects?"

"Eventually."

"You want to put your stamp on all the work?"

Alex looked puzzled, then a little angry. "That's an odd thing to say. Is there something more going on here than you told me last night? You're not just miffed about the job. Is it something about me in particular you distrust, or are you just paranoid?"

Paranoid? How many judgments did he intend on throwing around? "It's something about you, Dr. Blake."

"I see. I put your hostility yesterday down to shock. Is that still the problem?" When Susannah didn't reply, he continued, "I can take a certain amount of unpleasantness, but you're part of a team. This kind of behavior could sabotage the museum's work if it goes on too long. Care to have it out?''

That would be some conversation—make that some outburst. ''There's nothing to have out.''

''Then I suggest you hold your bitterness toward me in check. I wouldn't want it to be a barrier to the museum's functioning.''

It was a threat. How on earth had she gone from being Bruce's anointed successor to being seen as an expendable liability?

She stood up, as straight as she could. ''I'm not confident that you have this museum's best interests at heart, Dr. Blake. If you don't, you can expect a lot more than a few hostile words from me. It's really up to you how well the museum functions.'' She wished she could stalk out of his office, but lopsided hopping was the best she could do.

More than anything Susannah wanted to go home, but she was determined not to leave before closing. Or later. She was up to the rigors of her job, whether it was lying in the sand with a chisel or sitting at a desk with a keyboard.

Slowly and painfully, she made her way to the preparation lab. She detoured around a crowd of visitors pressed shoulder to shoulder at the observation window. Another group was inside the lab, being shepherded around by a public education staffer. Charlie wouldn't be happy. He didn't like sight-seers taking up elbow room, getting perilously close to the fossils under his care.

As she searched the long rows of metal shelves for specimens from the quarry, she couldn't help overhearing a snippet of conversation between Marie and Carol, lab technicians who had been at the museum nearly as long as Susannah.

"Did you notice his eyes?"

"Mmm. So blue—so kind and amused."

"He's got all that muscle and intensity of purpose and he just gleams with intelligence. I never could resist a brainy guy with a tan."

Marie raised her voice. "I hear Dr. Blake pulled you out of a sinkhole, Susannah. That must have made your day! Those strong arms wrapped around you. That broad, muscled chest—"

And that broad, muscled ego. "I'm afraid it was wasted on me. All I noticed was light and fresh air."

"Too bad." With pitying expressions barely hidden, the women pulled on their gear—gloves, masks, earplugs and goggles. Carol bent over a large chunk of rock. A quiet roar filled the air as she turned on a power drill.

"Susannah!" Charlie made his way through the rows of worktables toward her. They moved away from the noise. "You don't look much the worse for wear. Adventure must agree with you."

She gestured at the storage shelves. "I'm looking for my stuff."

He indicated one of the tables. "We've just unpacked the most recent specimens. Cretaceous flotsam and jetsam, most likely."

"I thought we crated some great specimens."

"At this point you've had a better look at them than I have," he admitted. "We'll see, once we get the plaster off and the rest of the rock chipped away."

"Is my skull ready yet?"

"Carol's been working on it. It should be ready sometime next week, I think. Unless Dr. Blake has lost it."

Susannah smiled at Charlie's aggrieved tone. "How would he have done that?"

"You can smile, but I'm serious. I found him in the storage room early this morning. He claimed to be doing an inventory. He left quite a mess."

"That's odd." Whatever she thought of him, she had trouble believing Alex would be careless with specimens. On the other hand, it hadn't bothered him at all to drive through the gully, probably crunching fossils as he went. Only half-joking, she asked, "My skull's still there, isn't it?"

"It's there." Charlie gave a sheepish shrug. "I'm exaggerating."

"Is it holding together all right?"

"So far, so good. It's fragile in places. You're lucky it got safely past your herd of dinosaur fanatics. How can you stand having all those kids milling around?"

"They slow down the work a bit, but they're lots of fun. They think we're an exciting bunch, you know."

"Naive little things."

"I don't mean to rush you with the skull. It would be awful if it broke—I'm beginning to think we might find a complete skeleton. That doesn't happen all that often."

Charlie smiled reassuringly. "We'll be extra careful."

THAT EVENING, Charlie drove Susannah home. "You going to do this to yourself again tomorrow?"

"I don't think I can." She was throbbing from head to foot. "I'll probably have to take some time off, like it or not. I hate to look weak in front of Blake, though."

"To tell you the truth, Sue, you don't come across as all that strong, wobbling around covered with bandages, looking like you're going to cry."

She glanced at Charlie, hoping he was teasing. "Is it that bad?"

He nodded.

"Shoot. I started today intending to make a good impression on Blake."

"You don't have anything to prove, Susannah." He pulled into the driveway, getting as close to the door as he could. "Maybe I should sprain my ankle so I can avoid him, too."

"You're still annoyed about the inventory?"

"Not just that." Charlie put the truck in park. "He's got half the women in the lab mooning over him. He and Carol were making eyes at each other this morning and then they disappeared for most of the afternoon. It was supposed to be a coffee break. I can't have him disrupting work like that."

"Are you going to speak to him?"

"I'd better give everyone a chance to settle down first, and get to know the guy, before I confront him about his behavior." Charlie looked as if he regretted being so sensible. "The welcoming party will be bad enough without that added tension."

"Welcoming party?"

"You haven't heard? It's Thursday night, at Diane's. Personally, I think they should wait a couple of weeks, until they're sure there's actually something to celebrate."

Susannah had to lean her weight against the passenger-side door to get it open. "Thanks for the ride, Charlie."

"Consider me your chauffeur for the duration." He reversed to turn the truck around, then rumbled out to the road.

For hours Susannah had longed to get home, but now that she was finally here she found that it wasn't as peaceful a haven as usual. Alex's presence seemed to linger everywhere. Last night, he'd moved quietly and confidently throughout the house, showing an unexpected kindness and domesticity. Twelve hours after straining the noodles from her soup, he'd threatened her job.

That wasn't so surprising. He had always tended to sharpness—pointed questions, sudden decisions, quick movements. She hadn't handled it very well in Australia and her university record had suffered for it. *Must learn to be more assertive if she is to survive in this field.* The apparently mild criticism had confirmed what a lot of the professors already thought, that a woman couldn't make it in paleontology. She'd spent a couple of years convincing them it wasn't true.

Keeping Blake's fingerprints off her work could be a problem. Whether it was intentional or in spite of himself, he became the focus of every job he touched. Would one visit to her quarry be the end of it? Maybe she would open *Canadian Geographic* one day to find a *Boy's Adventure*-style feature by Alexander Blake, Ph.D., starring Alexander Blake, Ph.D.

One-handed, Susannah prepared for bed. Pulling the sleeve over her left arm first, she struggled into her nightgown. It was robin's-egg blue, her favorite color ever since, years ago, the man she'd almost married had told her she looked beautiful wearing it.

It had been a departure for Craig, to actually look at a woman and notice her coloring and what she was wearing. They had gone to a concert in the park—a rare outing from the lab—and she had worn a robin's-egg blue sweater. It was fall, and they'd held hands and walked through crisp red and yellow and brown leaves, listening to the music. She had been delighted with the compliment—delighted with herself for looking beautiful in such a feminine shade, and delighted with him for telling her she did.

Soft light slanted from the west, bringing a pink tinge to the sandstone and accentuating the darker mudstone and coal layers of the hills. Soon mule deer or pronghorn would make their way to the river behind the house for a cool drink before dark. Susannah said good-night to the silent luminous beauties drifting in the aquarium and went to bed, conscious of an aching emptiness drifting inside her.

CHAPTER FIVE

ANOTHER OYSTER.

It wasn't that he didn't like oysters. Raw in the shell, smoked, wrapped in bacon—oysters were great. But he'd been digging for three hours in what used to be the bottom of the Bearpaw Sea, helping George Connery's team look for marine reptiles, and he'd found nothing but oysters. Kim Johnson was working a few yards away, and from her quiet sounds of disgust, Alex figured she was having the same results.

He peered at the section of dark shale he'd uncovered. In one corner, he saw a small raised area that might indicate a fossil just beneath the surface. His heart started to beat harder. It always did at moments like this, but the way the Bearpaw quarry was going, it should know better. Carefully he removed more of the layered shale, tapping his chisel with his rock hammer. A moment later, he heaved a sigh and sat back, giving his knees a rest.

Kim looked up from her digging. "Is the work not going very well, Dr. Blake?"

"If you want mollusks, it's going great."

"It's been like this the whole season." She flopped to the ground and sat with her legs stretched out in front of her. "There's a good shale base here. We know it was part of the sea floor. A couple of years ago George found a beautiful twelve-meter plesiosaur close by, but since then, there's been nothing. Nothing useful, anyway."

"That makes for a long, hot summer."

If Alex hoped to learn more about Kim by working at her side, he hadn't accomplished much yet. When she spoke she was pleasant, but she was quiet most of the time. Before quitting his job and the investigation, Bruce had gathered information about most of the people on staff, but he'd concentrated on year-round employees. Alex only knew that she was a geology student on summer field experience, and that she took more precautions against the sun than anyone he'd ever met, wearing long sleeves, long pants, sunglasses and a Foreign Legion-style hat with a flap that protected the back of her neck.

"It's been difficult," she agreed. "I won't have much to report to my prof when I get back to school." She pulled a tube of sunscreen out of her pocket and began rubbing the lotion into the few centimeters of skin her long sleeves and pants left exposed. "I'm afraid it's going to affect my grade, and if that happens, I might not qualify for all the courses I need. Then I'll have trouble getting a good field experience next summer."

The sun was getting in Alex's eyes. Rather than move, he pulled his peaked cap lower. "That's the snowball scenario. You've got to avoid that kind of thinking." Alex had never been prone to it himself, unless he counted his tendency to get more and more intense about experiences that got better and better. He'd been lucky every step of the way. Lots of friends, though, had been afraid their careers would crash and burn before they'd even started, every time the smallest thing went wrong.

"At this stage, it doesn't really matter what you find," he told Kim. "It's your technique that matters, and whether you know how to observe and record what's happening—or not happening—at the quarry. From what I can see, you do that very well."

"That's reassuring. I hope you're right." Her tired smile and look of gratitude made her seem very young, too young for the difficult work she was doing.

Her eyes moved, focusing on something past Alex's shoulder, and her expression changed. Pleasure, Alex thought, and something else—uncertainty or apprehension.

George's senior field technician was coming toward them, water bottles in hand. Paul Robbins. From the little Alex had observed, he seemed like a decent guy, and good-looking enough that he could understand the pleasure on Kim's face. Why the uncertainty, though? Unrequited attraction, one way or the other? Tension about the division of black-market profits? Disagreements about ultraviolet light? Paul seemed to dare the sun to do him damage. He wore a T-shirt and shorts, no hat. His skin was acorn-brown, his hair sun-bleached.

He came to a stop near Kim's outstretched feet. Trying, without much luck, to look stern, he asked, "Is this an authorized rest?"

"We rebelled," Kim said. George had been working as if his life depended on it, barely looking up from the ground all morning, and the rest of the team had followed his lead.

Paul handed Kim one of the bottles he was carrying. "I wish you'd keep some water with you. You're too small to stand any dehydration."

"I can go to the supply tent when I'm thirsty."

"But you don't. You shouldn't try to tough it out." He tossed a bottle to Alex.

"Thanks." Alex held the cool plastic to his forehead before unscrewing the lid and tipping his head back to drink.

Careful to keep away from exposed shale, Paul sat near

Kim. "George is in a state. I'm thinking we should rebury that plesiosaur from the museum, let him find it again."

"As wasted as he is, he probably wouldn't notice the difference. The baby's getting to him more than the quarry. George says she's a night owl. He's hardly slept since she was born."

"Maybe we should give him a hand. Stay at his house for the weekend, absolutely self-serve, no trouble at all. Play peekaboo or Monopoly all night, or whatever it is that six-month-olds like to do."

Kim gave Paul a small push with her foot. "Brilliant. Let's do that."

It was like watching kids in high school. They didn't try to exclude Alex, or make him uncomfortable, but he was clearly the older man on the outside as far as they were concerned.

"I didn't know about the baby," he said. "No wonder George is struggling."

Kim and Paul stopped smiling at each other and stared at Alex.

"George is doing fine." Kim sounded a bit indignant.

"You can see how hard he works," Paul said. "He's the best."

Alex had hoped to net more detail than that, maybe a declaration that George habitually worked until last light, even if he had to do it alone. A confident statement that he was usually seen caring for the baby in the evening would have been just as good.

Paul added, "We all work long hours during the summer, especially if we've actually found something to excavate. I have to admit we've been knocking off a little early lately, and trailing in a little late."

"Morale's at an all-time low," Kim agreed. She

glanced Paul's way. "Nothing to show for all this sunburn."

Paul banged a fist on his bare leg. "I've got it!"

Kim smiled. "What have you got?"

"The solution! We can turn the quarry into an overnight success. All we have to do is change our objectives." Paul pressed his thumb and index finger together and moved them back and forth on his leg. "Erase *Study marine reptiles and their environment,* and pencil in *Study oysters.*"

He leapt up, not bothering to brush the dirt from his shorts. "In case George doesn't agree with that idea, I'm going to look for a more promising site." He scanned the horizon. "Southeast. I sense mosasaur." Squinting into the sun, he headed off.

Still smiling faintly, Kim watched him go. "Paul is the only good thing about this quarry lately. He keeps our spirits up. Last week he even made George laugh."

"How'd he manage that?" Alex could see that the memory still amused her.

"He'd been digging away for a while, and he'd cleared a small rectangle, all very precise and neatly layered...then we saw him jumping around, grabbing the camera, getting pictures. So, of course, we all came running."

Kim paused, letting Alex's curiosity grow. "He'd excavated all these little tins of seafood—oysters, clams, mussels, snails, sardines. It was silly, but it broke the tension. George even sketched the tins on the grid map. We had a picnic."

"Sounds like an awful picnic."

"It was. Totally awful. The smell, the taste, even the thought of it. But it was a good day." She got up, rearranging the flap hanging down from the back of her hat.

"Paul's right. We won't get anywhere with this site, not if we dig all year. I think I'll just walk this afternoon, cover as much ground as I can. I'll see you at the party tomorrow night, Dr. Blake, if I don't get back here before you leave."

Alex took a long drink, then splashed some water over his face and neck. So, George had a new baby and was under significant stress. He was feeling pressure to succeed, enough that his assistant was joking about faking success. Did that add up to anything besides the need for an extended holiday?

According to the personnel file Bruce had written, George had the usual debts: remnants of student loans, a mortgage, a bank loan for a sport utility vehicle. Bruce hadn't mentioned the baby—a lifelong source of expenses. Did offspring make poaching more or less likely? You'd have to weigh the risk of fines and jail time away from your family against the benefit of a nearly bottomless education savings plan.

Alex didn't have much confidence in his ability to turn up clues through conversation, but he decided to give it a try anyway. He found George slouched on a crate in the supply tent, hands hanging between his knees. There was nowhere else to sit, so Alex leaned against a stack of crates. He pulled back when they moved under his weight. They were empty, waiting for specimens.

"Moping?"

George managed a small smile. "Never! Well...maybe a little." Right away, he backed away from the admission. "You know how it is. If we let the disappointments get us down in this business, we'd be moping all the time. Tomorrow could be the day."

"I hope so. I hear you have a new baby in the family. Six months old?"

With a resigned nod, George said, "She's at her best around three in the morning. Lisa and I take it in shifts, but we still can't keep up with her."

"Sounds tough. How's your team working out this year? Is there anyone you want to be sure to get back next summer?" Alex smiled. "Or sure not to get back?"

George didn't seem ready to think about next season. "Everybody's great. Paul's with me all year. He makes the staffing arrangements. He still has contacts at the university, even though he dropped out, so he's always got a line on which students are most interested in marine reptiles."

"Paul dropped out of school?"

"Not really. He has his master's. I think the expense got to be too much for him. You can have a good career without a doctorate, though."

If you didn't mind being someone's assistant all your life. "I'm surprised you're not finding any marine vertebrates. The location seems right. It's not like they can swim away."

George's look of distress deepened. "Maybe the area's more eroded than I realized. Specimens could have been lost that way. It doesn't take long once they're exposed."

Alex couldn't help feeling concerned about George. He really looked like a wreck. "Be sure to take some time off if you need it. There's no rush to find another plesiosaur." Unless, of course, you've promised one to a customer who just won't wait.

George seemed to take Alex's concern as a challenge. "I'll take time off when the snow falls. Not before." Looking grim, he picked up his tools and headed outside. Alex followed.

The three members of the team still at the site were removing another layer of shale, deepening the rectangular quarry about an inch at a time. They dug with all the ambition of moping kids scuffing their shoes in the dirt. Even unsuccessful quarries usually had a bit of life to them, a sense of optimism.

Was this a dummy quarry? Maybe the real work was going on somewhere else, with a shadow team, and someone was making sure this group didn't get anywhere near any important discoveries. Or maybe he was watching exhausted poachers putting in time, making it look good.

Alex started walking, the slow, heads-down walk familiar to any bone hunter. About four kilometers from the current site, hidden by a hill, he found what he was looking for—an area about fifteen meters by five meters, refilled and packed down, but still apparent. Big enough to have housed a plesiosaur, or a mosasaur. The ground around it was scuffed, as if someone had tried to hide footprints or tire tracks.

Damn.

There was always a chance it wasn't someone on staff. It could be an independent prospector.

But an independent prospector working this close to the quarry, unnoticed? Not likely.

SUSANNAH HAD ELEVATED her foot on the coffee table and tucked an ice pack under her shoulder sling. The enforced rest gave her a chance to focus on her article for the *Journal of the International Society of Paleontology*. It was her first piece for the respected journal, and some unexpected anxiety was slowing her progress. When the doorbell rang, she set aside the outline and, grasping her crutch, hobbled to the door.

"Diane! And Tim—it's great to see you, kid. Come in."

Diane's hands were full. "I've brought you a couple of

frozen dinners, a cooked chicken and the first ripe tomato from my garden."

"Thanks, Di. That's so thoughtful."

"I was afraid if you tried to do any one-armed cooking, you'd end up with more injuries." Diane went straight through to the kitchen to put the food away. Her head in the fridge, she asked, "Do you want a glass of this ginger ale?"

"It's probably flat, but sure."

Tim had tucked his hands behind his back. "I've got something for you, too."

Susannah sat at the pine table in the dining area. "Do I close my eyes and open my mouth?"

He grinned. "It wouldn't taste very good." He handed Susannah an already crumpled get-well card. This time his drawing showed her wrapped in plaster from head to foot, with the corners of her mouth turned down.

"It's beautiful, Tim. You've caught my mood exactly." She stood the card up in the middle of the table and pulled him close for a hug.

He patted her uninjured shoulder. "Are you going to feel better soon?"

"I feel a little better every day. Soon we'll be able to go swimming again. Would you like a cold drink?"

He shook his head. "Can I play computer games?"

"Sure. I installed Space Raiders for you."

"Thanks, Auntie Sue." Tim made it up the stairs to the computer nook in record time.

"That's the last we'll see of him for a while." Diane carried two condensation-clouded glasses to the table. "Not exactly quality time before school starts. I intended to be a perfect mother, you know."

"I remember."

"I just don't have the energy for leaf rubbings and puppet shows right now."

"Tim's happy and kind and curious, and he knows you love him. I don't see how you can improve on that." Susannah sipped the barely bubbling ginger ale, and looked at her friend with concern. The circles under her eyes were deeper and darker than they'd been two days ago. "Haven't you caught up on your sleep yet?"

"I'm fine." Diane sat straighter, as if she hoped to prove it. "Is the rest today doing you any good?"

"Some." It was obvious that Diane wasn't fine. It wasn't just the circles. Her whole body drooped. She didn't like being pushed, though, so Susannah decided to leave it alone. "It's a relief to stay off my ankle. I've been trying to do my journal article."

"Trying?"

"I can't think clearly. If I muff this, no one will take me seriously."

"You won't muff it."

"I don't know." Susannah shook her head in frustration. "Do you remember what it was like after Blake's evaluation? I had to work twice as hard to prove I could do the job. Now he's back in my life, and I feel like I have to prove myself all over again."

"That's just because you've got aches and pains," Diane said. "You have years of experience under your belt now, and you specialize in a different area than Alex does. I bet you could teach him a lot about herbivores."

"He threatened my job yesterday—"

"Are you serious?"

Susannah nodded grimly. "He seems to think the museum might be better off without me." She added, "I was being a bit hard to get along with at the time."

"He was just sounding off, then." Diane took a few

steps away from the dining area so she could see into the computer nook. "How are you doing up there?"

"Great! I've got three amulets already."

"Way to go." She returned to the table and sat quietly, moving her glass in little circles, watching the swirling liquid inside. Without looking up, she said, "I suppose you've guessed that something's worrying me."

"It seemed like something might be," Susannah agreed. "Can I help?"

"I don't think so." Glancing at the loft, Diane lowered her voice. "I've lost track of some specimens."

"Oh, Di." No wonder she couldn't sleep. "You've done all the obvious checking?"

"Ten times over."

"Are they missing from the quarry, or the lab?"

"The lab—unless the original cataloguing was wrong. I don't think so, though. My own records would have to be wrong, too. The labels on the drawers say how many of each specimen there should be, and they're not all there."

"What's missing?"

"Four Marella, two Hallucigenia and an Opabinia. I checked the circulation log. Anything I took out, I signed back in. I thought maybe I lent them to somebody and just forgot, but I would have made a note of that."

"Of course you would. Have you checked with Charlie?"

Diane shook her head. "He's such a stickler for procedure. I don't want to get that disgusted look from him. I was hoping I'd find them and no one would have to know. How could I have been so careless? I should be locked up."

"You don't even know for sure you're the one who

misplaced them. Lots of people besides you work with the specimens. You'll have to tell Charlie.''

"And Alex."

Susannah nodded. She thought about Alex's calm response to the news that she'd skipped his meeting because she wanted to avoid him, and about the gentle way he dealt with Matt after the boy ignored every rule of the science camp. "I'm not an expert in figuring out Blake's behavior—he's completely confusing and contradictory—but I think he'll be reasonable about this."

"I guess I'll face them both tomorrow." Looking a little uncomfortable, Diane said, "You might not be pleased to hear I'm having a party for Alex tomorrow night."

"Charlie told me."

"Everybody wants to welcome him," Diane explained. "James invited him to join their nightly campfire anytime he wants. Marie baked cookies for him, and Charlie says Carol can't stop batting her lashes long enough to look through a microscope—"

"That's no surprise. He'll probably have women coming out his ears before the week's out."

Diane managed a smile. "I'm sorry you and he have got off to a bad start. Things are bound to get better. Give him a chance, Sue."

"To do what? Fire me?"

"He's not going to fire you. I think you two just rub each other the wrong way. You're both a little headstrong. Maybe it's not surprising that you provoke each other."

Susannah tried not to dismiss the idea outright. "We act on each other, you mean. We're mutual irritants. We cause redness and rash and discomfort in each other. So my first instinct was a good one. Avoid the allergen."

"Or you could administer controlled doses of the offending substance until you're desensitized."

Susannah nearly laughed. "It's worth a try. I'll limit my contact with him. If there's still irritation, I'll just leave it alone—"

"That's right. No scratching."

"Eventually we'll adjust to each other. Working together will be no different from working with James or Charlie."

ALEX PRESSED the play button on his answering machine.

"Hi, it's Carol. I hoped I'd see you this morning. That was fun last night. I never had such a nice old-fashioned date. Dinner, a movie, walking home in the moonlight…right down to the chaste kiss at the door. But how about we fast-forward tomorrow night, after the party? Let me know."

Alex smiled. Carol's voice was warm and pleasantly flirtatious. Five years ago he would have called right back and asked what was wrong with tonight. Even now, he found he wanted to erase concepts like *old-fashioned* and *chaste* from her mind.

Her suggestion wasn't a surprise. He'd got the feeling she'd be glad to skip all the preliminaries of getting to know each other. It was tempting—no conflict, no strings, no expectations—but he didn't want to rush into anything intense right now. He should at least wait until she was off his list of suspects.

He moved on to the next message. It was from a friend who almost never left the field. Once a fossil was out of the ground, Riley didn't care what happened to it.

"I finally tracked you down! Chief of Dinosaur Research? Couldn't believe it when I heard, buddy. Do you need an intervention? I can have the guys there in two days! Or is there a female in the picture?

"Listen, we've been invited back to the Gobi Desert. The Science Academy in Mongolia is getting together an international team. I'm arranging everything. We leave in October. I know it's short notice. Tell me you're not going to let a desk job stop you from joining us. I'll give you the number…"

Alex thought of the dust and wind and heat and flies, of sand in his food and in his eyes and clogging the air intake of his truck. He'd expected it to be years before he got another opportunity to work in the Gobi Desert. Some of the richest fossil sites in the world were there—he'd give anything to go back. What were the chances he'd solve the case of the missing specimens by October? Maybe he could join the team late.

He poured a tin of spaghetti into a pot and left it on simmer. Before he got back to work, he needed a cool shower to rinse off the day's grime and bring down his body temperature.

He peeled off his T-shirt and socks and kicked his way out of his jeans and boxers. It was a few minutes before the water pressure built up enough so that more than a trickle came from the nozzle. Standing under the shower's spray, he worked up a good lather of soap in his hands and rubbed it briskly all over his body. Sand had got into his ears and somehow had found its way through his boots and socks to lodge between his toes.

His mind returned to the excavation site he'd found that afternoon. He didn't have any doubt a fossil had been stolen. Nothing big enough to come from that quarry had arrived at the museum from the Bearpaw Formation in the past two years, and the ground he'd seen today had been disturbed in the past couple of weeks. The board would have no reason to avoid calling in the police now.

He turned off the taps and stepped onto a towel. After rubbing the excess water from his hair and body, he strode naked into the bedroom, enjoying the cooling effect of air currents on his still-damp body. The few clothes he'd brought were in his duffel bag. He pulled on some clean boxers and jeans.

A bowl of spaghetti in one hand, he slipped a video-cassette into his brand-new VCR. When he pushed the play button, grainy, black-and-white images appeared on the TV screen. Small white letters in the bottom left-hand corner said it was 0800 hours, the fifth of June.

There was Charlie, recording something in the circulation log and lovingly putting some small specimens to bed. Alex turned to the log and looked up June 5. Charlie's precise printing informed him that some insect-bearing amber had been returned to its drawer. The next time Charlie appeared, he let himself into the locked mesh area where the largest fossils were stored. He slowly walked up and down the rows of shelves, apparently just checking specimens. After nearly half an hour, he left the room again.

Alex opened Charlie's personnel file. According to Bruce, Charlie was single and had no apparent debts—he had inherited a small house in town from his parents. He could be difficult. He was suspicious of new people, new ideas and new technology—all common in his line of work—but he tended the museum's fossils as if they were newborn babies. He didn't travel much. When he did, there was no apparent contact with fossil markets or geological fairs, where fossils were often sold.

Lifting the bowl of spaghetti closer to his chin, Alex brought a forkful of the pale, limp strands of pasta to his mouth and slurped them down. He was on his second helping when Susannah Robb appeared on the screen, opening a drawer near the Burgess Shale samples. He checked the date—June 25—and flipped through the circulation log until he found the right page. Her signature wasn't there.

She picked up a specimen, examined it, returned it to the drawer, then picked up another sample. Fossilized eggs, he thought. They'd fit in her blanket drawer without any trouble. She didn't take anything out of the room, though. She shut the drawer and locked it. Why had she bothered looking at them so briefly?

He checked the file Bruce had prepared. Dr. Robb was educated at the University of Calgary and McGill. She volunteered at local schools, and Girl Guide and Scout troops teaching kids about rocks and fossils. Debts—student loans and mortgage. Recent travel—UBC archeology department, the Royal Ontario Museum, The Field Museum in Chicago. With pencil, he added, ''Assortment of fossils observed at her residence. Source?''

So far, she'd been fairly hostile toward him. Her unscheduled trip to her quarry on Monday had let him, and everyone else, know she didn't plan to support the new boss. Had getting the job meant that much to her, or had she valued certain advantages that would have come with it? Being head of dinosaur research would clear a lot of obstacles from her path if she really were involved in fossil smuggling. He thought of those dark gray eyes, so serious and so angry. Had his arrival interfered with some master plan?

Everyone who worked at the museum was in and out of the storage room regularly. Charlie and the lab techs were the most frequent visitors. Bruce and Susannah usually went inside the locked mesh area, looking at large carnivore or herbivore fossils. George, Paul and Diane frequented the drawers of small fossils. So did Lynn Seton and Jeff McLean. She worked with fossil pollens; he studied ancient birds. They'd both left for their quarries right after Monday's meeting. They weren't expected back until fall.

Spaghetti forgotten, Alex sat forward, watching the television screen closely. The Bearpaw Formation and Burgess Shale drawers were side-by-side. When George or Diane opened one, he assumed they were looking at their own specimens, but he couldn't tell for sure which drawer either of them opened. His brain just supplied the information that made the most sense. What if someone performed some sleight of hand, in spite of the cameras? Could you sign out oysters and later appear to sign them in, while all the time you'd really removed a few Marella?

Alex sat back, rubbing his eyes. The board seemed to think he could figure out quickly whether the discrepancies Bruce had noticed were because of honest mistakes or stealing. He couldn't begin to estimate how long it would take to view all the security tapes. The inventory would take weeks. That was without visiting quarries, without checking computer files or researching fossil markets. So far, the board had refused his request for help.

He'd confirmed the inconsistencies Bruce Simpson had noticed. He'd visited the Bearpaw Formation quarry and found evidence of poaching. He hoped to get to the Burgess Shale quarry in a couple of weeks. The hadrosaur quarry would have to wait until Susannah Robb recovered enough to go back to work.

CHAPTER SIX

ALEX STOOD IN THE SHADE of a cottonwood that spread graceful branches over most of the McKays' front yard. Before the sound of the doorbell died away, a freshly scrubbed little boy in short-sleeved pajamas opened the door. Diane was right behind him.

"Alex! Welcome! Did you have any trouble finding the place?"

"None at all. That cottonwood is like a beacon." He smiled and, when he met the boy's gaze, his smile widened.

"This is my son, Tim."

Alex extended his hand. "I'm glad to meet you, Tim. I've been working with your mom at the museum this week." He was startled when the boy hid his face against his mother's leg. Had he been judged? Found wanting?

"It's admiration, Alex...the *National Geographic* cave explorer, life-size and breathing, right in front of us. Come in, please." When Diane moved away from the door, Tim slipped behind her but kept an eye on their guest.

Alex held out a bouquet of freesias. "I hope they haven't been out of water too long."

Diane lifted the flowers to her nose. It was good to see her face relax, even for that moment. When she'd come to him earlier in the day to report the missing fossils he already knew about, she'd looked so guilty and distressed, he'd dismissed any idea that she could be involved in their disappearance. No one was that good an actor.

"Thank you, they're beautiful," she said. "Come into the kitchen. I'll find a vase."

Alex followed Diane down the hall and around the corner into a large kitchen in which every surface was covered with food in various stages of preparation. She pushed aside a pile of fresh vegetables so she could put the freesias down near the sink. She seemed comfortable with the mess—she didn't ask him to excuse it, anyway.

Quiet amid mounds of food, Susannah Robb sat at the table, her left arm still in its sling. Alex was surprised how glad he was to see her. Not that her presence meant she was there to welcome him. In fact, she seemed to be making a point of ignoring him, giving far too much attention to forming perfect rows on a baking sheet of something threaded on toothpicks. When she looked up and saw him watching her, he smiled. She managed a nod in response. Not exactly friendly, but not a lacerating blow, either.

"Feeling any better today, Dr. Robb?"

"Much, thanks. Ice packs and four-hourly painkillers are very effective."

"Have you heard how Matt's doing at the quarry? Not sword fighting with femurs, I hope?"

She gave a flicker of a smile. "James called this afternoon, while the kids were resting. He says Matt's got a notebook, and he's keeping track of the two things he promised to do."

"Good for him. It'll be interesting to see how long he can keep it up."

A steady, muffled hubbub came from the backyard. Alex turned to Diane, still rummaging in the cupboards. "The party's out back?"

"Most people have gone out. I think George is brooding somewhere, and Lisa keeps coming in to check with the baby-sitter. It's their first evening out since their baby was born, and it looks like they might not make it till dinner. James and all the camp counselors are staying with the kids—they didn't want to be short-staffed after what happened on Monday." Diane found the vase at last and turned on the tap to fill it with water. "Kim and Paul aren't here yet, but I'm sure they won't be much longer...I guess you didn't meet them on Monday."

"I worked with them yesterday."

"Mosasaurs," Diane said dismissively. "Wait till you come to Mount Field." She turned off the tap and looked at Alex. "Is it too soon to hope you got anywhere tracing those specimens?"

Alex glanced at Susannah.

"Susannah knows."

He wished he had some good news for her. "This afternoon I double-checked all the places you'd already checked, and of course, there wasn't any sign of them. Charlie's on the trail, too. Don't get discouraged yet."

Diane's smile looked tired and not very hopeful.

"I noticed in the circulation log that someone by the name of Adams signed out some of your stuff. C.W. Adams."

She nodded. "Chris. He's a lecturer at the university. He borrowed some specimens for one of his classes. They often do. They keep them under lock and key, except while students are actually looking at them."

"You checked with him?"

"He said he took one of each specimen, except for the Hallucigenia and the Opabinia, since they're so rare." Diane turned back to the freesias. "I guess I should recut the stems. I'm so out of practice with flowers."

"I'll give you a hand." Alex reached for half the flowers, found a knife and began cutting.

"Diagonally, Alex."

"Sorry." He recut the stems he'd trimmed straight across. "What do I know? No one has ever given me flowers."

"Wait till you're a dad. You'll get dandelions all the time." She smiled at Tim.

The boy was still watching Alex closely. After handing the bunch of flowers he'd trimmed to Diane, Alex folded his arms, leaned against the kitchen counter and stared back. "So," he said, after a few moments, "is this a staring contest?"

Tim shook his head from side to side.

"No? Are you so scared of me you can't talk?"

Tim shook his head again.

"What could it be, then? Has an alien put a force field around your tongue?"

Struggling to keep his mouth straight, Tim nodded.

"Oh-oh. They're always doing that. Somebody should complain. Hang on a sec, Tim. I'll take care of it."

Alex scanned the kitchen for a likely looking utensil, something with buttons or switches. He spotted a hand-held electric mixer. Pointing it at Tim, he pressed the blade eject button and pushed the on switch back and forth between the three speed levels.

"Fortunately, they've just got you in a Level Two titanium-based force field with two-millisecond power bursts. I'll modulate the atomic structure of the titanium long enough to generate a barrier to its energy flow—there! Speech should be restored momentarily."

He turned to Diane. "I don't expect any lingering ill effects, but take him to sick bay if you suspect a problem."

She smiled, obviously pleased that he was willing to play with her son. He was happy to see amusement on Susannah's face as well.

Finally Tim spoke. "I bet you'd like my space game—"

"Hey, you're cured!"

"You want to play it?"

Diane intervened. "Dr. Blake wants to talk to the other grown-ups, Tim."

"I can talk to them anytime. I hardly ever get to play space games. Lead the way!"

"Just for a few minutes, Tim," Diane said to their departing backs. "It's your bedtime."

In the hall, Tim said confidingly, "She doesn't mean that."

"You don't think so? It sounded like she meant it."

"We can play till it's dark."

"Then it's lights out?"

"Nope. Then it's stories."

"And then it's lights out?"

"Then it's me hiding under the covers and Mom finding me."

"Do you *ever* go to sleep?"

Tim nodded. "After she brings my water and we rub noses." They had arrived in a small room with a computer, a desk and some bookshelves. "Do you want to be aliens or earthlings?"

"You pick."

"Okay, I'll be earthlings." Tim handed Alex a control pad and told him where to sit. He loaded a disk into the CD drive, double-clicked a few times to get the game going and waited until a uniformed character appeared on the monitor to tell him his mission. In short, it was to shoot down Alex.

It didn't take him long to do it. While Alex was still trying to familiarize himself with his controls, Tim's thumbs flew from button to button turning his spacecraft, evading the enemy and shooting phasers. A red, fiery blast told Alex he'd lost the first round.

"My Auntie Sue's better at this game than you are."

Auntie Sue? "I didn't know Dr. Robb was your aunt."

"Really, she's my godmother. She's good at this game."

Alex sat up straighter, grasping his control pad. "Well, you know, this is the first time I've played it. Just give me a little practice and I'll get better. Ready to go again?"

"Sure. Wait, I'll put it on beginner's mode for you."

Alex found there was more to the game than earthlings in white helmets fighting off space invaders in black ones. There were good and bad earthlings—heroes, pirates and spies. Alien pirates did business with earthling pirates and underground alien pacifists worked against their own kind. It was a complex game for a preschooler. So many levels of loyalty and betrayal.

Diane's inevitable interruption was unwelcome. Sadly Tim exited the game and put down his controls. Looking hopefully at Alex, he asked, "Can you read my bedtime story?"

"If your mom doesn't mind."

"Actually, it would be great. I could finish getting the food ready."

Rushing from the room, Tim called, "Last one there's a rotten egg."

By the time Alex found his way down the hall, Tim was already bouncing into bed, book in hand. He patted the edge of the mattress. "You can sit here." He handed Alex the brightly colored hardcover book.

Alex leaned against the wooden headboard, one leg

stretched out on the narrow strip of mattress Tim had allotted him, the other foot on the floor so he wouldn't fall. *"The Mystery of the Intergalactic Pirate.* Is the pirate the hero or the hero's enemy?"

"You'll see."

Alex opened the book to the first page and began to read. "'Tim knew he'd have no choice but to land his small craft in the deadly badlands—'" He glanced at the illustration and broke off. "Hey, the boy in this story looks like you."

"He is me." Tim bounced with eagerness. Alex could see he'd been waiting for the secret to break. "My Auntie Sue's cousin writes books and she said the badlands looked so weird they'd be great in a space story. And she made me the hero."

"Pretty nice." Alex looked at the cover again. Sure enough, the book was written and illustrated by Elizabeth Robb. He returned to the story, surprised when Tim relaxed in the crook of his arm as if he belonged there. One small hand rested on the page in front of them. Alex paused in his reading, silenced by a wave of affection that almost ached. So this was what it felt like. He didn't even have an urge to run to the nearest quarry.

SUSANNAH CLOSED the oven door. "That's the last of the appetizers."

Diane was frantically cutting vegetables. She'd just realized a doubled six-serving stir-fry recipe wouldn't be enough of a main course to satisfy the crowd in her backyard. "They make this look so easy in magazines. It's somehow supposed to be done already, and I'm supposed to be cool and charming outside, with my guests." She used the back of her hand to wipe sweat from her forehead. "Everybody must be starving. I shouldn't have planned such a late dinner. I thought it was a nice idea, though, to eat outside while the sun sets.''

"It's a lovely idea," Susannah assured her.

"I don't have a big enough pan to cook all this. I'll have to do it in batches and feed four people at a time. We'll still be at it by breakfast. When will I learn to just order pizza? Especially with everything that's happening now.''

"The fossils?''

"I can hardly think about anything else. At least Charlie was understanding. I mean, he gave me a pitying look, as if he expected nothing better from me, but he was kind. Alex surprised me completely.''

"He's good at that.''

"He asked some very calm questions, not accusing at all, just wanting to understand what happened. I think I'm going to enjoy working with him.''

"You haven't seen his controlling side at all?''

Diane pushed a mountain of carrots aside and began on the zucchini. "It's only been a few days, so it's hard to be sure. He seems a lot nicer than I expected. He's certainly energetic, and he's full of ideas for the museum.''

"I knew it! He's going to turn the place into Blakeland, right? There'll be bungee jumping into fake volcanoes and roller-coaster rides up and down a brachiosaur's back. And this is only day four.''

"I predict you'll be pleasantly surprised.''

"What's he planning?''

Diane smiled. "I think I'll let you find out from him.''

After the appetizers came out of the oven and were sent outside, Susannah limped to Tim's bedroom to say goodnight. As she approached the room, she heard Alex's voice rise and fall, sounding cruel, then brave; angry, then defiant.

She eased closer to the door. Two heads, one sandy and one auburn, were bent over Liz's book. They were getting to the good part. Soon Tim would take over, quoting remembered sentences until the story ended with the pirate bamboozled by the smaller but smarter hero. Quietly Susannah slipped away to join the party.

Late evening light slanted across the yard, full of museum employees and their spouses. Susannah headed for a small group sitting near Diane's struggling rock garden. Carol was there, swinging her sandaled foot to the music playing in the background. She looked restless.

"There you are, Susannah. Have you locked him in a closet?"

"Sorry…what?" She was still distracted by the image of Tim leaning trustingly against Alex's side.

"I heard Alex arrive, but he disappeared. What's he doing? This is supposed to be his party."

"He's getting to know Tim."

"Alex, Alex, Alex," Charlie said impatiently. He stood behind Susannah, steadying a lawn chair. "Sit, dear girl. Have we got something for you to put your foot on? How about that suitcase of a purse, Carol?"

"No way. It's brand-new." Carol pushed her purse under the chair.

"I'm fine like this," Susannah said. "Thanks, Charlie."

"Here, I'll sit on the ground in front of you. You can put your foot on my shoulder. No? Well, feel free to change your mind. Now, what can we all talk about besides Alex? There's no point circulating at this party. Hasn't anyone seen a good movie lately? Or even a bad one?"

Carol patted her boss's hand. "I know, I know, he messed up your specimens. So, not everyone's tidy, Charlie. When a guy looks at me like that, I don't expect him to pick up after himself.''

Charlie groaned. ''Why did Bruce do this to me? There were eight other perfectly good applicants.''

''I don't get it,'' Carol protested. ''What's not to like? Alex is fun, he's gorgeous, and he's the sexiest guy I've ever met. Don't you agree, Susannah? Isn't it worth losing the job to sit next to Alex on a hoodoo?''

There was a short silence.

''Really, Carol—'' Charlie began.

''That's all right,'' Susannah said quietly. ''The trouble is, Alex is the kind of guy who has a girl at every quarry. You have to ask yourself whether you're willing to fill that role.''

Carol smiled. ''I'd say I was born to the part. I get the feeling Alex thinks so, too.''

ALEX SCANNED THE YARD before going out. What did he hope to accomplish tonight? He'd had some idea that there were no secrets in a small community, that if he kept his eyes and ears open he might notice something useful.

Being suspicious of everyone was already getting uncomfortable. Faced with the friendliness of most of the staff, Alex felt like a snake coiled and waiting to strike. But that was the job. Anyone here who wasn't a poacher would understand. That didn't mean they'd ever trust him again, though.

A warm voice greeted him as soon as he stepped outside. ''Alex, I think? Richard McKay.''

Alex gripped Richard's outstretched hand. ''I've just been getting to know your son. He's a great kid.''

''He keeps us hopping, that's for sure. We've been trying to decide which of us he'll take after—will he be a journalist or a scientist? Lately we've realized the only option for him is to be a space warrior.''

"He shows definite aptitude."

"Here you are!" Carol appeared at Alex's side. "Marie and I have been waiting for you. We've been saving food. Honeyed-lamb-and-raisin strudel, chicken satay, grilled teriyaki tenderloin strips..." She almost crooned the list of appetizers, making it all sound like a naughty suggestion.

He smiled, enjoying the amused sparkle in her eyes. "I hope you saved lots. I'm starving." Across the lawn, he saw Marie guarding a plate heaped with food. Charlie and Susannah sat with her, deep in conversation.

Carol hooked her arm through his and, with a little wave, pulled him away from Richard. "Did you get my message yesterday?"

He nodded. "I nearly headed right over to your place."

"I wish you had."

Alex stopped walking. Quietly he said, "You're a lovely woman, Carol..."

"Oh-oh."

"And fun to be with..."

"Oh dear."

"I hope you can understand that I need to stay focused on my work right now."

She tilted her head to one side. "Well, I do admit to being a distraction." She let her hand drift from his chest to his belt. "I'm not talking about a time-consuming relationship, Alex, with problems to discuss and feelings to probe. I'm talking about pure enjoyment."

"That's a rare offer."

"It is," she agreed. "Fortunately, it's not a one-time thing. You'll get a second chance." She gave his arm a tug. "Let's get to the food before the flies eat it all." She raised her voice as they neared the others. "Look who I found, hovering around the door like the shy little thing he is."

At least Marie looked happy to see him. Susannah nodded stiffly, as if remembering at some point she'd been taught manners, and Charlie ignored him completely. There weren't any free chairs, but the wall of the rock garden looked sturdy. Alex brushed dirt from the stones and sat down. He helped himself to two of the little toothpick things, cubes of chicken, it looked like.

"Be sure to have lots of those," Susannah said unexpectedly. "Diane doesn't plan to serve dinner until sundown."

"Thanks for the tip." He could see fatigue in the line of her body and signs of strain around her eyes. She looked like she needed someone to wrap her in a blanket and hold her close. What was it about this woman? She prodded his protective urges in a way no one ever had. The trouble was, it really annoyed her when he acted on them.

Charlie was studying the rock garden as if botany were his passion.

"Hey, Charlie."

With obvious reluctance, he looked up. "Hey." After an uncomfortable moment he added, "I did some estimates this afternoon. There's no way we can afford to build those replicas you want for the Discovery Room."

Alex examined the plate of appetizers and chose a tiny piece of strudel. He finished it and took another. "You may be right, Charlie. I'll look at the figures tomorrow, and we can talk about it then."

Apparently Charlie didn't want to be placated. "I know you're in love with your plan, but I've been here for a long time. I know the museum. It wouldn't work."

"What's the plan?" Susannah asked, her voice tight.

"Alex wants to develop a children's activity room," Marie explained, "where kids can dig in real sand and find bones to wrap with real plaster. He's even suggesting they could put replica skeletons together."

"Real replica skeletons?"

"Just like we do in the prep lab."

Susannah looked at Alex with surprise and interest. "It's a wonderful idea."

"It wouldn't work," Charlie repeated. He leaned forward, eager to make his point. "Think about it. Putting the bones together takes manual dexterity kids just don't have. They couldn't manage the screws and wires and tools. It would take too long. It would be expensive. Anyway, we already have lots of things for children to do."

"Families are our biggest visitors," Marie reminded him. "The more we have for kids to do, the better."

Charlie heaved a sigh. "Sure, let's spend the whole budget on games. Why do we need to be a research facility, anyway?"

"Be fair, Charlie," Carol protested. "We can do both."

"Now you're ganging up on me."

Carol smiled and gave a little shrug. "When you're wrong, you're wrong."

"What about Bruce's pet project? The closed-circuit television system so tourists can watch what's going on in the lab? Are you ditching his plans as soon as he's out the door? Or do you hope to get funding for both projects?"

Alex suspected Charlie's indignation on Bruce's behalf was a bargaining tactic. He wouldn't be happy if either project went ahead.

The screen door opened and George came outside,

looking as dazed as ever. He stood silently on the step. As people noticed him, the conversations around the yard stopped.

Alex started moving toward the door. "George? Is something wrong?"

"I just heard from Paul. There's been an accident—out at the Bearpaw quarry."

"What kind of accident? Wasn't everyone gone for the day?"

"Kim was there. She's been hurt. She's at the hospital. Paul said it sounds bad."

CHAPTER SEVEN

THROUGH THE GLASS DOORS of the hospital, Susannah could see Paul pacing, a few steps one way, a few steps back, rubbing his neck as he went. He was wearing his usual party clothes, baggy trousers and a Hawaiian shirt. He looked up eagerly when she came into the lobby with Alex and George.

"She's still unconscious," he said, as soon as they were close enough to hear. Dark red smudges of blood contrasted with his shirt's blue-and-turquoise ocean scene. "Dr. Smythe is with her. They've been doing X rays and stuff."

"What happened?" Alex asked.

"I don't know. A crate must have fallen on her. That's the only explanation I can think of. I found her in the supply tent, with a crate beside her." Paul looked sick. "I thought she was dead."

George shook his head. "The crates are mostly empty. An empty crate wouldn't hurt her. Not that much, anyway."

Paul's shoulders jerked upward and his voice rose. "She was on the floor of the supply tent. There was blood on the ground and a crate—"

Alex led Paul toward a row of hard vinyl chairs. "You need to calm down. You can't do Kim any good in this state. George, see if you can find us something to drink."

"Hot or cold?"

"It doesn't matter."

Jingling coins in his pocket, George headed to a soft drink machine in a far corner of the room. Susannah sat beside Paul and put her good hand on his arm. "How are you doing?"

"I don't even know." He rubbed a shaking hand over his mouth. "I let her down."

Susannah thought she knew the feeling. When Matt had fallen into the sinkhole, she'd gone over and over all the things she should have done differently. "Sometimes you can't prevent accidents, even when you're careful."

Paul looked at her with a sad smile. "And sometimes you're not careful."

"Were you careless?" Alex asked bluntly.

"Alex," Susannah protested.

He ignored her and addressed another question to Paul. "Do you know why Kim was at the quarry after everyone else left? Diane thought both of you would be at the party tonight."

"We were planning to go. Kim was looking forward to it. You know, some fun in the middle of a lousy week. Then she decided to work all evening. She said she'd join the party later. She wanted to look over some rock concretions she found yesterday."

Alex nodded. "You both went hiking in the afternoon, looking for a new site."

"Yeah. I didn't find anything, but Kim was convinced she did."

"Did she tell you what she found?"

Paul gave a dismissive shrug. "She saw a few bumps in the rock that she thought suggested vertebrae, and a scattering of small bones on the surface. She hoped the two things were related. Based on the samples she brought back to the quarry, I told her there was nothing to get excited about."

"She thought she'd found a skeleton?"

"She's inexperienced and she's sorry for George and she wants to find something great this summer." Paul took a deep, shuddering breath. "I mean, seams of harder rock can leave bumps in soft rock. It doesn't have to be a fossil. And partly eroded bones strewn around..." He shook his head. "But she was too excited to listen. I don't blame her for losing objectivity. I do it all the time."

George returned with four canned drinks in the crook of his arm. He set them down on the wobbly veneer table in front of the chairs. "Sorry to be so long. I had to beg the person at Information for more change. What about Kim's family? Have they been notified?"

"I gave a nurse her home number." Paul's voice rose a notch. "The police have been here, George. They've been asking me questions, a lot of questions."

"That's just their job."

"It's procedure when something like this happens," Alex agreed. "Just keep your cool when they talk to you."

Paul made a wry face. "I wish I'd thought of that before."

Alex opened one of the drinks, then passed it to Susannah before taking another for himself. "So, Kim went back to wherever she found the samples. Do you know the location?"

"She didn't say."

"But you found her in the supply tent, not at the site she was checking."

"Yeah. She must have been finishing up, putting away her tools or maybe some more rock samples."

"Did you see tools or rock samples?"

"I just saw her."

"And why were you there?"

Resting his head on his hand, Paul said, "Jeez, Alex, you're as bad as that cop. You're giving me a headache."

"I'm sorry. I'm just trying to understand what happened."

Paul reached for a can of soda and popped the lid. He drank thirstily. "I didn't like the thought of Kim being at the quarry alone. You're not likely to cross paths with bobcats and coyotes, but you never know. Or she could have got lost out there after dark. I called her place a few times to see if she was back, but there was no answer."

"So you decided to skip the party and go back to check on her?"

Paul nodded. "I felt kind of overprotective doing that. I mean she knows how to take care of herself. But then there she was…so still and quiet. They seem to think she's been unconscious for hours and that's really bad news. That's all they'll tell me."

He looked at George. "I'm sorry. I should have gone after her earlier. I shouldn't have let her stay alone in the first place. No wonder the police acted like I did something wrong. But the way they look at you, like you're a worm. I mean, I found her. I brought her to the hospital."

"And thank goodness you did," Susannah said. "Imagine if she'd been out all night, until the team got there in the morning."

George stood up. "I can't do anything here. This is the colic hour. Lisa's probably at the end of her tether by now. I'll check in with you tomorrow, Paul."

Almost as soon as he'd gone, a nurse approached. "Your friend is conscious, Mr. Robbins. Just barely, but you're welcome to speak to her." She glanced at Susannah and Alex. "One visitor at a time, I'm afraid."

ALEX HUNG UP THE PAY PHONE. He couldn't believe what he'd just heard.

His contact on the board didn't want him to overreact. Accidents happened, apparently. It was dangerous work. There was no need to upset the staff yet, or have police all over the museum and stories in the paper. They needed real proof of a crime before stirring things up.

Fine. As far as he was concerned, he had real proof.

A ward clerk told Alex the policeman who had questioned Paul was still somewhere in the hospital. He roamed through the emergency waiting room and the first floor corridors until he saw an RCMP officer in conversation with a nurse.

"Constable?"

The nurse tactfully moved away. The officer looked at Alex with a reserved, questioning expression, as if he assessed each person he met for criminal tendencies. He was taller and broader than Alex, and almost crackled with self-confidence. "Yes, sir?"

Alex introduced himself. He was surprised when the Mountie shook hands.

"Constable Sherwood. What can I do for you?"

"I wonder if we could speak privately."

"You're here about the woman with the head injury?" Sherwood looked up and down the corridor. "We can borrow a treatment room, if it doesn't take too long."

He found an empty room and motioned for Alex to go first, then followed him inside. There was only one chair and an examining table, so neither man sat down. Alex stood between a sink and a two-tier metal table full of medical instruments and petri dishes. The constable stood in front of the closed door. Alex was almost sure he didn't mean to bar the exit.

"Is there something you wanted to tell me about the incident tonight?"

"Indirectly. The museum board hired me because the previous head of dinosaur research thought some of our fossils may have been stolen."

Sherwood hadn't quite perfected his poker face. Alex saw a flicker of interest. "May have been?"

"Honest mistakes can happen. My job is to decide if we've got cataloguing problems, or a thief."

"And?"

"I think the missing fossils have been stolen. I haven't found enough proof to convince the board yet."

"What kind of proof do they want?"

Alex gave a frustrated smile. "I'm beginning to think it'll take a thief in hand." He thought the constable looked sympathetic. "Yesterday, I came across an excavation site in the Bearpaw Formation. It looked as if a large fossll had been removed, close to the place where Ms. Johnson was hurt tonight. If we've got poachers, and if they're taking complete skeletons, the stakes are huge."

"Define huge."

"A saber-toothed tiger skull went for over $30,000 recently. A triceratops was sold for $150,000. With prices like those to look forward to, poachers are ripping whatever they can find out of the ground. Under the circumstances, it's hard to believe Ms. Johnson's injury is accidental. If there are poachers here, they're likely part of a larger ring. This is a national, possibly international, issue."

The constable had drawn a notebook from one of his pockets, and flipped it open. He found a pen in another pocket. "Are you an investigator of some kind?"

"Not at all. The board heard that I'd helped with a joint RCMP-Interpol investigation a couple of years ago—"

"Helped how?"

"They needed someone who could identify recovered fossils and locate fossil sites."

"Uh-huh. Who headed the investigation?"

"The Canadian side was headed by a Sergeant Beaubier. Henri Beaubier."

The constable nodded as though the name was familiar to him. He turned to a new page of his notebook. "What fossils are missing?"

"Some of our Burgess Shale specimens. They're rare marine invertebrates found in a small area of the Rocky Mountains—not the kind of thing people usually imagine when they think about paleontology."

"Invertebrates," the officer repeated. "They don't have backbones?"

"Right. They don't have bones at all."

"So how did they turn into fossils?" The constable's expression had become less guarded. Now he was just curious, like anyone Alex talked to about fossils for more than a couple of minutes.

"That's a good question. Did you know the Rockies used to be part of an ocean floor?"

The constable's eyebrows went up. "You're kidding."

"Nope." Alex glanced around the room looking for paper. "Can I have a couple of pages from your notebook?"

The constable hesitated briefly, then tore two sheets of paper from the back of the book. He watched as Alex laid them flat, side by side, on the examining table.

"This is the bottom of an ocean hundreds of millions of years ago," Alex said, indicating the paper. "Maybe a reef collapses, burying some unlucky creatures in clay. No oxygen, no decay. Two things happen, geologically speaking. Over time, intense weight turns the mud into rock, sandwiching the organisms between the layers and forming remarkably clear impressions.''

''And the second thing?'' the constable prompted when Alex paused.

Alex placed his hands firmly on the papers, and with a quick movement pushed them together. Irregular folds and ridges formed, raising the middle half of each sheet higher than the rest. ''Earth's plates collide, forming mountains and forcing the buried organisms high above the ocean floor. And now Diane McKay finds the sandwiched fossils. And somebody else steals them.''

The constable looked like a kid watching a magician. ''Why didn't my science teacher do that?'' he muttered. He leafed through the pages he'd written on. ''And if something was collected illegally from—where else did you say?''

''The Bearpaw Formation…land that was covered by an inland sea until about seventy million years ago.''

''Okay. So, what would have been taken from there?''

''Some kind of marine reptile.''

''This would be quite a bit bigger than the invertebrates you mentioned.''

''A lot bigger. About twelve meters long.''

''And heavy, right? How would thieves move something like that?''

''They can cut it into smaller blocks, then move it by flatbed truck, or even by helicopter.''

''Well, I guess we can start by seeing who's been renting helicopters.'' The constable closed his notebook and returned it to his pocket. ''I appreciate you taking the time to talk to me, Dr. Blake. Give me a call if you come across any other information.''

KIM LOOKED TERRIBLE.

There was nothing gory; no blood or noticeable bruising, but there was a worrying heaviness in her limbs as she lay listlessly in the hospital bed. When she spoke, it sounded like the words were being dragged out of her.

She told Susannah she didn't know what had happened that evening. "They say I worked late. Something hit me."

"Paul found a crate on the ground beside you. I suppose they're piled too high in the supply tent. It's not safe."

"No." The word disappeared in a sigh. The effort of talking and the struggle to keep information in sequence obviously exhausted her. Kim closed her eyes.

Almost soundlessly, a nurse came into the room and started the series of checks she'd been doing when Susannah had arrived fifteen minutes before. Blood pressure, pulse, respirations, checking pupils with a flashlight, telling Kim to squeeze her hands. The nurse had to repeat her request a few times before Kim roused herself enough to respond. Susannah watched, but she didn't see much movement. Almost none in the left hand. From what she could remember of a long-ago physiology class, that suggested an injury to the right side of the brain.

When the nurse left the room, Susannah followed, hoping to ask about Kim's condition. By the time she reached the hall, the nurse had already disappeared, but Dr. Smythe was sitting at the nurses' station. It looked awfully far away. She leaned against the wall, a few tears trickling down her face.

"Susannah?"

Of course, Alex would turn up right now. Always when she was at her worst or weakest.

"I didn't realize you knew Kim so well."

"I don't." She wiped a hand over her cheeks. "It's

awful, that's all. Last week, Kim came to my office. She told me she was worried about something.''

Alex's attention sharpened. "Did she say what?"

"She said it was work related, but then she decided not to tell me. I can't help wondering if it's connected to this accident. Maybe she was worried about the way George organizes the Bearpaw quarry. Too many crates kept at the site, piled too high—but would she have come to me about something like that?"

"I doubt it. A word to George would have been enough. She didn't give you any idea what was on her mind?"

"Just that she didn't want to get anyone in trouble. I thought there might be something awkward going on at the quarry, gossip or some kind of power struggle." A few more tears escaped. "This doesn't mean anything. I'm just tired." She sniffed loudly.

Alex found a cotton handkerchief in one of his pockets. "It's clean, more or less. I just use it to rub dirt off specimens."

"Thanks." Susannah dried her face without worrying about the smudges of dust on the cloth, then blew her nose. "None of this makes sense. After all the planning and care setting up a quarry, how could something as simple as a falling crate do so much damage?"

Alex ignored the question. "Why do you keep pushing yourself?" he asked quietly. "The more you use your shoulder and your ankle, the longer it'll take them to heal. Why don't you give yourself a break? Your quarry will still be there in a week or two."

"I've got this new boss…"

"Oh," he said, nodding slowly. "He's tough to please?"

"If not impossible."

"Really?" Alex looked genuinely surprised. "Maybe you should talk to him about it. He probably doesn't have any idea he's making you feel that way."

"You think it's unintentional?"

"I'm sure of it."

"Hmm," she said. "That's something to think about." She pushed away from the wall and got her crutch ready. "I'm going to hike over to the nurses' station and talk to Bob Smythe. Want to come?"

"I'll look in on Kim, then I'll join you."

Bob looked up from the chart he was writing in when Susannah approached. "Resting the ankle, are you?"

"I have been, as much as I can tolerate, anyway." The front of the desk, equipped with built-in shelves, rose to the middle of Susannah's chest. She leaned her weight on her good arm. "Can you tell me how Kim Johnson's doing?"

Bob's expression changed. "She took quite a blow to the head. It caused a generalized cerebral contusion. You could say she has a bruised brain. She's in and out of consciousness, and we're watching for complications."

"What sort of complications?"

"With a blow like this, there's always a chance that a subdural hematoma could develop. We'll keep a close eye on her. If there's any change in her vitals, or her level of consciousness, we'll airlift her to Calgary. What are you people up to out there, Susannah? The boy from the science camp, you, now Kim Johnson—all of you injured within a few days of each other."

"There must be a full moon this week."

"The phases of the moon don't seem to be part of the police investigation."

Susannah stared, surprised. "There's an investigation? Paul said the police had asked him questions, but we thought it was just routine. A crate fell, right? It might have been careless storage, but it wasn't a crime.''

"A crate was found on the ground beside Miss Johnson, but that isn't what knocked her out. She was hit by a round, blunt object.''

"Was hit?'' Susannah repeated. "You make it sound as if *someone* hit her.''

"That's right. Someone did hit her. Hard.''

That wasn't possible. The Bearpaw quarry was in the middle of nowhere. Violent people didn't just go hiking in the badlands looking for trouble. "But we heard that a crate fell. Paul saw it on the ground.''

"The new fellow—Alexander Blake. I saw him talking to the police. He should know all about it.''

Susannah looked down the hall, toward Kim's room, and saw Alex on his way to the nurses' station. She had talked to him about the crate, about how such an accident could happen, and he hadn't said a word. Why didn't he want to tell her what he knew?

CHAPTER EIGHT

"WELL, LOOK AT YOU. I heard about you jumping into a sinkhole after a kid who should've known better. Come to think of it, *you* should have known better."

"Morning, Dorothy." Susannah shuffled up to the gleaming counter, hoping the storekeeper wouldn't put too much energy into the upcoming lecture. "It looks like it's going to be a lovely day."

"For some." Behind Dorothy were rows of jars filled with candy—spearmint leaves, licorice babies, marshmallow strawberries, jawbreakers, humbugs. Dorothy still sold them for a penny each, although most stores charged a nickel. There were jars of polished stones, amber collected from local shale, and dime-a-dozen fossils—shark's teeth, brachiopods and small ammonites. Old photos on the wall behind the jars showed teams of straining horses pulling fossil-laden carts out of the badlands, and barges loaded with dinosaur bones floating down the Red Deer River. Dorothy's father, a grinning turn-of-the-century version of Alexander Blake, stood over the spiked skeleton of an ankylosaur. "Not such a lovely day for you, by the look of it. All because of a careless child."

It was Saturday morning. Susannah had kept her foot elevated and her shoulder on ice since getting home from the hospital Thursday night. "I need a few groceries and some company. I've started talking to myself."

"You know what they say. As long as you don't answer—"

"I've been answering."

Dorothy shook her head, with its immovable armor of dyed black hair. "Come sit down at the lunch counter, Susannah. I've got some fresh-squeezed orange juice. Vitamin C is good for healing." She pulled at the top-opening door of an ancient icebox and extracted a pitcher of pulpy orange juice. She filled a small glass and set it on the counter in front of Susannah. "I don't know why this boy's still here, when he thinks he can line up all the rules you tell him and break them one by one."

Susannah smiled. "Not one by one, really. All at once."

"And you pay the price."

Sipping the juice, Susannah said, "It's his first time away from home, Dorothy. He tries. You should see him. He's such a serious little guy, but so eager and interested in everything. He just gets carried away."

"You're soft with kids. What you need is to get some of your own."

"Before or after getting a husband?"

"However you want to accomplish it. You're a natural-born mother."

Susannah laughed. She had expected a push down the aisle.

The door chimes tinkled. A white-haired man leaning on a cane stood in the doorway waiting for his eyes to adjust to the dimness of the room after being out in the August sun.

"Morning, Arthur. Look who's here, almost in one piece."

Arthur waved his cane at Susannah's crutch. "I see you

and I have something in common these days, Doctor. Went bungee jumping without the cord, did you?''

"That's right. You know me, I like living dangerously.''

He gave a gently snorting laugh. "I've noticed that about you. Reckless.''

"Excuse me, Arthur." Dorothy walked out from behind the counter. "You're going to have trouble carrying a shopping basket this morning, Susannah. I'll go around for you. What are you looking for today?''

"Just a few essentials. Chocolate milk. Something to read. And I was wondering if you have any sponge toffee—do you remember that stuff? That little butterscotchy square that sort of melts in your mouth? I've been craving it.''

Dorothy frowned. "Do you need a copy of the *Canada Food Guide*, dear? I've got some extras somewhere." Dorothy's opinions on nutrition were usually restricted to a few comments at the cash register. Having her in control of the shopping basket was a new experience.

"Give the girl some sponge toffee, Dorothy.''

"I don't have any, but I can order some. Be here in a week or so. How about some nice bran flakes?''

"Sure, I'll take a box.''

"And of course chocolate milk won't go very well with that, so we'll take what nature gives us." Dorothy tucked a liter of plain milk into the basket. "What else? Some fruit? I just got a fresh batch of Okanagan peaches.''

"A couple of chocolate bars would be nice.''

Dorothy looked at Susannah sadly. "I tell you, I don't know why I carry the stuff. Sometimes I feel no better than a drug pusher. They do say chocolate is like a drug, don't they? A mood elevator. All right. One chocolate bar, since you've been feeling bad. And some peaches?

They're so sweet, you won't even want candy after you've had one.''

"Two chocolate bars, and I'll take the peaches."

Dorothy walked back to the counter with the basket containing very little of what Susannah had planned to buy. "Now, what's all this about the Johnson girl? Did you hear about that, Arthur?"

"I heard." The old man shook his head. "Senseless. Poor girl."

"I couldn't believe my ears. I thought that sort of thing only happened in the movies. Next thing we'll hear she witnessed some atrocious crime like they have in the city all the time and somebody'll be out to get her to keep her from testifying. It's not safe out there for you girls anymore." Dorothy started to ring Susannah's purchases through the cash register, an old carved wooden one with tall black keys that had to be pushed down with a bit of muscle.

"Have you heard how Kim is doing, Susannah?" Arthur sounded worried.

"She has a bad concussion. They're watching her closely."

"She visits me sometimes, you know, for tea and a chat. We talk about the Depression and the war. Not too many people her age are interested in the past. Maybe I'll go see her in a day or two, when she's feeling a little better."

"You can take her some peaches," Dorothy suggested. "More sensible than flowers." She turned to Susannah. "That's twelve dollars, fifty-nine cents. Now tell me about this Alexander Blake. Looks like a nice enough fellow."

"That seems to be the consensus."

Dorothy cocked an eyebrow at Susannah's tone. "He's

been in a few times for groceries. Doesn't get much. A man like him, with that build? He's mistaken if he thinks he can hold it together with a box of sugary cereal and a ham sandwich. You probably don't see this side of him at work, Susannah, but he's a bit of a rascal. Teases me and thinks I don't know it. Oh! You wanted a book.''

Dorothy reached behind her, where a shelf under the jars of candy and fossils held the latest bestsellers. ''Have you read the new Grisham? One of his best, people are saying, although I haven't read it yet so I don't have an opinion one way or the other.''

A familiar voice broke in. ''I don't believe it. Ms. MacDonald is declining to express an opinion?''

With a pleased sparkle in her eye, Dorothy turned to her new customer. ''I've told her about you, Alex. Always teasing. Look at you this morning! You're worn right out.''

He did look exhausted, Susannah thought. If anything, he looked sexier than usual, in a gray and gritty way.

The tired blue eyes came to rest on Susannah. ''Good morning, Dr. Robb. On your feet again? Shouldn't you be home resting?''

''I think that's her plan,'' Dorothy agreed. ''She's bought a book and some chocolate bars. Not that candy will build her strength or her immune system.''

''Good morning, Dr. Blake.'' With both of them putting in their two-cents worth, Susannah was surprised she managed to sound as businesslike as she did. ''I'm feeling much better. I'll be back at work soon. Monday, I think.''

''Good. With the report on the hadrosaur quarry complete?''

She had forgotten all about the report. ''You're joking.''

''Preparing it seems like an ideal way to pass the time

while you have to keep your foot up. I've had everyone else's for days. I assumed you'd be concerned about getting yours finished."

Susannah couldn't tell if he was serious. Out of the corner of her eye she saw Dorothy turn and walk toward the back room. Leaning heavily on his cane, Arthur moved to examine the bread shelf. Despite the show of tact, both remained within hearing distance.

"Still flexing your muscles, Alex? Marking your territory?"

"I'm just trying to do my job. I think I understand, though. Preparing a report for me offends your dignity."

"Of course it doesn't!" He made her sound foolish. The magazine picture flashed into her mind again: Alex standing in front of huge, curving ribs like a big-game hunter triumphant over his trophy. It was just his way, she supposed, and it *was* paranoid to equate herself with the kill. More calmly, she said, "You might have a point. Having to prepare a report for you makes me feel like a kid in school."

He watched her, an intent expression in his eyes. It was disconcerting. Maybe it had nothing to do with her. Maybe he looked at everything that way, people and fossils and chessboards. "Did you mind when Bruce behaved like your boss, or did he have to walk on eggshells all the time, too?"

"Too? When was the last time you walked on an eggshell? Anyway, with Bruce, it was different."

Alex leaned against the store counter, a move that brought him closer to her. "How was it different?" There was no challenge in his voice. Just interest. "No one else had any trouble giving me a project report."

"No," she agreed. Her heart began to thud.

"You could pretend it's for Bruce."

"I don't have that good an imagination. You're nothing like Bruce."

"Too bad for me. I really admire the man." Alex peered into her shopping bag. "Bran flakes and one percent milk? That's no good. You need protein. Want to go over to the greasy spoon for breakfast?"

Breakfast? She wasn't sure she wanted to spend that much time alone with him. "Breakfast would be nice."

He picked up the shopping bag. "I'll take this out to your car, and you can follow me to Helen's."

Dorothy hurried from the back room to the cash register. "With the book, that comes to twenty-one dollars and ninety-nine cents, Susannah. Let's call it twenty-two and I'll put a penny in the jar for you."

While Susannah counted out the money she owed, Dorothy told Alex, "Don't let Helen hear you calling her restaurant a greasy spoon. She was telling me just the other day her place is actually more of a tea shop. She considers her oat cakes her specialty."

"Her oat cakes, as warm and wonderful as they are, are just a footnote, Dorothy. Her specialty is the Hungry Man's Farm Skillet—three fried eggs, three sausages, a mound of bacon, pan fries, pancakes and toast."

"You wouldn't, Alex. You might as well eat a plate of arsenic. Do you need a copy of the *Canada Food Guide?*"

THE AIR AT HELEN'S WAS TINGED with the smells of coffee, grease and cigarette smoke. Susannah and Alex sat at a table for two in the far corner of the restaurant, an area Helen was determined to call the nonsmoking section. Alex leaned his folded arms on the red-and-white checked tablecloth and looked at Susannah over a bouquet of plastic flowers. He'd rolled up the sleeves of his shirt.

She tried not to notice the contrast of sun-bleached hair against tanned skin.

"You didn't order the Hungry Man's Farm Skillet."

"I was just pushing Dorothy's buttons, I'm ashamed to say."

"You don't sound ashamed."

"She doesn't mind. She thrives on it. I haven't decided yet if she really is a tough, mean old bird, or if it's just an act. She lectured me about my contract with Matt, you know. Said it was nothing but bribery."

"Isn't it? More or less?"

Alex shook his head firmly. "I explained what he'd been doing wrong, and what he needed to do instead. I told him there were consequences—punishment for doing wrong and reward for doing right. That's what we all do anyway, but Matt has trouble seeing that pattern for himself."

"So you made the pattern clear and the incentive stronger."

"Exactly. People do the same thing when they're trying to quit smoking or to lose weight."

"Dorothy's kind, though. If Matt had been there this morning she would have been all over him—"

"With offers of whole-grain cereal and cod-liver oil?"

"Something like that." Susannah's smile faded. "Alex, about Kim. I couldn't believe it when Bob Smythe said the police are investigating what happened."

"You don't think they'd be interested?"

"It's hard to believe she was hit intentionally." *By a round, blunt object.* The words gave Susannah a chill. "Was she hit by an object that fell, or by someone wielding an object? What if a rock hammer was on top of a crate, and both things fell?"

Alex just looked at her.

"If she was attacked, why? Was she robbed? Was the site vandalized? What happened?"

"I don't know any more about it than you do. The police will figure it out." Alex looked past Susannah. "Here's our breakfast."

Snow-white-aproned, Helen swept up to the table. "Piping-hot fluffy pancakes for you, Dr. Blake. And oat cakes warm from the oven for you, Susannah." She leaned closer and pointed to two little dishes beside the biscuits. "My very own preserves. Apricot. Serviceberry."

"Everything looks delicious."

"It's good to see you out and about, Susannah. This can be a very, very dangerous area. I hope you'll be careful."

"I will, Helen. Thank you."

"It makes me wonder whether those children really ought to be camping out there. Something to think about, isn't it?" She smiled and rushed away. Susannah watched her go, struck by the fact that yet another person had felt free to give an opinion about the choices she made. Maybe Alex had had a point all those years ago.

He peered at Susannah's plate. "Serviceberry? What's that?"

"Saskatoons. They're like blueberries, but woodier. They grow wild in the river valleys. There's a beautiful spot where Serviceberry Creek meets the Rosebud River—you'll have to see it sometime."

"Maybe you could show me the way, when you're feeling spry enough."

First breakfast, now a day in the country? "I'm sure someone would go with you."

"But not you?"

"I mean, I'm sure you'll have a chance to explore the area, whoever goes with you."

"So you're not avoiding me."

Susannah's teacup clattered onto its saucer. "Maybe having breakfast together was a mistake."

"If it was, it's been an enjoyable one."

She took a deep breath and let it out slowly. "What do you want?"

"That's difficult to answer. Too metaphysical for me at this hour, Susannah."

She stared at him in frustration. Half the time, he annoyed her; the other half, he made her want to laugh, and all she really wanted was to be completely unaffected by him. "Why did you suggest breakfast?"

"I'm just trying to make friends."

"You really don't remember me, do you?"

One sandy eyebrow twitched. "We've met before? I thought you seemed familiar. Where was it, a conference?"

She already regretted telling him. "We worked at the same site once."

He looked surprised. "Where and when?"

"Australia. Thirteen, fourteen years ago."

"That long?" She could see him thinking and coming up empty. "We were hardly more than kids. I think I was doing graduate work then." He smiled. "You must have been in high school…that's quite a field trip."

"I'd just finished second year university. I was on field experience." She played with an oat cake, her appetite gone. "I was lucky to get a chance to travel to a major quarry that soon." Or maybe not so lucky. She obviously hadn't been ready for it. "You weren't impressed. Less than impressed, I suppose, since you don't remember despite all this jogging of your memory."

"I think I understand. We argued? And you're still angry?"

"No, of course not." She shouldn't have said anything. She didn't want Alex to remember what he'd thought of her that summer. "I'd better get home and get this foot elevated. Thanks for suggesting breakfast." She pushed back her chair and put a five-dollar bill on the table before hobbling away.

Alex watched her go, handling the crutch more expertly than she had a couple of days before.

After a few minutes of comfortable conversation, the tense voice and flustered, angry manner had returned. Something must have happened when they were both in Australia, and she wasn't going to forget it, whatever it was. She would keep tending the dikes she'd built between them, determined to keep him out. It was an odd dance. Neither of them wanted anything more than a good working relationship. She kept pushing him away, though, and he kept minding.

He put some money on the table, more than enough to cover his part of the bill, and went outside to his car. Just as he was getting in, a police cruiser drove by slowly. He recognized the man in the passenger seat. Henri Beaubier.

ALEX CAME FACE-TO-FACE with the Queen when he stepped into the lobby of the RCMP building. It was an old portrait, showing Elizabeth II in confident middle age. On either side there was a flag—the red-and-white maple leaf to the right, and Alberta's blue flag with the crest of mountain, foothills and prairie to the left.

A young woman sat near the door, behind a glass partition. Before Alex reached her desk, she spoke into the telephone. "He's here, Sergeant."

From somewhere down the hall came the sound of a

chair scraping against the floor, and Henri appeared from around the corner, grinning. "Alex, *bonjour*. Good morning. I saw you on the road. Thought you might head this way."

"Henri. It's good to see you." The two men shook hands warmly. "What are you doing here?"

"I'm doing what I always do—protecting dinosaurs from those who would do them harm."

Alex smiled. "So, while I've been stumbling around looking for signs of theft, you were already watching the place?"

Henri seemed to enjoy that picture. "We've been watching a number of fossil-rich areas. When we heard you were involved here, I headed right out."

"We were a good team two years ago."

Henri nodded. "With me knowing how to investigate, and you identifying fossils."

"Give me a break, Henri. It wasn't my idea to be a detective."

"That's what I thought. You're a sensible man with a good grip on reality. Come on back to the office. I want to show you something." Henri led the way to a back room, and pointed to something cloth-wrapped that half covered a desktop. "What do you make of that?"

Alex pulled back the corners of the cloth. Inside was a piece of sandstone the size of a hockey bag. A fossil was embedded in the rock.

"Well?" Henri asked. "It looks like a tiny tyrannosaur, doesn't it?"

"I suppose it does. But the forearms are longer, and the teeth are different. This one has canines and molars, not a mouthful of serrated knives. It's heterodontosaurus."

"Never heard of it. It was found in the back of a tourist's van last week."

Alex straightened up. "Here?"

"Entering Banff National Park. A family going home to British Columbia. The father claimed his children found the fossil while hiking. He said he didn't know it was illegal to take it home. I'm told the kids were heartbroken when the park warden confiscated it."

"They may have been heartbroken, but they didn't find this fossil on a hike. It wasn't picked up off the ground. It was chiseled out." Alex pointed to the clean edges of the fine bones. "Some excellent preparatory work has been started, most likely in a museum."

Henri didn't seem surprised. "The park warden took down the license plate number. When I ran it through the Department of Motor Vehicles, you can guess what I found."

"It was a stolen plate?"

"It was indeed. The question is, how did the happy family get their hands on this fossil?"

Alex was silent, considering the possibilities. "I don't know for sure that it's ours. I've been checking inventory since I first arrived. I haven't found any record of a heterodontosaurus yet, but I'll keep looking."

"But if it is yours?"

Alex shrugged. "We allow visitors into the lab on guided tours, but no one could wander off with something this size and weight. There haven't been any signs of break and enter. If it's from our collection, someone on staff had to give it to them."

"Does that scenario point to any particular employee?"

"Not really." A lot of people had access to specimens in the prep lab and the storage room. Technicians, cataloguers, artists, any of the paleontologists. "A fossil as large as this couldn't be removed surreptitiously. Even if there were no witnesses, the security cameras would catch it leaving the storage room." Alex folded the cloth back over the specimen. "This is from the Triassic. It's older than the fossils I usually excavate. Rarer, too. These people aren't wasting their time."

Henri moved to the chair behind the desk and motioned for Alex to choose a place to sit. "You told the constable your predecessor had become aware of discrepancies in the museum's fossil collection."

"Right. He was supposed to keep tabs on staff, notice unusual expenditures, or trips to areas known for fossil marketing, things like that. Then the board asked him to get everyone to take lie detector tests."

"A fairly common practice when employees are suspected of theft, but not foolproof."

"Bruce couldn't bring himself to do it. When they suggested he go first, that was it. He figured after all his years at the museum they should know him and trust him."

"Where is he now?"

"He took off somewhere, no forwarding address."

"Interesting."

So much for being known and trusted. "My understanding is he was sick of the whole business and wanted to dig on his own."

"We'll look into it. I suppose you did the polygraphs when you arrived? Did they suggest anything?"

Alex hadn't done them. He didn't know if he would have if asked. Fortunately, his employers had changed their strategy. "The board decided to be more discreet."

"Good. I'd rather not alert any poachers that we're watching." Smiling, Henri added, "It's easy enough to find the rib. I want the whole skeleton."

He referred to a file on the desk. "It troubles me that

this Paul Robbins happened to be at the quarry to find Ms. Johnson. His explanation is convincing, and just as a cigar is sometimes just a cigar, a fellow who goes miles out into the badlands on the chance that a colleague may be in difficulty is sometimes just a fellow who goes miles out into the badlands..."

"Paul's concern for Kim seems genuine."

"Perhaps it pained him to have to clobber her. In his favor, he has no criminal record, he's worked with Dr. Connery for a number of years without incident, and his university records are exemplary. There's no reason to single him out."

"Except that he was there."

"Exactly."

"There's another thing to keep in mind," Alex said. "Kim thought she'd found a promising fossil, but Paul dismissed it. Because of his assessment, the team won't be looking for the site, or digging there."

"You're thinking it's convenient Ms. Johnson isn't able to disagree with him?"

"I'm thinking I'd like to find her new site. I looked all day yesterday, without any luck. I plan to spend the rest of the weekend looking."

"Leave it to us, Alex. I'll send out some officers. I have a couple of people who made a point of getting sunburned in preparation for this assignment."

"Your officers won't find their way around the badlands without help."

"Certainly they will." The detective changed direction. "Who knows? Perhaps Ms. Johnson had a different reason for staying late at the quarry. Perhaps she arranged to meet a fellow poacher and they became argumentative."

Alex had considered the possibility, but had trouble

seeing the soft-spoken student in that role. "A dissatisfied customer?"

"It could happen. Everyone at the museum is a fine upstanding citizen, as far as I can see. There are no convenient ex-cons or cat burglars to focus our attentions on. It's a good policy to suspect everyone."

"Do you still want my help, now that you're involved?"

"Of course! That's the whole idea. I want you to continue what you're doing. Don't forget to be head of dinosaur research, though. If you've got poachers on staff, they'll notice if you aren't doing the job."

"I'm glad you're in town, Henri. You'll keep me posted?"

"Absolutely. You're my Watson."

When Alex stepped outside, the sun felt at least ten degrees hotter than it had when he'd left Helen's. No doubt, when he was back in the Gobi Desert, he would remember this as pleasantly cool.

Suspect everyone. How did a young paleontologist still paying off student loans afford a home like Susannah Robb's riverside cedar house? As soon as he asked the question, Alex became aware of a deep reluctance to think the fossils he had seen in her cupboard might be part of the answer.

CHAPTER NINE

ON MONDAY MORNING, Susannah squeezed past a television van blocking the staff entrance, and followed the sound of voices into the galleries until she reached the carnivore exhibit. There she saw Alex, surrounded by tripods holding lights, a camera and a microphone.

She stood in the corridor, near the wall, where she was sure Alex couldn't see her. Behind him prowled the tyrannosaur skeleton, jaws ready. Beside him, a pack of knife-clawed dromeosaurs cornered a lone triceratops. In front of him, just outside the camera's range, was a woman who held his complete attention.

"Isn't museum work a bit tame for you, Dr. Blake?" In an effort to meet Alex's eyes, she tilted her head, pointing a delicate chin toward his chest. She looked graceful in heels Susannah knew she couldn't balance on, sprain or no sprain, let alone walk.

"A new experience is never tame, Ms. Hall."

The television producer was persistent. She'd found what she was looking for, someone willing to do a semifictional program in which the real results of their work were beside the point. Susannah didn't know why she was disappointed. It was what she had expected of him.

Smiling, the woman said, "Somehow I can't see you enjoying the challenges of office administration."

"You think a desk diminishes me?"

She laughed, low in her throat. "Come to think of it, I'll bet you make a desk look downright exciting."

Give me a break.

The woman continued, "So, by this time next year the museum will unveil several new exhibits?"

"That's right, but not just finished displays. We hope to make the process more accessible as well. One of the ways we'll do that is by videotaping our excavations."

Videotaping? Susannah loved the camaraderie at the quarry, and she loved the intense nature of the isolated work. Video cameras would ruin that.

"You've had just one week on the job, Dr. Blake, but you've already had some exciting moments. We heard you rescued a staff member who fell into a sinkhole?"

Susannah tensed. Now her public image would be set down in stone. Not just a dusty academic—a careless, child-losing one.

"I'm afraid you've got the wrong impression. One of our scientists rescued a child who found his way into a sinkhole. I just gave her a hand." Alex glanced at his watch. "Our time's up. We can talk again another day, if you need anything more. Feel free to film the galleries."

He stepped away from the lights. For the first time, Susannah was glad of his steamroller tendencies. Ignoring a request for another ten minutes of his time, he moved past Sylvia Hall and the cameraman, and into the corridor, where he stopped, just an arm's length away.

"I wondered if you'd manage to get in today. You're feeling well?"

"Much better. And I see you managed to get some media attention."

Her remark seemed to puzzle him. "The interview should be good for the museum. Ms. Hall's original plans were too lightweight for my liking, but she agreed to modify them. The piece will be part of a science series.''

"Focusing on the glamour of our work?"

"That's what she was looking for, but it's going to be more of an overview of what we're doing here. The science, the educational programs, funding challenges…''

Maybe he hadn't arranged a quick media fix after all. From the little contact she'd had with the producer, Susannah was surprised she was willing to change her plans. "I'll be at the quarry today—you mentioned you'd like to go out with me.''

"You're sure you're up to it?"

"I'm sure I'm able to make that decision.''

"Good. On the way, you can fill me in on what you've found so far.''

"Of course," she said pleasantly. "I'll welcome your suggestions.''

After a fraction's pause and an appraising glance in her direction, Alex said, ''Give me half an hour to clear my schedule and I'll be ready to go.''

TWENTY MINUTES LATER, Alex stopped by Susannah's office, with a backpack over one shoulder and a Vancouver Canucks cap pulled low over his eyes. He watched while she hobbled around, collecting her backpack and crutch.

"If it gets to be too much for you out there, let me know. I can bring you back early." He held the elevator door so it wouldn't close on her as she limped through.

Let him know? "I've already lost too much time. I hope to stay all day.''

When they passed the prep lab, Carol called Alex's name and glided to the door to meet him. "I was going to look for you later, Alex. Some friends of mine are getting together tomorrow night. Just dinner at the pub,

maybe catch the football game on the big-screen TV. I
thought you might like to go. It would give you a chance
to meet some more people.''

"Sounds good. Can I get back to you about it, Carol?''

"There's no rush. It's just a casual thing.'' She seemed
to notice Susannah for the first time. "You could come,
too.''

"Thanks, but by the end of the day, it'll just be me and
my bathtub.'' Trying not to mind Carol's obvious relief,
she asked, "How's the hadrosaur skull coming along?''

Carol looked blank. "What hadrosaur skull is that?''

"Charlie told me you were working on it last week. I
thought it might be ready.''

"I wasn't working on a hadrosaur skull last week.''

"The week before, then.''

"It must have been somebody else, Susannah.'' Carol
flashed another smile at Alex. "I'd better get to work, or
Charlie will frown. I hope I'll see you tomorrow.''

Alex reached the driver's-side door of the blue pickup
before Susannah, and climbed in, seemingly unaware that
she had intended to drive. He turned the key in the ignition, and the engine started easily. "I cleaned the spark
plugs and carburetor. The fuel filters were dirty, too. This
old truck really needs to be babied, doesn't it?''

It wasn't that she was jealous, Susannah thought, as
they pulled out of the parking lot. It was natural to be
irritated when your rival got comfortable in your job, with
your friends, with your godson and with your truck.

She felt uneasy sitting so close to Alex in the small cab
of the truck. Even when she leaned against the door and
concentrated on the view through her window, she was
aware of his body a few inches from hers. He seemed as
composed as ever, unaware of—or indifferent to—the tension between them.

"I went to see Kim yesterday," he said. "They think she's out of the woods, but she seemed very weak and vague. She can't remember seeing anyone on Thursday night." Alex glanced at Susannah, then looked back at the road. "Will you feel vulnerable at the quarry if her attacker isn't found?"

"It had to be an isolated incident. I doubt it's open season on paleontologists."

The truck slowed. Alex shifted gears and turned, nosing down the steep decline from the Cenozoic road onto the Cretaceous floor of the badlands. "Do you want me to drive into the quarry?"

"No, thanks. The walk will do me good." She could put some weight on her ankle now. She wasn't sure it was up to a fifteen-minute hike—in fact, she knew it wasn't. But if she was going into the quarry, she wasn't doing it in a fossil-crunching truck.

Alex parked beside the science camp's school bus. "Maybe I should carry your backpack, then."

"I can manage." Susannah stepped carefully out of the truck, and experimented with putting equal weight on each foot. Her left leg didn't give way. Encouraged, she leaned her crutch against the truck to free both hands and shrugged the knapsack onto her back. Right away, a gnawing pain set in.

"All right?"

"I just need a minute to get organized." She eased the pack off and slipped it over her right shoulder instead, letting it dangle on one side of her body. She stood, leaning on the crutch and wishing there was something she could do besides ask Alex for help. At least he was looking out at the badlands and not at her struggles. "You know what? I can't carry my stuff and walk. Chew gum and walk, yes, but not this."

"No problem." He added her backpack to his own load.

They walked at Susannah's pace. She moved awkwardly, picking her way around rocks strewn over the ground the way marbles spill from a bag. They were glacial erratics, carried thousands of miles south by the glaciers of the last Ice Age. Sometimes she came across the stones arranged in circles, remnants of a time when Plains Indians used them to secure the bases of their tepees.

Now and then Alex paused, picking up a fragment of bone or a rock to examine. He rubbed one small piece of smooth, concave ironstone with his thumb. "Makes a good worry stone." He slipped it into his pocket.

"You don't strike me as someone with worries."

"No? I'd need a very limited imagination to have no worries."

"I thought you just..." She stopped, wondering if he minded a discussion of his personality.

"Just what?"

"I don't know...went out and grabbed life by the throat."

He laughed. "I suppose I do, in a way. It can be risky, though."

"So the next time you're dangling from a mountain precipice you can rub that stone and find peace of mind?"

"That's the idea. Or the next time I have a run-in with Charlie about casting extra replicas for the Discovery Room." He looked grim just thinking about it.

"He's giving you trouble, is he? Charlie doesn't always like new ideas."

"So everybody says. Whatever I suggest, he comes up with nineteen reasons it won't work."

The day was already hot, without even a breath of wind for relief. Alex looked up, examining high wisps and puffs of cloud. His tilted head exposed the line of his tanned throat and the curling sandy hair at the neck of his shirt. Susannah's imagination wandered, picturing the continuing path of curls over his chest.

"Looks like there could be a storm," he said.

She pulled her attention away from Alex, to the potential problem of the weather. The blue of the sky still stretched for miles, but high cirrus clouds and lower altocumulus clouds were moving in. "Mare's tails and mackerel scales," she quoted. "We don't get many rainstorms here, but when we do they tend to be sudden and intense. I hope the science camp is prepared."

"I got the impression from James they were prepared for everything except Matt."

Alex stopped walking again, this time to inspect a modern bone, probably a pronghorn femur. Susannah was beginning to wonder if he was stopping for her benefit.

"You seem to know the area well," he said. "What the sky portends. Where to look for bones and serviceberries."

"I've worked here for years, one way or another. When I was in university the museum was like a second home. They paid me when they could, and I volunteered when they couldn't."

"No wonder you have trouble accepting a newcomer, especially one armed with changes."

Susannah stiffened. "I don't have a problem with change."

"No?" The obvious lie seemed to amuse him.

They were in sight of the quarry, when she stopped and leaned tiredly on her crutch. "You can see where the river turned and the current slowed. That's where we're digging. The bonebed is much more extensive than we've uncovered so far. We'll probably be digging for another year—or longer.''

''It's a major project.''

''And all to be preserved on videotape.''

''I hear a note of displeasure.''

A note? Displeasure had oozed from every word. No wonder he thought she was bitter. ''You know being observed changes the way people behave. I don't want my team to feel they have to censor themselves.''

''They won't be put under a microscope. You can decide what's worth taping.''

''I can decide?''

''Of course.''

Was she always misjudging him, or did he keep backtracking to avoid criticism? Turning again to the quarry, she said, ''We're looking for several things. The size of the herd, the ratio of mature to juvenile skeletons, possibly a trackway.'' As she talked, Susannah forgot her discomfort with Alex. ''With a trackway, I could estimate from the depth and spacing of the prints how quickly the animals moved, and we might get an idea of the group's organization. Did the juveniles bunch together, or did each one stay close to its own mother? We're getting a picture here of a social group, living and traveling together. This site should provide some very valuable data.''

The blue eyes pivoted from their study of the landscape to Susannah's face. Azure? What shade was azure, anyway? ''That's possible.''

''Possible?'' It was certain.

''Sometimes we take quite a leap from what we've actually found to the conclusions we make. Do you ever wonder if your interpretations are fact or fiction?''

Indiana Blake was suggesting that *she* might be careless

about scientific details? "Never. I don't make unwarranted hypotheses."

"That seems a little overconfident—"

Her voice sharpened. "Dr. Blake, I agree some paleontologists prefer adventure and the limelight to academic rigor—"

He smiled. "And some paleontologists rigorously misinterpret the clues they find. Look at the oviraptor—"

"Not the oviraptor again." The dinosaur was an object lesson trotted out for every student. Because the first example of the species was found beside a nest of fossilized eggs, scientists concluded it must be an egg-eater, and so it got its name. Later they'd realized the skeleton was of a parent caring for the eggs. "I'll admit mistakes have been made. They've taught most of us to be more cautious."

"I'm not sure they've taught us well enough."

"Meaning?"

"Well, look at some of the early ideas about fossils. A few centuries ago, Europeans thought they were the bones of animals killed in the Flood…North American Plains tribes thought they were the bones of the mythical ancestor of the buffalo."

"What does that have to do with our work?"

Alex gave a little shrug. "I'm just saying, their reasons for thinking so must have seemed as convincing to them as radiometric dating and stratigraphy are to us."

He couldn't be serious.

"But we confidently call their ideas myth and ours truth—"

"We call our ideas theories."

"—till we find something new and realize our old truths were, in part, old stories—"

"You're distorting the process and you know it."

"—and, that by putting them in journals and textbooks for others to read, we've created modern myths." Alex smiled. "Do you ever feel like a fiction writer, Dr. Robb?"

She knew she should just ignore him. "I take care to develop reasonable ideas about the evidence I find. If that's not what you're doing, maybe you should get the librarians to recatalogue your writing and shelve it with the rest of the teen fantasy. Science isn't about spinning delightful stories designed to gratify your own ego. It's about observing, measuring and interpreting data. It's about creating order out of chaos."

Alex seemed unmoved by the lecture. "To make everything small and manageable? To make us feel like we control the universe? Is that how you use science, Dr. Robb?"

Who was he to talk about control? As Susannah struggled with her indignation, and before she could voice a denial, a small figure looked up from the excavation site, then hurtled toward them.

"Dr. Blake!" cried Matt. "Come and see the bone James found. It's huge!"

Matt and Alex hurried to the site, leaving Susannah standing alone.

She wandered over to examine the work area. As Matt had said, they had found a very big bone—the distal end of a femur or thigh bone—and it was in good shape. She felt a stir of excitement. What if the pelvis was there, too, still enclosed in the rock?

James noticed her watching the excavation. "Good to see you back, Sue. I think we're going to find the whole animal, from head to toe, just like you said!"

Susannah moved away from the bone and the workers. She knew the entire expanse of this curve of the old river hid more specimens. With a perception that came with experience, she eyed the ground, picking out the subtle lineation that told her where the river had wound. There was a trackway under here somewhere. She knew there was.

She could see the herd of dinosaurs in her mind's eye. Alert for danger of a different kind, some genetic programming telling them there was safety in numbers. Choosing the wrong moment seventy-five million years ago to cross a floodplain.

She heard the crunching of sand underfoot, and turned to see Alex watching her.

"Are you all right?" he asked. "You've seemed out of sorts ever since we left the museum. It's not just your sprains."

"I'm…excited to be back at work."

Alex nodded slowly, a small crease between his eyebrows. They were close to the color of sandstone. She found herself wondering how his lips would feel on hers. The thought of it was enough to send a wave of warmth through her body.

How could this happen? She was in the same fix she'd been in thirteen years ago. Despite his opinions about her personality, and despite her concerns about maintaining control of her work, the mere sight of him was enough to turn her inside out. She wasn't alone. She'd been one of many females distracted by his presence at the Australian quarry; she was one of many now. It could be explained scientifically. Even amoebas laid a pheromonic trail to attract other amoebas.

"Is this too much for you, Susannah?" He sounded concerned. "The walk into the quarry must have been difficult in itself, never mind trying to work."

She welcomed his explanation for her discomfort. "Maybe I did rush things."

"I could get the truck—"

"No, thanks, I'll sit here for a bit and rest."

"Do you mind if I just look around as I please?"

"Help yourself." She watched him walk away, striding confidently over the uneven ground. He *would* help himself, of course. That was the problem. To Matt's admiration, to the quarry, to anything else he wanted.

ALEX WATCHED Matt painstakingly keep track of the time and his own behavior. The boy had made a chart in a pocket-size notebook. There were two columns—one labeled "Stay Off Hills," the second, "Stay With Group." A long list of numbers trailed down the page marking off the hours in the day. Each hour, Matt pulled out the notebook and ticked off the two things he'd agreed to do. Alex was glad to see that the contract really did help focus the boy's attention.

Matt and Melissa were working together. She used a chisel to chip at the soft rock around a long, narrow bone, and he brushed the loose dirt away. They knew they nearly had the fossil and its surrounding matrix out of the ground. Alex could see it in the tension in their bodies. When they had cut around the sides of the specimen, so it sat like a statue on a pedestal of rock, Matt looked around, his face alight.

"Dr. Blake! We got it!"

Alex went closer to the pair. "So I see…and what is it you've got?"

"An arm bone, maybe? Humor-something?"

"Humerus? I don't think so." Alex held the boy's hand out so it lined up with the specimen. The fossil, glistening from the preservative they had painted over it, stretched beyond Matt's fingers. "It's a phalanx. A finger bone."

"No way! A finger?"

Melissa pretended to shudder. "I wouldn't want a hand that size wrapped around me at lunchtime!"

Matt took her seriously. "It wouldn't be interested in you, Mel. Hadrosaurs ate plants."

Alex intervened before the inevitable argument began. "What's your next move?"

"Burlap and plaster," Melissa said.

"And then?"

"Undercut to get the fossil off the rock pedestal, turn it over and plaster the bottom."

"That's right. Good job." The kids were flushed from the heat and the effort of digging. "How about a break first? We'll sit in the shade and have a cold drink. Then I'll give you a hand plastering."

WHEN SHE WAS SURE her heart rate and respiration were under control, Susannah hobbled back to join the group.

"That's our Sue," James said. "Makes it to the work site just in time for coffee."

"Actually, I'm hoping for the clink of ice and the haze of condensation on a cold, cold glass of iced tea."

Alex emerged from the supply tent, holding a pitcher in each hand. "You're in luck." Raising first one, then the other, he said, "Ice-free lemonade. Ice-free iced tea."

"I'm tired of traveling third-class," James complained. "Starting tomorrow, things are going to change around here. I'm going to bring another cooler, and that cooler is going to be full—full, mind you—of ice."

Alex looked disappointed. "I thought you were going to say a cooler full of beer."

James leaned close to Alex. "Four more days of science camp and then this quarry changes its spots—coolers of beer every day. German, Japanese, English. Around the world in eighty brands of beer. My favorite way to travel.'' He lowered his voice. ''She doesn't have to know.''

''As long as you don't drop the bones, you can do what you like. I'm more interested in your productivity, James. How many coprolites have you dug up?''

''None.''

''None?''

''Zilch. No dung.''

Alex looked from one earnest face to the other. ''You're looking for coprolites? Isn't there enough evidence about the hadrosaur's diet? What point are you trying to make?''

''She's not trying to make a point, Alex. She's trying to make her fortune.''

Alex looked at Susannah for such a long time that she finally said, ''It's a joke. We're fooling around. There was an article in the paper—''

''I know. I saw it. Coprolites going to private collectors for huge sums.''

''We thought it was funny...'' Her voice trailed off. Alex wasn't laughing. Not even smiling. ''You've got to admit it's funny,'' she pressed. ''Thousands of dollars for droppings, even if they are antique droppings.''

''So you haven't really gone into business on the side.''

''Of course not.''

''Good. I'll take the drinks to the shelter.''

STORM CLOUDS WERE BUILDING in the west, towering mounds and columns that echoed the badlands terrain. Still, there was no relief from the baking sun. With her collar turned up to protect her neck and her hat brim pulled down over her face, Susannah knelt by the ancient riverbed, studying depressions in the ground. She brushed sand away, then felt gently with her fingers, probing, searching the undulations for a pattern. She concluded the unevenness in the ground was the result of erosion, not the passage of a community of dinosaurs on its way to disaster. Carefully she began to chisel, removing a thin layer of sediment. She worked until she had uncovered an area about one meter square. Then she brushed and probed again.

A tall shadow appeared, obscuring her view of the ground. Susannah looked up, her glance passing over sand-dusted jeans and broad shoulders until she reached the eyes, their piercing color shaded by the Canucks cap. "Do you want something?"

"I'm surprised you're not all over that femur."

"Time will tell if more of the hadrosaur is there." She bent her head to resume her examination of the ground. "Could you move out of my light, please?"

The shadow repositioned itself as Alex flopped down on the ground near her. "Need some help?"

"Not really."

"Back to that?"

She looked at him, then wished she hadn't. His face was very close. "I'm back to work, but I suspect that's not what you mean."

"No," he agreed. "I mean that you're back to being prickly. It reminds me of a joke I heard once."

Susannah's hand, brushing debris, paused. He sounded good-natured, and he probably had no intention of hurting her. Keeping her voice calm, she said, "I know the one you mean."

"About the baby porcupine and the cactus?"

"Is that you, Mama?"

The shadow hovered. "I guess that wasn't as funny as I thought it was going to be. Sorry."

"No problem. Nothing bothers me. I have three brothers." She squinted at the ground, trying to think of nothing but the indentations she hoped to find. After a moment, the shadow stood tall and moved away.

SHE WALKED STIFFLY to stand beside James. "Hey," she said.

"Hey, yourself. You look all done in, kiddo." He held out his arms. Susannah moved closer and rested her head on his shoulder. He patted her back. "Nothing to show for a day's digging but creaking joints?"

She nodded.

"You've had quite a week. On the bright side, the femur is in excellent shape. I'm beginning to hope for a pelvis."

Susannah straightened up. "That's great. I'm being greedy, I suppose, hoping for a complete skeleton and a trackway from one site."

"It's a natural hope. Things will look better after a good sleep."

"You're right. Thanks for the shoulder."

"Anytime." James grinned. "My body parts are always at your disposal."

She found Alex sitting on a rock, talking to a group of kids who were hanging on to every word. "Am I interrupting?"

"Yes," Matt said. "We're in the middle of a story about Dr. Blake in the Gobi Desert."

She caught Alex's eye and pointed out the approaching clouds. "Can they get the second installment tomorrow? I'd like to get back to the museum before the rain starts, and we've only got one truck between us."

"I'd rather stick around here for a while, if you think you can manage the truck." He reached deep into his jeans pocket for the keys. "I'll get a ride with James later." Speaking more quietly, he added, "You two seem close."

"We are. Very close." Susannah was surprised he was interested. Maybe he wasn't. Maybe it was idle conversation. She was glad to mislead him, though, to have him believe she was attracted to another man and had no reason at all to give him a second thought.

CHAPTER TEN

TRYING TO IGNORE the rumbles of thunder that were getting louder and closer, Susannah stared at the first page of her *JISP* article. Until she could manage the stairs up to her computer nook, she was working in longhand at the table in the dining area. She had finished the outline, but the article wasn't going well.

"Evidence regarding social and familial patterns in herbivore vertebrates during the Late Cretaceous." That was the title. And that was as far as she'd got. She knew what she wanted to say—she had the research, the notes, the outline—but she couldn't say it. Was there any chance Alex had a point? In her stack of meticulous research might there be a trace of fiction?

If she could go full tilt and really get into her work, her confidence would come back. It was frustrating to be slowed by sprains right now, when the bonebed was living up to its promise. Every day it looked more likely that the main specimen in that jumble of bones would be a complete skeleton. *From head to toe,* James had said, and then Matt and Melissa had uncovered a phalanx. That was a turning point. The smaller bones often didn't survive. Now she just had to track down the skull she'd thought Carol was working on, or she'd end up with a headless hadrosaur. That might be all right for a Halloween exhibit—something Alex would no doubt get behind with great enthusiasm—but she was hoping for something a little more conventional.

And that was the problem. If Alex were to describe his ideal woman, the words *hoping for something conventional* weren't likely to be part of the description. Susannah found herself thinking about emerald eyes and ivory skin, the two things she'd most wanted when she was twelve or thirteen. That would get his attention.

What was she thinking? She didn't want to get his attention.

It was about sex, she reminded herself, pure and simple. His values and what he thought of her meant nothing to her hormones and neurotransmitters.

A few drops of rain splashed against the window. It was already dark outside, hours sooner than it should be. Storm clouds hovered ominously, like an army waiting for the order to attack.

A bolt of lightning, as thick and yellow and jagged as a child's drawing, cracked from the clouds toward the ground. Before the flash of light faded, thunder shook the house and water poured down. Susannah couldn't see the distant hoodoos. She could barely see the trees in the yard. Hard-driving rain beat the ground, forcing loosened soil toward the river. She'd watched summer torrential rains from this spot before. For the first time, she felt a stir of alarm. The tents at the science camp wouldn't hold up to this. Were the kids out of the rain?

She reached for the phone. She'd try the museum first. Imagining footsteps hurrying from another part of the building or counselors shushing children, wondering if they'd heard the phone, she called the staff room, the front lobby and the preparation lab, letting each number ring ten, fifteen, twenty times. There was no answer.

Flipping open the yellow pages to "Hotels and Motels,'' she continued dialing, running down the list of names. The campers hadn't checked in anywhere. James must have got them away from the camp, though, away from the rising river.

For a moment, she felt helpless. They would probably be all right, but she couldn't go through the night without knowing. There wasn't much time—ditches could fill and roads wash out in as little as half an hour, flash floods just as sudden now as they'd been seventy-five million years ago. She pulled a handful of oversize plastic garbage bags from the cupboard under the sink, then moved as quickly as she could to the stairs. Step by step, she made it up, leaning hard on the banister.

All her clean pajamas, nightgowns, T-shirts and sweats went into one bag, sheets and towels into a second, pillows into three more. She scooped blankets into the last two bags, careful not to bang the fossils nestled in the drawer. After tying the bags securely, she dropped them to the floor below.

One by one, she dragged the bags to the back door. She pulled on her hooded raincoat and a pair of high rubber boots, and went out to load the supplies into the car. She couldn't hear anything but the rain, and the water rushing in the river. How long had she been? Ten minutes? In that short time, the river had risen higher than she'd ever seen it. Torrents of silt-laden water surged between the banks, individual waves leaping and tumbling like people in a panicked crowd pushing forward. To the southeast, where the river usually idled down an eight-foot slope, a dark waterfall gushed—a mudfall.

The car's headlights showed her muddy grass and the muddy driveway just ahead. Beyond that, there was nothing but rain. She drove slowly on a road she couldn't see, steering between channels of rushing water.

At the corner, she eased to a stop, tires sliding in the muck. She blinked and squinted, looking for the smaller road that led to the museum. Finally she just pointed the car where the stop sign suggested the road should be, and eased forward. The tires spun, then gripped the ground, and the car moved. "Okay," she muttered. "Nearly there."

As she went, she reached slightly higher ground, enough that the difference between ditch and road was visible again. Susannah risked going faster. Turning onto the access road, the car floundered in the deepening mud. "Nearly there," she said again, as if she could encourage the struggling car.

Finally, the parking lot. Susannah steered through posts that marked the entrance. There, thank goodness, was the school bus, right near the staff door. They'd made it. She stepped out of the car into ankle-deep water and sloshed her way to the steps.

Alex stood just inside the door, dripping wet. "Susannah." His voice was blank with surprise. "What on earth are you doing out in this?"

She pushed back her hood. "I had to be sure you were all right. Not you. Them. Are they all right?"

He smiled. "They're having a great time."

"I have some supplies in the car—"

"Great. I'll get the stuff. Go on in. The kids are in the galleries."

Susannah didn't argue. The past half hour had been a shock to her ankle and shoulder. She made her way along the corridor, toward a clamor of high-pitched voices. When she reached the carnivore exhibit, she found wet children, wet counselors and stuffed-full plastic bags piled in puddles on the floor. Everyone talked excitedly, no one listened…Matt fit right in. At the edge of the action, Amy comforted Julia, sitting quiet and still, frowning at her waterlogged shoes.

"Sue!" James found his way out of the maze of children and joined Susannah at the door.

"Alex is getting some supplies from my car. Blankets, towels, clothes."

"Wonderful." He sounded a little breathless. "We managed to get some of our stuff into bags before the sky broke open, but we can use whatever you've got.

"Oh, great," he said, when Alex appeared, weighed down by the bags. James began untying knots. "You're better than a Saint Bernard, Susannah. I've always said so."

"I didn't have any food to bring."

"I'll unlock the gift shop and the cafeteria," Alex said. "Take whatever you need, James. Just keep a list, and I'll straighten it out later."

Alex was dripping on the bags, so he moved away and began a new puddle in the hall outside the galleries. His shirt clung to his skin, showing the lean curve of his chest muscles. His hair, darkened by the rain, was plastered against his forehead. Rivulets of water ran down his face. Susannah's hand twitched with the urge to brush the water away. She rummaged through the bags and found him a towel.

"Thanks." He patted his face, then started rubbing his hair. "How were the roads when you came?"

"Bad. They're probably under water by now."

"So we're stuck." He spoke quietly enough that only Susannah could hear. "I was looking forward to getting home. I can't take much more of this racket."

"Why don't we hide upstairs, in the staff room?" she heard herself suggest. "Maybe we can find you some tea towels to wear while your clothes dry."

THE STAFF ROOM WAS SO QUIET they might have been alone in the museum. Standing in the carpeted area, surrounded by two sofas and several mismatched armchairs, Alex looked down doubtfully. The thin, cotton-blend lab coat barely reached his knees. "This looks kind of silly."

"Yes."

He shot her an expressive look, sheepish and annoyed and amused.

"You look fine," Susannah assured him, achingly aware of the meager strips of cloth that covered him. Latching onto her grandmother's cure-all, she said abruptly, "We need tea."

"Isn't it a little warm for tea?"

"It's never too warm for tea."

While she waited for the kettle to boil, Susannah prepared a tray, setting out two mugs, some milk and sugar, and a pot with two bags of Darjeeling. Alex rummaged in the cupboards for a snack. He found a tin of store-bought cookies and arranged some on a plate. The institutional room felt homey. Did pheromones do that?

Susannah set the tray down on the table in the middle of the room and poured the tea, not bothering to wait until it was fully steeped. Choosing the chair farthest away from her barely dressed boss, she sipped the hot drink, glad of something to do with her hands and something to look at besides Alex.

"You seem edgy. Are you okay?"

"It's the storm," she said. "I'm worried about my house. The river was rising quickly when I left."

"Have you ever been flooded?"

Susannah shook her head. "The gully is wide enough and deep enough there to hold a lot of extra water. I think the house is far enough from the river that it'll be all right."

"That's a one-in-a-million spot you've got. I envy you."

"Most people think it's kind of desolate."

"But not you?"

"I love it. It's stark, but that can be beautiful. I like the way life takes hold wherever it can...pincushion cacti and great horned owls out in the sand, an oasis of trees and songbirds along the riverbank."

"A place like that must have cost a bundle."

Surprised by his bluntness, Susannah didn't answer right away. "I just bought the house and yard—I don't own the river, or a single hoodoo."

He smiled. "Too bad."

"The view is free."

Just as Alex reached for a second cookie, there was a sharp crack of thunder overhead, and a too-near flash of lightning illuminated the room. The lights went off.

"They'll come back on in a minute." Alex's voice was calm.

She pushed back her chair. "I think there's a box of emergency candles in one of the drawers."

His hand found her arm. "I'll get them."

"They should be in a drawer near the wall. Candles and matches." She heard him leave the table. There were clanking sounds as he felt around in a series of drawers, then a flashlight glowed.

He directed the light toward the table. "Better?"

"Much. It's amazing how little wattage it takes to make a person feel safe."

"Do we want the candles, too?"

She nodded. "Flashlights go out. I don't know if we have any candleholders, though."

A cupboard door creaked open, and the flashlight shone on the dishes inside. Alex chose a plastic juice glass and dropped one of the candles into it. When he lit it, the leaning candle began to drip wax on the table.

He sat across from Susannah. "I don't feel as naked in this light."

She decided not to tell him he looked just as naked as before, only more enticingly so in the flickering light and shadow. He seemed more approachable, his toughness softened, his skin all too touchable. What would happen if they did touch, if their bodies pressed against each other as they had by the sinkhole? Maybe she'd ignite on the spot, leaving nothing but a handful of ashes. Think of the posthumous notoriety. Spinster Spontaneously Combusts! Pop Paleontologist's Touch Toasts Fossil-Hunting Female! She reached for her cooling tea and spent an unnecessarily long time taking a sip of it.

Alex shifted in his chair. "We got off to a rocky start, Susannah. Our conversation in my office last week has been on my mind."

"I've thought a lot about it, too."

"I said some things that were really out of line. I'm sorry."

Susannah hadn't expected an apology. "I wasn't exactly an innocent bystander."

"I understand it was a shock for you when I was hired. You were straightforward about that." He gave a small smile. "In spite of that, every now and then we manage to get along for a few minutes. Could we try for more?"

"More?"

"Well, for example, maybe we could get along for half an hour."

"I'm willing if you are."

"Then it's unanimous." He lifted his mug, as if in a toast.

She gently touched her mug to his. "I heard the end of

your interview with Sylvia Hall this morning. Thanks for not trying to make a better story of the sinkhole incident.''

"I just told the truth. You saved Matt. I helped you out.''

"The story could have been given a less complimentary spin.''

The pleasant mood was already evaporating. "Why would I try to embarrass you on television?''

"I don't know why. I just thought you might.''

Alex looked baffled. "Why are you so suspicious of me, Susannah? You see hostility where there isn't any. Isn't that a little paranoid?''

Her voice sharpened. "I wish you'd stop labeling me.''

"Labeling you?''

He sounded as if he didn't know what she was talking about. How could he not know? "Timid. Hostile. Paranoid.''

"I've never seen any evidence of timidity,'' he said dryly.

"Your exact words were 'Timid. Must learn to be more assertive if she is to survive in this field.' ''

Alex stared at Susannah blankly. She saw the moment when he finally remembered. "Oh…that.''

"That,'' she agreed firmly.

"I was an idiot in those days. It was an accurate assessment, as far as I can recall, but I wish I'd expressed myself differently. I'm sorry if it hurt you…and it must have if it's still an issue now.'' He went on, "It seems to have done the trick, though. You've certainly become assertive, and you've survived.''

"I've more than survived,'' she said angrily. "Are you saying my less-than-timid behavior now is your doing?''

"Isn't it?''

Susannah's mug hit the table with a thud. "I can't believe your arrogance. That evaluation didn't do anything to help me. I spent the next few years living it down—''

"My point exactly."

"It was my first quarry, my first trip abroad. I was young and overwhelmed and you made things worse. You intimidated me and judged me, and you really haven't changed, have you?"

"I still intimidate you?"

"Of course not! But you still judge me."

"I've just been trying to figure out how to work with you."

"I've been working perfectly well with everyone here for years—"

"Exactly. For years. That's the problem, isn't it? I'm on your turf." Alex pushed out of the chair and took some quick strides away from Susannah, his body radiating tension. He stood at the window, staring into the darkness, looking as if he would step right through the glass if he could, into the rain and the mud, and be happier than he was inside. After a moment, his voice quieter, he asked, "How did I intimidate you?"

By being so sexy I could hardly see or breathe or talk.

When she didn't answer, he came back to the table and said, "I don't know if you can understand what my life was like then. I was running my first quarry, and I wanted it to be good. There wasn't any room for uncertainty, not mine, not anyone else's."

"I noticed."

"But part of my job was helping you learn yours. A critical evaluation at the end of the summer wasn't the way to do that. I'm sorry, Susannah."

She nodded. "Okay."

His eyebrows went up. "Is it as easy as that?"

"I think so." She waited for the little worm that had

been gnawing away inside her since she'd heard Alex had got the job. There was nothing, no twist of anger, no ache of resentment. "In the articles you write, you don't sound so intense. You always sound as if you're having nothing but fun."

He grinned. "That's right. Intensely serious fun."

She sat forward suddenly. "Do you have a key to the prep lab?"

It took him a few seconds to adjust to her change of mood. "Why?"

"I want to look for my skull."

"The hadrosaur skull," he said. "You want to look now, while the power's out?"

"Why not? We're here."

"What do you expect to see by flashlight?"

She looked at him without speaking until he gave a short nod and said, "All right. I'll get my keys."

Susannah blew out the candle and followed Alex as far as the door. The corridor was darker than she'd expected—darker than the sinkhole had been. She waited until he returned, keys jingling, from his office, where he'd left his clothes to dry. Leaving her crutch behind, she unlocked her office door and retrieved a second flashlight from her backpack. On the way to the lab she stuck close to Alex, her eyes on the two bobbing circles of light ahead of them.

They stopped outside the galleries to check on the children. A soft red glow came from the floor in front of the tyrannosaur skeleton, a flashlight under crumpled red paper. The children had circled pillows and blankets and rescued sleeping bags around the fire. His voice soft, James was telling a story.

"Good job," Alex whispered. "Without your supplies we'd still be wringing them out."

Susannah held both flashlights while Alex sorted through the keys on the ring, looking for the right one. When they were inside the lab, Alex locked the door behind them. "Where do you want to check first? The shelves out here, or the storage room?"

Searching through the thousands of bones in the main storage room would be a nightmare without electric light. "Here."

He opened the mesh doors that enclosed the fossils after hours. Slowly he let the light trail along the length of the shelves, playing over plaster-wrapped bundles and glistening bones. When the light found a hand-printed sign that said Hadrosaur Quarry, Alex stepped deeper into the cavelike space. Without thinking, Susannah reached out and felt in the air until she found his lab coat. She closed her fingers around a handful of cloth.

"I don't know about this after all," she said. "This was a crazy idea."

"Yeah, it was." Alex sounded like he was having a good time. "Scared?"

"Not exactly."

"My sister doesn't like the dark much, either."

Keeping close together, they turned a corner and examined the next set of shelves. Most of the specimens were still wrapped in plaster, but the technicians had begun work on a few pieces.

"No skull so far," Alex said, moving to another row.

"I don't understand why Carol didn't remember the skull. Even if she wasn't the one working on it, you'd think she would have noticed it."

"Maybe they've misplaced it."

"Charlie said—" Susannah stopped abruptly.

Alex shone his flashlight near her, illuminating her face. "Charlie said what?"

She hesitated. There was already plenty of tension be-tween the two men. But maybe Alex deserved to hear the story that was going around the museum. "He joked that you might have lost the skull."

"Did he suggest how?"

"He said you made a bit of a mess doing inventory. He thought the specimens might have got so disorganized that it's hard to find them all now." She repeated, "He was joking. You wouldn't be careless with fossils."

They stood with the flashlight's glow between them. Alex'd had a long day, and it was beginning to show. She wanted to place her thumb at the corner of his eye and stroke away the tiredness she saw there. She wanted to kiss the soft skin, feel his eyelids close under her lips. Did he feel the pull between their bodies, or was it all one way? Did magnets feel the attraction they exerted?

"Do you want to check the storage room?"

"Not right now."

Alex nodded. "You must be worn-out. Think we can make ourselves comfortable upstairs for the night?"

"Those sofas aren't quite as hard and lumpy as the ground. We'll be all right."

He locked the mesh and the door of the lab. They were quiet going past the galleries—the flashlight campfire still glowed, but the children seemed to be asleep. Climbing the stairs, Susannah needed to lean on Alex.

"There should be a sleeping bag in the staff room closet," she told him. "I'll get one from my office."

When she returned, Alex was already stretched out on one of the sofas. He had set the flashlight on its end, lamplike, on the coffee table. Glowing concentric circles lit the ceiling.

She limped to the second sofa and unrolled her bag. "I got a letter from my mother today."

"Oh?"

"My grandmother's going to sell her house and move into a seniors' home."

"You don't sound happy about that."

"It's the original family house, the one my great-grandfather built. My grandmother says she can't take care of it now, even with the help the family gives her."

"Isn't there anyone in your family who can take the place over?"

"My brothers' wives prefer new houses. It's a big, old, drafty place. We half lived there when we were kids. Grandma never minded how many of her strawberries and raspberries we ate. We picked peas and ate them raw from the pods, and played games on the veranda, and watched the spiders spin their webs."

"It sounds like a wonderful place."

She nodded. *Times change,* people always said with a shrug, when things like this happened. You were expected to change along with them. Walking to the quarry, she had told Alex she didn't have a problem with that. There was something about him that made her tell bald-faced lies.

"A few years ago," Alex said, "my parents sold the house where I grew up, and moved into an apartment. I still miss the place sometimes."

"Do you? I can't see you missing a house. I think you'd be happier living at a quarry."

"It doesn't take long for me to get cabin fever," he agreed.

Alex clicked off the flashlight, and they lay in darkness. She heard him moving around just a few feet away, trying to make himself comfortable on the narrow couch. It seemed like hours before the downpour subsided and a gentle rainfall lulled her to sleep.

CHAPTER ELEVEN

"ALEX?"

At the sound of Susannah's sleepy voice, Alex turned from the staff-room table, a couple of bowls in hand. She was sitting on the sofa, all soft and tousled. "Good morning!"

"Do I smell coffee?"

"You do."

"Wonderful." She winced when she stood. "I guess I made things worse last night." She reached for her crutch, leaning against the side of the sofa. Alex found himself wishing he could pick her up and carry her to the table. Instead, he made himself look away from her tired hobbling, and filled their mugs with coffee.

He'd never met a woman before who didn't start smoothing her hair self-consciously as soon as she got out of bed. Susannah rubbed her eyes a little, but then she was happy to just sit with her chin on one hand while she waited to wake up. She took a slow, thankful sip of her coffee and, after a few more, began to take notice of what he'd put on the table. There was orange juice, cereal, muffins and cinnamon buns, bananas and tinned fruit cocktail.

"What a feast, Alex. Did you raid the cafeteria?"

She sounded impressed with the provisions. Alex felt as pleased as if he'd gone out to the woods and wrestled the meal to the ground with his bare hands. "There was a chocolate cake, but I left it for the kids."

She smiled, then rubbed her eyes again and yawned. "Are they awake?"

"Sound asleep, last time I looked, with their campfire still shining."

She pulled a watch out of her shirt pocket. "It's only six-thirty."

"Is it? The clocks are wrong or flashing all over the building. I just knew the sun was shining, and my clothes were dry enough to wear, so all's right with my world." He offered Susannah the muffin plate. "There's banana, or apple cinnamon."

She took one, without checking to see what kind it was. Her hands weren't bandaged anymore, but they still looked sore. He'd noticed that she liked working without gloves—he did, too. The ground and the fossils seemed to communicate more information that way—but until the scrapes on her palms healed, he wished she would protect them.

"How are you this morning? You sounded homesick last night, talking about your grandmother's house."

"I'm sorry I went on so much about that. It was all those bones, glowing at me out of the dark." She bit into her muffin.

"Is your family far away?"

"Most of them farm in Manitoba, about an hour and a half from Winnipeg. I get home for a visit a couple of times a year. My cousin Liz lives in Vancouver. She moved there right after high school."

Alex liked the way Susannah's face softened when she thought of her cousin. "I enjoyed her book. *The Mystery of the Intergalactic Pirate.*"

The calm expression she'd worn since she woke up wavered. "Oh, that's right. I saw you reading it to Tim."

Had he stepped on her toes again? The woman had

lived alone too long. "He sure enjoys being the inspiration for a storybook hero."

"It's an experience I might share with him."

"Oh?" Alex poked a knife along the dotted lines of a single-serving cereal box, and poured on too much milk.

"Liz is thinking of writing a book about a little girl who falls into a sinkhole and finds a subterranean world of living dinosaurs."

"Will I be in it?"

"Oh, no. It won't have a hero. Storybook heroines have to save themselves."

"Maybe I could be the villain."

"The tyrannosaur?"

He grinned. "Typecasting?"

"Well, you *are* a hunter."

"That's true. A big, crafty and very successful hunter."

"And you *are* a carnivore."

"Not entirely." He waved the cereal box in the air to emphasize the point.

"Do we know for certain that T-Rex didn't enjoy the odd cycad leaf?"

"With those teeth?"

"Then I'm afraid you don't qualify to be the villain of the piece."

What was happening to him? A gorgeous blonde had offered him complication-free fun and pleasure, and he'd turned her down. Now he was pleased that this touchy woman didn't think he had much in common with a T-Rex.

He needed to get rid of his lingering doubts about her involvement with the missing fossils. His attempt to find out how she'd paid for her house hadn't got him far. The fossils in her cupboard were still unexplained. "Do you want to look for your skull again this morning, now that we can see?''

"I'd rather get out to the quarry right away.''

That was reasonable. But now he had another question nagging at him. For all her eagerness to search the lab last night, why, once they'd got there, had she hardly bothered to look?

Susannah spooned some fruit cocktail into a bowl. "Have there been any hints yet about what happened to Diane's specimens?''

Alex shook his head.

"It's so odd. Usually everything runs smoothly around here. It's not unheard-of for a bone or two to be mislaid occasionally—not that I think my skull has been mislaid. I just don't know where it is at the moment.''

"Maybe I did make a terrible mess in the lab after all.''

She smiled. "No, you're free and clear. Diane's been looking for her stuff since before you arrived. At first, I wondered if she could have misplaced the fossils herself. I think she's lost everything but Tim at one time or another. She's looked everywhere, though, and checked with anybody who might have worked with them.''

"What do you think happened?''

She isolated a grape from the other fruit in her bowl, and bit it with a satisfying crunch. "Maybe when Bruce left our routine fell apart, just enough that a few mistakes happened. His decision was so sudden. We were all worried about him and scurrying to get his projects finished before he went.''

"You think people just weren't as careful because of the hoopla?''

Susannah didn't look all that impressed with her own suggestion. "Charlie would be devastated to think his fossil-storage system could fail, but he can't be everywhere. A lot of people are in and out of the lab all day."

This seemed like a chance to steer the conversation where he wanted it to go. "That's a good point. I know Diane trusts her team, but they work without her for long periods. They could be making decisions she doesn't know about."

Susannah's friendliness faded abruptly. She looked at him disapprovingly. "Diane likes to spend as much time as she can with Tim. Sometimes she takes him up to Mount Field with her, but it's not a great place for a little kid."

"I'm not criticizing Diane," Alex said quickly. "I'm just looking at the possibilities. Maybe someone on her team borrowed the specimens for independent observation, but didn't remember to record what he or she was doing."

"And hasn't wanted to admit it? That's hard to believe. Anyway, we've all asked our teams not to do that. Fossils have to be available for everyone to use, not hoarded by one person."

Oh? "But we all do it—take fossils to our offices or tents or homes to work on."

Susannah gave a one-sided shrug. The longer she was awake, the more she seemed to be favoring her left shoulder. "It's worth checking. I have trouble believing anyone on Diane's team would keep it from her if they did that." She glanced from her fruit bowl to Alex's face. "What is it? You're staring at me."

"It's nothing." Had she forgotten the fossils in her cupboard? Was she lying? Bruce probably wouldn't have given them a second thought if he'd seen them. Alex didn't want to, either. He'd got a good idea yesterday how deeply she cared about her work, and she seemed to care a lot about Diane, too. Deep down, he didn't believe she would hurt either of them. Unfortunately, he was being paid to deal with evidence.

"Morning, guys!" Paul paced through the staff-room door and collapsed into a chair across the table from Alex. "You two look like an old married couple, sitting at the breakfast table, staring at your coffee, nothing left to say." He took a muffin. "Is this a private picnic?"

"Help yourself," Alex said.

Susannah frowned at Paul. "My parents often sit quietly at the table. It's not that they have nothing to say, it's that they don't need to talk all the time. They understand each other."

A look of mischief crossed Paul's tired face. "And you and the boss have already reached that higher level of communication? Impressive." He turned his attention to the plate of cinnamon buns. "Kim's parents have set up a line of defense around her. They don't want me to visit her. They don't want the police to ask her questions. They're mad at George. They think the hospital isn't equipped to take care of their daughter and Bob Smythe doesn't know what he's doing. It looks like they're going to take her to Calgary."

"I met them on Sunday," Alex said, "and they seemed reasonable. Something must have happened."

"Oh yeah, something happened. Kim got really upset yesterday when that constable tried to jog her memory. That set them off. Dr. Smythe wasn't too happy, either. She can't remember anything about Thursday evening, and she's got an elephant of a headache, and this guy keeps at her."

"Maybe her parents have the right idea, then." Susannah began to gather dishes. "I'm not being antisocial,

Paul. I just want to get to the quarry as soon as I can."

"You two go ahead," Paul said. "I'll have breakfast and take care of the dishes."

THE FLOODWATERS HAD NEARLY disappeared, quickly drained into the Red Deer River and soaked into the perennially dry ground. Tree branches, tin cans, pieces of drenched cardboard sat here and there, deposited by the rushing water. The road was still damp enough that dust didn't sift in through the floorboards and windows as Susannah and Alex drove to the quarry.

Once again, they sat too close for Susannah's comfort in the small cab of the blue truck. Alex's shoulder was just inches from hers, his leg so close on the dusty seat. Even after their weather-induced intimacy and his friendliness at breakfast, he didn't seem aware of her at all. It was a bit much. She didn't want to be this job's conquest, but she would like him to notice she was female. The night he'd wrapped the tensor around her ankle, he'd been almost insultingly impersonal, as if she were an injured dog, or a fossil he was wrapping in burlap.

Alex slowed the truck before the turnoff into the gully, where the road ran parallel to the river. "I'll bet the early fossil hunters went right by here on their barges. They'd float along with the current, weighed down by huge bones—mostly going out of the country, unfortunately." He seemed of two minds about the old fossil collecting methods. He clearly wasn't happy that fossils had left the area, but he sounded almost wistful that they'd left by barge. "Someday I'd like to retrace their route. Would you go with me?"

Susannah looked at him in surprise. Was he inviting her on an adventure? Carol could be the lover, and she could be the sidekick. "It depends how unsinkable a barge is."

Impatience, or something like it, flickered over his face. "There wouldn't be much point doing it if it was like a bicycle ride down a country road."

"Have you ever ridden a bicycle down a country road?"

Smiling, he asked, "Are you suggesting it's risky?"

Susannah nodded emphatically. "You have to anticipate loose gravel, broken beer bottles, frogs and garter snakes—and let me tell you, you really don't want to run over a frog or a snake with your bike."

They had arrived at their usual parking area. Alex turned off the engine, but they didn't get out of the truck. They sat in silence, looking out at the haystack hills and mushroom pillars, and the snaking gullies in between.

"It's a world within a world," Susannah said quietly. "Another time preserved and contained within ours."

"Like those nesting Russian dolls."

Susannah liked the analogy, but it surprised her that Alex would think of it. "I always wanted a set of those dolls."

"Me, too. My sister had a set. Of course I couldn't play with it."

"Wouldn't she share?"

"She would have. But I was a tough guy."

"I can believe it."

"Then one Christmas my mother gave me nesting Santas. That was great—even self-respecting tough guys can play with Santas."

Susannah tried to ignore an ache of fondness. "You remind me of Matt."

He looked at her curiously. "Oh? Does he have a secret yearning for Santas?"

"Both of you are tough and playful at the same time."

His gaze intensified.

"I mean, you both have that focused enthusiasm for whatever gets your attention. It could be a mountain, or a hill to slide down when you shouldn't, or a fossil you've found—"

Increasing interest warmed his eyes. Susannah decided to steer back to a safer path. "I suppose your teachers had to devise contracts—"

Alex leaned toward her, his body full of tension, as if he were drawn to her and pulled away from her at the same time. Slowly he came closer, until she felt his breath on her cheek. His lips touched her skin, moving lightly from the point of her jaw to the hollow of her neck where her pulse throbbed. Her eyes closed. She turned her head so her lips touched his hair, but then he moved away. With an effort, she pulled back, letting her hand trace the length of his thigh before it fell onto the seat between them.

She forced a smile. "He cooks, he cleans, he kisses…" Trying to head off a feeling that something momentous had happened, she added, "It was just a kiss, after all."

"Technically, no. Technically, it was more of a caress."

"Still," she said, consideringly.

"Still," he agreed. "If we're going to call it a kiss, I wouldn't say it was *just* a kiss. A kiss communicates something. We communicated a fair bit with that one."

"Maybe that it's a beautiful morning after a frightening storm," she said quickly. "And that you made a wonderful breakfast and it's been so nice not to have been fighting with each other. And that it's stimulating to wonder what we'll find at the quarry—damage from the storm or more fossils uncovered?"

"All of those things. Maybe something more."

Susannah stared at the dashboard. If he thought he had

guessed her feelings, she had to persuade him he was wrong. "It may have been some kind of outlet. There's been a fair bit of...agitation between us. It's partly you, I think."

"No doubt."

"I'm not trying to blame you. Obviously it's partly me, too."

"Obviously."

"But...you can be quite provocative. You've pushed the bounds of my privacy, coming into my house uninvited, deciding what I need."

"Haven't I stopped doing that?"

"Have you even tried?"

"Absolutely...but you keep needing me."

"Needing?" The word finished an octave higher than it began. "That's ridiculous. I don't *need* anyone, at least not more than anyone needs anyone. I didn't need you last night—you needed me. Well, you needed someone, you needed...towels."

"When the power went out, you were afraid of the dark. You needed company."

"I didn't *need* it," she protested.

"You were glad of it."

"Of your company?"

"I think you were."

"I think you enjoy provoking me."

Alex was quiet for a moment. "I suppose that's true. Partly true, anyway. I enjoy the tension between us. It's stimulating."

"Stimulating!"

He tried to explain. "Like finding a perfect fossil or going through a tricky stretch of white water. You test yourself, you feel more alive."

So he was playing a game. It was like exercise, something to stretch the muscles and get the blood flowing. Luckily she had known not to take the kiss, or whatever it was, seriously. The same went for the arguments and the kindness and the friendly conversations. If she kept that in mind, things would be less confusing from here on in.

With just a trace of a smile, Alex said, "Maybe we need to look at why we provoke each other and figure out whether we want to respond—"

"That's unnecessarily analytical," Susannah said quickly. "We just need to stop bothering each other. Then this commotion between us can settle down."

"Is that what you want?"

"Of course. As you said yourself, this sort of thing can interfere with the museum's functioning. We'll both be much happier, and more productive, when we establish an appropriate working relationship."

"So we focus on the job." She thought he looked disappointed, but that didn't seem likely. "That sounds like a good plan."

JAMES AND ALEX HAD FASTENED a protective tarp over the bonebed before the downpour started. Some rainwater had flowed under it, washing away loose sand, but the exposed specimens had been well protected from the driving rain.

Near the site, where Alex and James hadn't protected the ground, the rain had gouged into the sandstone. Susannah crouched to look closer. Gently she ran her fingers over ridges that hadn't been visible the day before.

"Look. Ribs."

Alex nodded. "Here, too. It's quite a pile. Ribs, vertebrae, femurs, fibulas. It looks like fifty skeletons were put in a box, shaken up and let fall."

"Like pickup sticks."

They moved on. Susannah tensed as they approached the prehistoric riverbank. At first the ground looked no different from the day before. She ran her hand over the sandstone as if she were reading Braille. Anticipation building, she took a brush from her backpack and swept away grains of sand, then crumbling stone to reveal an indentation.

"Here," she said, hardly breathing.

"Yes."

"And here."

"You've got it, Susannah."

She rested her hand gently inside one of the tracks. It was big, four times as big as her hand, as deep as her little finger was long. She could see the pattern left by the flesh that had covered the three-toed foot. It looked like a maple leaf.

"Look," she said urgently, brushing some smaller tracks with her fingertips. "A juvenile."

Together, she and Alex crawled along, sorting out blurred and muddled prints, trying to read the story of the animals who had traveled there.

"Susannah, these tracks are different."

"A carnivore."

Alex nodded. "Bipedal, smaller than the hadrosaurs by far. From the depth of the print I'd estimate less than two hundred pounds. It's probably a dromeosaur—there's a suggestion of that long claw on a few of the prints. It was just skirting the herd, I think, waiting to find a careless parent, or an animal past its prime."

"Revolting creature. I hate it," Susannah said vehemently.

"That's a little strong, isn't it?" His tone was light, the way it sounded when he wasn't taking things as seriously as she would like. "There's no good or evil in the animal kingdom. Just hunger."

The morning's tensions flared. Susannah hissed, "I'll be glad when I see an end to your supercilious so-called humor, your little lab coats and your jokes about prickles and your professorial pronouncements!" They were nose to nose, furious gray eyes glaring into amused blue ones.

He whispered, "I can see down your blouse."

Susannah suppressed a surging impulse to swing her fist into his face. "Enjoy the view, Dr. Blake. I'm sure it's rare that you get to gaze upon real flesh and blood, rather than dust and bone." Even as the words came out of her mouth, she wished she could take them back. They made no sense at all.

"You're projecting. I'm not the one who's let myself turn into stone."

Another voice broke in. "Look, children. Dr. Blake and Dr. Robb are butting heads."

Still on their hands and knees, Susannah and Alex turned to see James and the science camp kids standing nearby.

James continued his explanation. "It's a ritual some members of the animal kingdom, like bighorn sheep and deer, use to prove their superior strength and eligibility. Thank you for the demonstration, doctors. Most enlightening."

CHAPTER TWELVE

ALEX SAT BACK ON HIS HEELS and smiled widely at the group of staring camp counselors and children, apparently not the least bit embarrassed. "She's found the trackway!"

Ignoring the hand he offered, Susannah struggled to her feet. She stepped away from him, widening the distance between them by following the path of footprints. He wasn't an allergen, he was poison. You couldn't become desensitized to poison. You had to put a big skull and crossbones on the bottle and store it safely out of reach.

"No kidding? A trackway?" James said excitedly. Quickly followed by the others, he dropped to his hands and knees, examining the ground more closely. Susannah anxiously shooed some children off the tracks themselves, imagining a stampede of twenty-first-century sneakers destroying the millennia-old footprints just minutes after they had been revealed.

"This is where they really walked?" Julia asked. "The dinosaurs we've been digging up?"

"They walked right here where we're standing, drinking from the river and looking for plants to eat," Susannah said. "The way herds of bison or wild horses do today."

"Then a flood came. Poor guys."

"If the rain uncovered all this," Melissa asked, "why don't you just wait to find fossils? Why bother digging?"

"Because it's fun," Matt said.

"It's fun," Alex agreed, "but that's not the only reason. Dr. Robb knew if there was a trackway to be found, this was a good place to look for it. What if we hadn't been here? What if we'd been miles away sitting on deck chairs waiting to see what the rain exposed?"

Melissa was quiet while she worked out the implications. "You mean with more rain and wind the trackway could keep eroding? Until it's gone? Without anybody ever seeing it?"

"That's right. We'll never know how much has been lost that way."

They gave the children time to explore and fit their hands into the huge fossilized footprints, then Alex led them back to the original bonebed and the femur they'd been excavating the day before. He looked intently at Susannah as he went by, as if there was something he wanted to say if he could just get the privacy to say it. Whatever it was, she was sure it would be very nice, because it was time for something kind or sensitive. That seemed to be part of the game.

James stayed behind. "Are you all right, Sue?"

She was so far from all right she didn't want to look at him. "I'm fine."

"You looked upset when we got here. Still do."

"It's nothing. I can't figure the guy out, that's all. Diane says we just rub each other the wrong way." She glanced at James then, and was relieved to see he looked like he usually did, just a few degrees from laughing.

"I'm going to defy biology here," he said, "and go against my own best interests."

Susannah couldn't help smiling. "That doesn't sound wise."

"Here's the thing. I'd say Alex is falling for you."

"You can forget that idea. Do you know what he's called me in the past two days?" One after another, she held up three fingers. "A stone, a cactus and a porcupine."

"Well," James said slowly, "I'll grant you I would have expected a smoother technique from the guy, but all that only proves my point."

"It proves he thinks I'm cold, hard and prickly." As other possibilities came to mind, she gave a little shrug. "Maybe brittle, too. Sharp. Heavy. Volcanic, I suppose, if he wants to overstate things."

"Uh-huh. And why would any of that bother him?"

She had expected vehement protest. Didn't James disagree with that description of her character?

Lowering his voice, James asked, "Do you want me to let the air out of his tires? 'Cause I'm happy to do it, much as I like the guy."

"I'll let you know."

He jerked his thumb toward the new bonebed. "I'll be checking out that pile of bones, if you need me."

Aware of the children's chatter in the background, and of Alex's deep-voiced responses, Susannah knelt beside the trackway. She started the painstaking process of drawing a grid to scale, and sketching the last steps of a family of herbivores and the hunter that had shared their fate.

WITH ONLY A FEW DAYS LEFT to dig, the children had elected to keep working through the afternoon. Alex knelt beside Matt, who was chipping happily in the area of the emerging complete skeleton. "What have you got there?"

The boy looked up with an eager expression. "Maybe another rib."

Alex peered at the specimen. "You're right. Good job."

"You could take some from that new mess of bones."

"I suppose we could. Mix and match skeletons."

Matt laughed, and sat up from his work with a delighted expression, as if several ridiculous-looking dinosaurs had immediately suggested themselves to him.

"James says you're doing great with our contract, Matt."

"Yeah, well, we made a deal."

"You want that afternoon in the lab, do you?"

Matt nodded energetically. Then, just as quickly as the excitement had lit his face, it disappeared. "It's not just the lab."

"No? What else is it?"

Matt glanced around at the other campers, then sidled closer to Alex and said quietly, "Falling in that sinkhole was the scariest thing I ever did."

"I'll bet. You were brave climbing out of there."

"I coulda died and never got out, but Dr. Robb found me, and she got hurt."

"You feel bad about that?"

"Yeah. Really bad."

"The main thing is you learned from your mistake. That's what we all do—try to, anyway."

Matt and Alex sprawled on the ground, long and short blue-jean-clad legs stretched out behind them, and took turns chiseling and brushing around the specimen. At first, Alex listened to every word Matt had to say, but gradually his mind began to wander.

He kept seeing Susannah beside the trackway, her guard down, her body nearly vibrating with contained excitement. Gently she had run her broken-nailed fingers over the fossilized footprints. Her sentimentality when she saw the predator's tracks had surprised him. Whatever she wanted to believe, her enthusiasm for her work didn't all stem from cool, logical science.

In Australia, he'd hardly noticed her—that was hard to believe now. Every time he saw her, he wanted to help her or protect her or make love to her. He needed to stay objective. He needed to keep his mind on the job.

"Hey, Dr. Blake," Matt said, "are you thirsty?"

"I'm parched. And you look like you got caught in a dust storm." Alex hooked his chisel to his belt and hauled himself up off the ground. "Let's see if we can find a cold drink."

"Maybe we can find chocolate-chip cookies, too," Matt suggested. He hurried toward the supply tent, circling back whenever he got too far ahead of Alex. When they went in, Amy was just putting the lid on one of the larger coolers. She lifted a second cooler and piled it on top of the first.

"Hey, Amy," Matt said. "Lookin' for cookies, too?"

"I don't eat cookies, Matt. They interfere with my silhouette." He looked at her doubtfully, so she explained, "I'm going over our supplies. Plaster and preservative and picks and shovels."

"We won't get in your way," Alex promised. "Maybe we should get enough for everybody, Matt. Check that blue cooler."

Amy took a quick step to Matt's side. "Here. Let me help." She pulled off the lid and peered inside, then held it out so Matt could see.

"Orange slices." He sounded disappointed.

"Not as great as chocolate-chip cookies," Alex said, "but not bad. And here's some lemonade already mixed up. Somebody was planning ahead."

"There should be oatmeal cookies somewhere. They're

in a brown paper bag." Amy looked around the crowded tent. "Here they are."

"Great! C'mon, Dr. Blake." Clutching the bag, Matt hurried out of the tent, calling to the other campers as he went.

Amy shook her head. "It tires me out just watching that kid."

"He's a bit of a whirlwind," Alex agreed. "I'll miss him, though."

"Not me." She tapped a box of plaster. "Are there any supplies you'd like me to order while I'm at it?"

"Thanks, but I'll leave that to James or Susannah." He picked up the orange slices and the lemonade and went outside, nearly running right into James. "I'm afraid Matt and I have started a stampede to the dining shelter."

"It's a good time to get the kids out of the sun. I don't think Susannah will take a break, though. Wild horses couldn't drag her away from that trackway right now."

"Maybe I can."

James looked at Alex sternly. "How furious are you trying to make her?"

"Furious?"

"I've worked with Susannah for the better part of five years, and I've never seen her as upset as she was this morning. If I were you, I'd change my technique, or leave her alone. She doesn't seem to appreciate your current methods."

"True enough." Alex handed the lemonade and fruit to James, and headed to the trackway. Susannah didn't look up from her work, but he saw her body stiffen before he even got there.

"Susannah?"

Her movements controlled and precise, she put down

her tools and stood up to face him. "Is there something you want?"

Gently Alex said, "You're pushing it today. That doesn't seem like a good idea, considering how sore you were when you woke up."

She stared at him. "Do you enjoy the back and forth, the roller-coaster game? Is that it? You try to inject that sort of erratic excitement into relationships?"

"I'm not sure what you're talking about."

"Oh, come on. Are you so out of touch with your own behavior?"

"Apparently. Explain it to me."

"There's a clear pattern. You must have noticed. You alternate kindness with meanness. Over and over again. Like someone enticing a bird closer and closer with bread crumbs and then making a noise or sudden movement to scare it away just when it thinks it might be safe."

Alex raised his eyebrows. "And you see yourself as the timid bird hoping for crumbs? That's interesting."

"Of course I don't! That's not what I meant at all. How like you to twist what I say, rather than trying to understand!" She paced a few steps away from him. "How can you make breakfast for me and kiss me, or whatever that was, and share finding the trackway—" She took a deep breath, then continued more quietly. "I don't know what you're trying to do. I don't like games."

"Believe it or not, I'm not playing any."

"Then you're a very mixed-up individual."

Alex gave a frustrated laugh. "Not usually. I'm usually very straightforward. Since I got here, I haven't known if I'm coming or going half the time." He moved closer. There was a tight knot of suspicion between them, and he wanted to get past it. "Susannah, I don't intend to be mean, or erratic. What if I try to stay off the roller coaster and you try not to think the worst of me? Does that sound fair?''

"It sounds familiar."

"If at first you don't succeed…"

"All right," she agreed. "We'll try again."

"Thank you." He wondered if he should leave it at that or push his luck. She didn't pull away when he took her hands in his, checking the scrapes on her palms. Most had been shallow and had already healed, but one deeper scrape had opened again. "Look. Dirt's getting into the wound. At the least, this should be cleaned and taped up. Why not go home and take care of yourself?"

She looked tempted. "I'm too far behind to stop working."

"You're a week behind. As long as the specimens are protected from the wind and rain you can take your time. Science camp is almost over. When your team isn't doing double duty, the work will go a lot faster."

"Dr. Robb! James! Dr. Blake!"

Melissa's voice, unusually shrill, got them both moving. Not even thinking about whether he might be stepping on dinosaurs, Alex ran. Heart thudding, ready to wrestle monsters, he slipped past James and the other counselors, who had been closer and had got there first. He quickly saw that excitement, not fear, had pitched Melissa's voice so high.

"We've trenched to the end of the femur! And look, the pelvis is here, too, right?"

Alex dropped to his knees and slid his fingers into the depression the girls had dug. "It's here, all right! Good work!" He looked around for Susannah. It had taken her longer to reach the site, but she was there, at the edge of the group. The look on her face stopped him cold.

She made her way through the crowd that had gathered

around the fossil. "Not so close, kids," she said quietly. "Remember to be gentle with what you find." They moved back about half a step.

"Melissa and Julia found the pelvis," Alex told her. He had no idea what was wrong now.

Susannah wouldn't meet his eyes. She smiled at the two girls. "You've done a beautiful job."

Beaming, Melissa said, "I'll get the preservative."

Julia gave an excited little jump. "I'll get brushes."

As the others drifted back to their own work, Alex checked for a fossil-free spot and sat down near Susannah. Softly he asked, "What happened just now?"

She had already started widening the trench that exposed the pelvis. Harder than her usual caution allowed, she banged her chisel with the rock hammer, and a chunk of sandstone jolted loose. "I don't want to get into it. I'll just make it clear that this is my quarry."

"I'm aware of that."

"You get excited and carried away. I understand. That's your nature."

He didn't think it was so, but this didn't seem like a good time to deny it. Whatever the misunderstanding was, he wanted to clear it up quickly, before Melissa and Julia got back from the supply tent. "Look, Susannah, these are your bones. I don't want them. I don't even study herbivores."

Finally she looked up at him. "Do you remember Billy Dane, in Australia?"

"Of course. I worked for him."

"Did you?" She tilted her head as she asked the question. "Because after the journal articles started to appear, it looked more like Billy worked for you."

Startled, Alex said sharply, "Wait a minute—"

"Did he even get a mention in your *JISP* article?"

The girls were getting closer. "Are you suggesting I stole his work?"

"You got a lot of mileage out of that quarry, and you didn't give Billy the credit you should have." Looking at his face, Susannah softened. "I believe you didn't mean to take over his find. But you did it, Alex. And whatever we say about getting along, and whatever we mean by that, I'm not going to let you do it here."

ALEX GOT BACK to the museum before the end of Carol's shift. He wanted to talk to her in person.

When she saw him striding toward the table where she was working, her face lit up. "Poor Alex," she said warmly. "You look like you've had quite a day."

"It's been productive, though. The storm helped uncover a trackway at Susannah's quarry. We had wall-to-wall excitement out there. I'm finding out I'm a quieter man than I realized."

"Lucky for you, I know three kinds of massage." Watching him, Carol's smile faded. "You're not coming tonight, are you?"

"No, I'm not. I appreciate the invitation—" he smiled "—both invitations."

She kept her tone light. "I suppose you have to go to a funeral?"

"No."

"A sudden trip out of town, then? One of those emergency paleontology conferences? I know! You've taken a vow of celibacy." She gave a very slight nod.

"That's right," he agreed. "Otherwise…"

"Of course. You've really missed something, you know."

He nodded. "I know."

She turned back to the specimen on her table. He stood

indecisively for a moment, wishing there had been a way not to hurt her. The day seemed full of things he'd done wrong.

Taking his keys from his pocket, he let himself into the storage room. There were two things he wanted to check.

First, he looked for the drawer containing hadrosaur eggs. On the security tape, Susannah had handled a few of them, but apparently not borrowed them to study. There wasn't any reason she shouldn't take a seemingly point-less peek at the eggs, but he'd feel better checking that they were all still there. He hadn't reached the drawer yet in his inventory, and he couldn't wait any longer for it to come up in the orderly sequence he was following.

There should be eighteen of the melon-size eggs. Gently he pulled the drawer open. It looked full. Five…ten…fifteen… He exhaled slowly. He hadn't even realized he'd been holding his breath. Eighteen. He pushed the drawer shut and locked it.

Next he approached the Bearpaw Formation drawers. He chose one that was beside some Burgess Shale spec-imens. Carefully he removed a piece of shale with oyster imprints and placed it in a carrying crate. He locked the drawer and went to the entrance, where he wrote in the circulation log.

He waited a few minutes, then, standing directly under the camera, he transferred the piece of shale into a second crate. There were other cameras in the large room, but he'd studied the angles they covered, and he was fairly sure none of them would record his actions.

Carrying the first crate in front of his body, with his back to the camera, he unlocked the drawer he'd opened before, then slowly put his hands inside, holding them as if he carried something. He closed and locked the drawer, recorded the time in the log, then left the storage room, locking the door behind him.

On his way past Charlie's desk, he said, "I'm borrowing the circulation log."

Charlie looked as if he was considering standing in Alex's way. "What if we need it?"

"I'll just be a minute." He walked briskly along the corridor and around the corner to the security office.

A guard looked up from a small wall of monitors. "What can I do for you, Dr. Blake?"

Alex set the circulation log on the guard's desk. "I'd like you to check the log against the videotape for the last transaction in the fossil storage room."

"No problem." The guard checked the time Alex had borrowed and returned the fossil. He rewound the appropriate videotape by a few minutes, then set it to play. When the grainy image appeared on the monitor, he said dryly, "Well, as you probably know, that's you, Dr. Blake." He tapped the paper in front of him. "You borrowed some Canadapsis imprints from the Burgess Shale at 1705 hours and you returned them at 1708 hours."

"Can you play that again?"

"Sure." The guard rewound the tape for a few seconds, then pressed the play button. They both watched Alex remove and return the fossils.

"Does anything look odd to you?" Alex asked.

The guard shrugged. "That was just you doing what you guys always do. But you did it a little faster than usual. Three minutes to study a fossil." He sounded curious, but he didn't ask what was going on.

"Thanks very much. You've been a big help."

Alex hurried back to the preparation lab. Again he let himself into the storage room. With a small sense of accomplishment, he returned the oyster imprints to their drawer. Finally he'd found a way that a poacher might take small specimens from the lab.

An ache was beginning to gnaw away behind his eyes, but he had one more chore. He made his way up the stairs, more slowly than usual, and found the staff secretary. "Can you try to find out where a paleontologist called Billy Dane, or William Dane, is located these days? If you can find me a phone number, I'd appreciate it."

"Certainly. You've got a message from a Sergeant Beaubier. He said he'd like you to call him no matter what time you got in."

"Thanks." Alex went into his office and closed the door.

CHAPTER THIRTEEN

SUSANNAH VISITED the preparation lab first thing Wednesday morning. Now that they had the hadrosaur's pelvis, she wanted some reassurance about the skull.

Carol's voice greeted her. "I hear you found a trackway yesterday. Alex told me about it last night. Congratulations." Her tone was almost accusing. With a cool smile, she turned away.

Of course, Susannah thought. Carol had invited Alex to meet some of her friends on Tuesday night. There was no reason he shouldn't have gone. His kindness to her hadn't been anything more than that. But he'd looked at her with an unguarded, searching expression that had made the skull-and-crossbones label seem ridiculous. His eyes—apparently the only flashes of color in the entire badlands—had first seemed to caress her, and then they had convinced her to listen.

What had happened to common sense? Of course his eyes seemed to caress her—he had that kind of eyes. Whatever he'd said to the contrary, he *had* to be playing a game. He probably couldn't help it. No doubt it was entrenched in his DNA. The idea was to make your heart beat a little faster, to throw around a few outrageous compliments, and to remember that it all meant nothing.

"Sue!" Charlie called. "I heard your news! It's great. Just great! Will you want to get casts of the tracks soon? Let me know when and what you need."

"Thanks, Charlie." His enthusiasm helped restore Susannah's good spirits. "It's an amazing site. An apparently complete skeleton and the jumble of other bones you claim are mostly flotsam and jetsam, but who knows? There's the second bonebed, and there's the trackway." *There's the trackway.* She'd said it so calmly, as if finding it had been a sure thing. "You'll have to come out and see it."

"Maybe I'll do that. Should I wait for an invitation?"

"Of course not, come any time. Oh! I've been wanting to ask you about the skull, Charlie. Carol says she hasn't worked on it—"

Charlie's expression changed.

"What's wrong?"

"I hate to give you bad news this morning, when things are going so well. The skull broke, Sue. Not the whole thing," he added quickly. "Just the lachrymal and ethmoid bones."

"Can it be fixed?"

"Of course! I'm not going to let anybody else lay a hand on it."

"I'll just leave it to you, then. You're an artist. I know the repair won't even be visible." Before continuing to her office, she added, "You remember Matt, from the science camp? It looks like he's going to earn his afternoon helping put a skeleton together. We'll be bringing him to the lab on Friday."

"Great. Somebody to spill the hydrochloric acid."

"I had the same thought. It might be a good idea to lock it up."

"And the power tools, anything with a sharp edge, anything fragile. The whole lab, in fact. That's it. I'll lock up the lab."

"Come on, Charlie," Susannah said encouragingly.

"I've seen you handle clumsy students, packs of touring Brownies, hundreds of kilograms of tyrannosaur—you can handle Matt for a few hours."

He gave a bleak smile. "I'll keep telling myself that."

As soon as Susannah stepped off the elevator, Diane was there, giving her a hug that made her sore shoulder numb. "Way to go! I nearly jumped up and down like a kid when I heard. Everybody's excited. When I got in this morning, one of the cleaning guys was even talking about it."

"There's something about a footprint. It's more personal than a bone."

"What do we do, break a bottle of champagne over it?"

"Over the trackway?" Susannah's voice nearly squeaked. She couldn't laugh about something like that. Looking down the hall, she saw that Alex's door was closed. There was no reason it shouldn't be, but it worried her. She half regretted mentioning Billy Dane yesterday. Alex had steamrolled over him a long time ago, and he couldn't fix it now. When he'd realized what he'd done, he'd looked like somebody had punched him in the stomach.

She'd only glanced at the door, but Diane noticed her interest. "Alex isn't going to be in today." She cocked her head. "Now, what could be going on, that the guy even enters your consciousness the day after finding a trackway?"

Susannah unlocked her door. "Shall I make enough coffee for you, Di?"

"You think you can distract me with the promise of caffeine? What's going on, Sue?"

Susannah avoided her friend's curious gaze by measuring out coffee and water. "What's going on with Alex, do you mean? Nothing."

"Gotcha." Diane drew her fingers across her lips in a zipping motion.

"That's enough," Susannah told her sternly.

"Absolutely. And I'll pass on the good word. There's nothing going on."

"You mean people think there's something going on?"

"Paul saw the two of you having breakfast yesterday, alone in the staff room, when everyone else stayed in the galleries."

"For Pete's sake." Coffee in hand, Susannah closed the door and sat down behind her desk.

"You know how everybody can be," Diane said, settling into the other chair. "We haven't had a good love affair around here for ages. The fact that it's frosty Susannah who's involved—or not involved, as I'll tell them—is particularly titillating."

"Frosty!" Susannah exclaimed. "First he says I'm letting myself turn into stone, then you tell me people think I'm frosty!"

"He said that?" At first, Diane didn't seem to know whether to be annoyed with Alex, or amused. "When? Did you hit him? Or display immovable dignity, like a rock?"

Susannah tried to answer the questions in order. "Yesterday, after he looked down my blouse and I challenged him to enjoy the view because all he usually gets a chance to look at is dust and bone. I didn't do anything, because James turned up with the campers and made fun of us. Who called me frosty?"

"He looked down your blouse? Isn't that a little juvenile?"

"He is juvenile. He's an overgrown kid digging in the sand. My main concern now is to remind him it's my sandbox, before he sends an article somewhere telling how he found a bonebed and trackway all in one day. With a chesty babe on his arm, no doubt."

"Babe, sure, but chesty?"

"Maybe he'll cast Carol in my part." Susannah leaned forward, elbows on her desk. Even though the door was closed, she lowered her voice. "Yesterday, before we found the trackway, we kissed. Sort of."

Diane raised an eyebrow. "Sort of?"

"We agreed it was more of a caress."

"Sounds nice."

"It was. But he only wants to play. He's dating Carol."

"Are you sure?"

"Charlie and Carol both said so, more or less. Anyway, my feelings for Alex are a generic thing..."

"Generic how?"

Susannah was relieved Diane hadn't pounced on the admission that her feelings were part of the equation. "You know. Generic in that he's good-looking and sexy to everyone and therefore it's meaningless and I might just as well go to the movies and lust after some wall-size projection while eating popcorn. I don't even like him." Her voice softened. "Sometimes he seems like such a nice person and I enjoy being with him so much—"

"But you don't like him."

"I don't know if I do or not. Whenever I'm around him I get angry and weak at the knees at the same time. And it's getting worse, not better."

Diane sighed. "This is more convoluted than I expected. Let me recap to see if I've got it. You're attracted to him and you enjoy his company, but you don't like him. He's acting as if he's attracted to you, but it's meaningless. He just likes women, all women, any women.''

Susannah ignored the sarcasm. ''Right. So what do I do?''

''You could sleep with him.''

What kind of advice was that? It was an urge she'd felt and dismissed at least once a day for the past week and a half. ''No, I couldn't.''

''You'd get it out of your system, and he'd move on to the next woman and leave you alone, if everything you say about him is true. No? You don't like that solution?''

''You know I can't do that.''

Diane nodded. ''It's got to mean something. Did it mean something with Craig?''

''I thought it did,'' Susannah said unhappily. ''All it turned out to mean was that I'm not cut out for relationships, long-term or otherwise.''

''Do you want me to tell you what I really think?''

That was exactly what she wanted. An objective observer to tell her to stop behaving like a schoolgirl with a crush.

''You like Alex. From the little I've seen and heard, I don't think he's playing. Lots of women around here have noticed him, but he's not caught in an emotional tangle with any of them. Just with you.'' Diane spoke intently. ''You keep pushing him away, Sue. What if you succeed? Have you thought about that?''

THE POACHERS WORKED under a large piece of tan canvas. Even from the air, it was unlikely anyone would have spotted the group. The camera's motor whirred as Henri took picture after picture. ''I've got close-ups of each one,'' he told Alex, not bothering to speak quietly. They were a good distance from the excavation site, lying in a hollow.

"Recognize anyone?"

"They're all new faces to me. I'll run the photos through our computer."

When Alex had returned Henri's call the night before, the sergeant had admitted that his officers hadn't been able to find Kim Johnson's fossil site. That morning, the two men had headed into the badlands together. Henri had tried to blend in, wearing jeans and a T-shirt and carrying his equipment in a knapsack over one shoulder, but Alex thought he still looked like a Mountie. It wasn't only the haircut. It was his posture, and a constant air of alert watchfulness.

Alex had a general idea of the direction Kim had gone. He avoided areas he or the officers had already checked, and keeping his eyes open for the kind of rock formations Kim would have looked for, he had found the poachers after only an hour of hiking. Henri had insisted it was luck.

Eyes on the quarry, he asked, "Still no information from Kim?"

"It doesn't look like we're going to learn anything from Ms. Johnson. Her memory is improving—she's clear about the day and who the prime minister is and so on—but Thursday evening is still a blank. Dr. Smythe says that could be permanent."

"I'd better arrange more security."

"Don't do that, Alex."

Alex looked from the poachers to Henri. "We've had a person attacked, and a complete skeleton is being stolen right in front of us."

Patiently Henri said, "If you suddenly have guards at

every quarry and extra surveillance at the museum, you'll warn the poachers. At the least, they won't surface to take anything and we won't find them all. At the worst, they'll take off, lie low, start somewhere else, and we'll be back to the drawing board.''

"You want to make it easy for them to steal our fossils.''

"You've slipped one of my people into the Bearpaw team as Ms. Johnson's replacement. She'll keep an eye on everything there. Perhaps it's not too soon to put an officer in place somewhere else.'' Gradually, as staffing needs made it workable, they planned to add a Mountie to every team.

"Things are going slowly at the hadrosaur quarry because of an injury. No one would question extra staff there.''

"Good, then. I can have a man ready in a day or two.''

Alex understood what Henri was trying to do, but it was hard to sit back and watch fossils disappear. "So, we let them finish here? We watch how they remove the skeleton from the area, and follow it as far as we can?''

"And along the way, we identify more of the poaching ring.''

"Someone's coming.'' Looking through binoculars, Alex studied a truck keeping just ahead of a dust cloud. "It's a half-ton. Black. I can't make out the license plate.''

The truck came to a stop near the quarry, and one of the poachers hurried to meet it. His back to Alex and Henri, he leaned an elbow on the open driver's-side window.

"He's in the way,'' Alex muttered. "I can't see the driver.''

Henri put out his hand for the binoculars. "Chev Silverado, '88 or '89, I think…extended cab, box…and, of course, the license plate is too dirty to read." He shook his head, and muttered, "Are you trying to keep a low profile, or are you just lazy? Come on, help your friends, this is heavy work." But the truck went into reverse, wheeled around and headed back the way it had come. "Oh, I see. Just visiting. You've got more important things to do."

"Think it's the boss?"

"Middle management, I'd say."

Alex pulled a water bottle out of his backpack. He took a long drink, then rubbed some of the water over his face and neck. He handed the bottle to Henri.

"Thanks."

In as casual a tone as he could manage, Alex asked, "How would I find out how someone arranged financing for a house?"

"Why? More to the point, who?"

"Why and who don't matter," Alex said. He felt as if they were beginning a vaudeville routine. "I need to know how."

"We're working together, are we not?"

"I don't think this is related to the investigation."

"Protecting someone?"

Alex didn't answer.

"I see." Henri nodded. "You're aware that women, even attractive women, sometimes break the law?"

Alex smiled. The men were about the same age, but sometimes Henri acted like a world-weary uncle. "I'm aware of that."

"If what you found regarding this person and this house concerned you, would you tell me?"

"If it concerned me enough."

Henri looked at Alex with new interest. Without further argument, he explained how to do a land titles search. "I hope you'll be happy with what you find, Alex." He put his camera in its case. "Let's get out of here. I'll send some officers back. I hate the sun."

A SMALL WHITE TENT STOOD near the trackway. Inside, there was a folding cot with pillows; beside it, a table and chair; under that, a small cooler holding ice packs. On the cot, there was a note. Susannah recognized Alex's handwriting.

> "Welcome to your new home away from home. Now you can get as much rest as you need, without leaving work. I'll be away from the museum all day today. I hope we can talk soon."

Susannah smiled at the paper in her hand. No one would work this hard at a game. Pushing away a stirring of excitement, she put the note in her pocket and went outside. James met her, and together they walked around the site, evaluating the next stages of the job.

"Let's get a tarp secured to protect the second bone-bed," Susannah said. "We won't be touching it this season."

"We can take care of that today. There are some extra tarps in the supply tent."

"I want to focus on the pelvis and the trackway for the next few days. We should have a couple of counselors and a group of five or six kids working on the pelvis, and another group with me at the trackway."

"They'll like that—helping with the two main excavations before camp ends."

"Dr. Robb?" Julia, her eyes damp with tears, stood waiting for attention.

"What's the matter, sweetheart?"

Julia struggled to control the trembling of her mouth before she answered. "I broke a fossil."

Once fossils were exposed, they could be surprisingly fragile. When Susannah had agreed to let the campers work at her quarry, she'd accepted that their inexperience might lead to more damage than usual. "We've all done that at one time or another. Let's take a look."

Julia led her to the tarp-shaded quarry and stood sadly beside a small, crumpled bone. "It's in pieces. It's ruined. I ruined it."

Susannah crouched over the specimen. "It was probably cracked already. We can still save it, you know."

"How?"

"We'll pour on preservative to bind the pieces, then we'll package the whole thing. The technicians at the prep lab can fix it. By the time they're done, the repairs will hardly show." She dug in her pocket, found a clean tissue and dabbed Julia's tear-and-dust-stained face. "Better now?"

Julia nodded, but she didn't look much happier.

"Is something else wrong?"

"Camp's nearly over."

She had been homesick for the whole two weeks. "Are you sorry it's ending?"

"Kind of. It's scary here. Everything's dangerous. You know, like the sinkhole. Matt told us about the snakes that nearly bit him."

Susannah's eyebrows jumped in surprise.

"But I really like finding bones," Julia continued. "When you see a bone sticking out of the ground, and you think about a real animal walking here, when everything was different, that's cool. I'm going to miss that.''

Matt joined them, his foot just centimeters from the broken fossil. ''Dr. Robb, could I ask you something?''

''Of course.''

''I was just thinking, what if dinosaurs didn't really become extinct? Couldn't small ones live in a jungle far away from people? I mean, don't they still discover live animals they didn't know about before? What if we just don't see dinosaurs anymore because they're really, really rare?''

All the campers within hearing looked up from their work, ready to join in.

Matt continued, ''Why isn't a Komodo dragon a dinosaur? And if crocodiles were around at the same time as dinosaurs, why aren't they dinosaurs?''

Susannah opened her mouth to explain the anatomical differences, but no one waited to hear an answer. Another boy said, ''Yeah, what about the Loch Ness monster?''

''What about Ogopogo?''

''Those aren't real,'' Julia said, almost whispering.

''They could be dinosaurs, couldn't they? Plesiosaurs, right?''

''Don't they think birds are dinosaurs?''

''Matt said he saw dinosaur tracks in the sinkhole, fresh ones—''

''No way!''

''I did too. Didn't we, Dr. Robb?''

''There aren't any dinosaurs,'' Julia protested quietly. ''Not anymore. That's right, isn't it?'' She looked at Susannah, worried doubt creeping into her eyes.

Susannah smiled reassuringly. ''That's right. Not that Komodo dragons and crocodiles are much cozier than dinosaurs.''

"But they're far away." Julia shuddered contentedly.

"It looks like we've found our topic for campfire," James said. "Are dinosaurs really extinct? Did they evolve into something else? Among living species, are there remnants of the dinosaurs? You can be thinking about all that until tonight."

Susannah caught James's eye and smiled. The work might go faster when the kids were gone, but she'd be just as happy to have them stay.

After lunch, James stopped Susannah on her way to the tent to lie down. "I need some help." He indicated the clipboard he held in one dusty hand. "I'm having trouble tracing a few specimens. They're on the list, but they're not in the crates."

Susannah reached for the clipboard. "How many specimens are involved?"

"Several—all relatively small ones. A few vertebrae, and the bones of a foot."

"You're sure they weren't in crates we've already sent to the museum?"

James nodded. "We haven't sent a load since the missing bones were excavated."

Missing bones. The words gave Susannah butterflies. "For now, let's stick to the idea that these are bones we're having trouble tracing."

"Sounds better," James agreed.

"It's probably a cataloguing mistake." Together they studied the grid maps and lists of specimens for each day of the past couple of weeks. "Here." Susannah pointed to a discrepancy. "The grid map for the fifteenth of August shows two cervical vertebrae at E-5, but four are listed in the inventory for that day."

"So the find was listed twice and now it looks like two vertebrae are missing?"

''That must be it.'' Susannah stared at the list. ''But how could we make that mistake more than once?''

''Maybe we've let the kids help with the cataloguing more than we should. I'll keep checking the map and the inventory against the crates.''

Silently thanking Alex, Susannah went into the tent and stretched out on the cot, her foot raised on pillows. Cataloguing mistakes could certainly happen, especially, as James said, with so many children helping. It was hardly an epidemic. A few of Diane's fossils, now a few of hers.

What if the specimens really were missing, though? She knew fossil poaching was a problem. Scientifically important specimens were disappearing all over the world, or being damaged by thieves who were overeager and untrained. For some reason, she had never expected it to happen here.

''There's no reason to think the worst,'' she muttered. Maybe her suggestion to Alex, that a few things were going wrong because Bruce's departure had shaken their routine, was worth considering.

Right. Someone attacked Kim because the routine fell apart?

Could all three things happen at once and not be related? Could her team suddenly get careless cataloguing fossils? Could Diane suddenly lose specimens? Could Kim be attacked at the Bearpaw quarry? And could all three of those things happen at roughly the same time and not mean anything? Whoops, guys, we've sure had a run of bad luck?

''Susannah?''

She shot up off the cot. There was a shadow at the entrance to the tent. Even if she hadn't heard his voice, she would have known Alex from that outline. She lifted the canvas flap and tried not to feel so happy to see him.

"Come in. Thank you for the tent. It's a great idea. Really thoughtful."

"I can hardly stand half a day in the office myself." He was standing just inside the tent, as if he wasn't sure of his welcome. "I've got some news I think you'll like. I've hired a new field worker for you. He starts Friday."

"That's terrific. Another pair of hands will really help."

"I just have something quick to say. Do you want to sit down?"

A little nervous, she sat on the edge of the cot, leaving the chair for Alex.

"I talked to Billy Dane last night. He agreed with your assessment of events that summer. I haven't decided what I'll do about it. I could reissue the article, and give Billy the credit he deserves. I could write a new article, and do the same. Or I could write a letter to the editors of *JISP*, admitting what happened."

"Did you ask Billy what he wants?"

"He told me to forget about it. I couldn't believe how decent he was. He said there have been a lot of quarries since then. He claimed he would have written a counter-article if he'd cared enough about it. He said everyone has a little growing up to do in the beginning." Alex looked at the floor. However appealing he was in dinosaur hunter mode, he was even more so like this, slightly wounded. He cleared his throat. "What kind of person would do what I did?"

"Write an article about a quarry without giving its leader credit?"

A shadow crossed Alex's face. "I didn't realize I was doing that…"

She nodded. "I know. You just wanted to go a little

way along the riverbed on your own, but you ended up going too far."

He smiled sheepishly. "You're never going to let that analogy go, are you?" Elbows on his knees, he rubbed his face then sat with his chin in his hands. "Do you believe I don't have designs on your quarry?"

"I never thought you had designs on it. I just thought you might not be able to help yourself." She hesitated briefly, then asked, "Have you spoken to James?"

"I came straight to the tent. Why?"

"He's having trouble tracing a few of our specimens."

Alex's air of uncertainty disappeared. He wore a familiar expression, the intent, searching one that always flustered her. "What happened?"

"We agreed it was most likely a cataloguing mistake."

"A cataloguing mistake," he repeated. "Diane is missing specimens, James is having trouble tracing specimens, and you don't know where a hadrosaur skull is—"

"I do," she said quickly. "Charlie told me this morning. A couple of the bones broke, and he's going to fix it."

"So you think any losses or discrepancies are accidental?"

"Of course!" For some reason, she didn't want to admit what she'd been thinking before he'd arrived. "If not, then—"

"Exactly. If they're not accidental, then someone is stealing fossils."

Maybe. Maybe someone was stealing fossils. "Slow down, Alex. It's a huge step from scratching our heads over a few bones to concluding we've got poachers." To her relief, Alex didn't argue.

"I'll go have a word with James."

When he was gone, Susannah closed her eyes. Too much had happened in the past few weeks. She hadn't had time to absorb it all, and now it was catching up with her. The pieces of her life just wouldn't stay in order, no matter how many times she tried to rearrange them.

THE MUSEUM WAS CLOSED. Bright lights, turned on for the cleaning staff, cast eerie, giant shadows of sharp-toothed carnivores and cringing or combative herbivores on the walls and floors. The droning of vacuum cleaners and floor polishers was a strange counterpoint to the skeleton-filled galleries.

Alex was too restless to sleep, so he had returned to the prep lab to continue his inventory. He was only a third of the way through the collection. So far, nothing else was missing. Maybe the act of counting was enough to discourage poachers.

He couldn't figure out how they were able to remove specimens while surrounded by staff, cameras and security guards. Henri had liked his experiment showing how fossils from the Bearpaw Formation and Burgess Shale drawers might be taken, but how could something larger, like the heterodontosaurus, be removed?

Alex walked from the storage room to the main work area, picturing the way it had been when he'd stopped in that afternoon. Carol had given him injured looks from her worktable, turning them into overly bright smiles every time he caught her eye. Marie had used a drill to remove stubborn bits of rock matrix from bones sent down from the Ellesmere Island site. Charlie and several technicians had been busy with the triceratops assembly. There was a bit of a crowd at one point, when a tour group came in, and he had been concerned to see one tourist who had consistently lagged behind the others. Alex had already recommended to the board that they stop allowing visitors inside the lab. Letting ten or twenty tourists roam around, even with supervision, was asking for trouble.

Let's say you signed out a few Marella, he thought, *while fooling the camera into thinking you'd taken oysters. You slip them to a loitering tourist. She drapes her sweater over the piece of shale you've given her, thanks the guide for the tour and ambles out to her car.*

You'd need a different sort of go-between for a larger fossil. A deliveryman, say. Someone with crates on a dolly. You leave the cart with the block of stone. He brings in boxes, sets one over the block, leaves with boxes...an enlarged shell game. The people working around you would miss what happened, because they would accept the actions of a businesslike person in a coverall.

Alex sat at Charlie's desk and reached for the phone. He dialed the number of Henri's hotel room. The Mountie answered after the first ring.

"Some more fossils are missing. This time from the hadrosaur quarry."

"Who's in charge there?"

Alex found that he didn't want to answer the question.

"Alex? Who manages the site?"

"A very experienced woman. Bruce trusted her absolutely. Susannah Robb. She's been here for years."

"Lots of opportunity to make marketing contacts, then."

Alex couldn't argue with Henri's reasoning. He hadn't done the land titles search yet—his need for proof that

Susannah wasn't part of the poaching ring was fading rapidly—but now he decided it was a priority. If the police were showing an interest in her, he wanted to stay a step ahead.

CHAPTER FOURTEEN

AT ONE O'CLOCK on Friday afternoon, Susannah and Alex stood with Matt outside the door to the prep lab. Alex pointed across the room to some worktables covered with bones. "Those are the replicas we'll be putting together."

"They look real."

Alex nodded. "You can hardly tell the difference until you pick them up. The replicas are lighter and easier to handle."

For once, Matt seemed hesitant. Encouraged by Alex and Susannah, he stepped through the doorway and edged forward. Alex whispered, "Still afraid he'll raise hell?"

"He's just getting his bearings. Give him time."

Charlie came to greet them, hand outstretched. "You must be Matt. Congratulations! Come on, I'll show you around."

"Are you going to join in the fun, Susannah?" Alex asked.

"Not this time. I have a journal article that's begging to be finished." Finished? She'd hardly started, unless the title counted as a good week's work. "I'm tempted to come along, though, if only to say I told you so." She met Alex's amused gaze. Indigo?

"If anybody's going to say I told you so, it'll be me. And I'll raise the stakes. If I'm wrong I'll chauffeur you to the science camp windup tonight."

Susannah wasn't sure whether to hope she won the bet, or lost it. "Then I'll see you around nine o'clock, in my office."

SHE HELD AN ICE PACK to her shoulder, and read an e-mail from Liz.

"Did you hear that Grandma's planning to sell the house? We should go for a farewell visit, as soon as I finish *Susannah and the Three Tyrannosaurs* (working title only) and you've finished digging for the year. Agreed?"

The news about the old house being sold must have thrown Liz, too. She hadn't been home since high school, not even for weddings.

"Agreed," Susannah typed. "Let's go as soon as the ground freezes or the snow falls. We can help Grandma go through her things before the move. There must be three lifetimes of stuff stored in that house. Imagine the stories you could find there!" Now that she thought about it, it was odd that Liz had never written a story about their grandmother's house. Even though Susannah only wrote dusty articles that no one wanted to read she could see the possibilities. Most of the people and places Liz knew became grist for her mill—why not the house where she'd spent so much time as a child?

She clicked the mouse a few times and the title of her *JISP* article stared back at her from the monitor. The rest of the screen was still empty. She had started to write several times during the week, but the sentences had seemed hollow from excessive caution, or bordering on the edge of fiction. Were those her choices? Sink the article with academic prudence or join the ranks of the edutainers?

She began to write, typing and deleting, trying to find a balance between the two extremes. It was impossible to concentrate, though. Her mind kept wandering to Kim Johnson, in a Calgary hospital now, behind a protective wall of parents and siblings, still in precarious health. Would they ever know what happened that night?

A fragment of conversation from her last trip to Dorothy's store popped into her mind. Arthur, talking sadly about visits from Kim—a cup of tea and a chat, he'd said.

She grabbed the telephone directory, found Arthur's number and phoned. When he answered, she explained the reason for her call. "A little while before she was hurt, Kim told me she was worried about something, but she wouldn't say what. I wondered if, when she last visited you, she said anything about problems at work?"

"I don't think so."

"Are you sure? Did she suggest there were problems of any kind at the quarry?"

"She didn't talk about the quarry at all. We talked about the war. Like I told you, she's interested in history." He sounded troubled. "Come to think of it..."

"Yes?"

"Maybe she did say something. I thought she was just making conversation." There was a long pause.

"What did she say, Arthur?"

Worry slowed his voice. "She asked me about the black market, when we were still in Europe after the war. She wondered what I would have done if I thought someone I trusted might be a black market racketeer."

Susannah felt like there was a rock in her stomach. "What did you tell her?"

"I said I'd watch until I was sure. I wouldn't just report the person in case I was mistaken...oh dear...I never thought...I should have asked her if there was something wrong." There was grief in his voice. "Things have sure changed. It used to be like picking berries, or lumps of coal. You just went walking in some gully and the bones were scattered for the taking. Now, it's all new people, strangers I suppose. No one ever got hurt in the old days. Those geology fellows never minded what we did—''

''Arthur?'' Susannah broke in, not completely surprised by what she was hearing. If Arthur still dabbled, it might be better for him if she didn't hear any more. ''Thanks for your help. I'll let you know what happens.''

She hung up and swiveled her chair so she could see out the window. A family with two young children and a baby walked out of the museum toward the visitor parking lot. The children walked along the curb as if on a tightrope, souvenirs dangling from outstretched hands. Their parents smiled good-naturedly. They'd had a good time, or they'd be scowling and telling the kids to get off the curb.

Kim had noticed someone she trusted doing something suspicious. She had decided to watch whoever it was, and he—or she—had stopped her watching in no uncertain terms. Had the person lashed out in fear and surprise, or was it someone who had been willing to silence her for good?

DISTRACTED BY A SMALL SOUND, Susannah looked up from her desk and saw Alex leaning against the door frame.

''You told me so.''

''How bad was it?''

''Nothing spilled or broken. He was all over the place, though. Apparently he felt the rule about staying with the group didn't count indoors. He handled fossils like they were toys. I'm afraid I lost my patience, and possibly my hero status.''

Susannah smiled.

"He wore me out. There wasn't a question about paleontology he didn't ask. We must have covered two years' worth of university in one afternoon." Alex sank into the chair next to her desk, his legs crossed so that one ankle rested on the other knee.

"You told me so, then. I thought it would be disastrous, not educational." His beard had grown in the past few hours, and she could see individual whiskers, some sandy, some red. His face would feel rough if she touched it, smooth if she brushed her hand the way the hair lay, rough if she rubbed her cheek against his. She rolled her chair away, widening the distance between them. "I talked to Arthur today."

"Oh?"

"About Kim. She visits him sometimes, and he remembered something about their last conversation."

Alex's eyes focused on hers, alert. "She told him something about the quarry?"

"Not directly." Susannah looked down at her desk, wondering how to voice her fears. She might as well jump right into the middle of the problem. "With all that's happened, I've started to wonder if someone could be stealing fossils. You mentioned that possibility when we talked on Wednesday. Was it just a thought, or do you have a reason for suggesting it?"

He didn't answer right away. Finally he said, "Someone is stealing fossils. That's why I'm here."

Her face went blank with surprise. "Are you an investigator of some kind?"

Briefly Alex explained his past relationship with the RCMP. "Henri Beaubier is their main investigator into fossil theft."

"So…this has been going on for a while?"

"Bruce only noticed it recently. That's the reason he

left. He didn't want to investigate his friends. But I want to go back to your conversation with Arthur.''

Susannah explained Kim's roundabout way of asking Arthur's advice.

"I see. So she stayed at the quarry alone, trying to find out whether someone she trusted was breaking the law.''

"I can't believe anyone on the Bearpaw team would hurt Kim.''

"It's hard to grasp at first,'' Alex agreed.

"But, Alex. What about the hadrosaur quarry?'' In nature, what worked for one organism usually worked for another. Susannah was trained to look for patterns. "What about the Burgess Shale site?''

"I'm sorry, Sue.''

She shook her head. "I trust everyone on my team. I trust them absolutely.''

"How well do you know Amy?''

"This is the third summer she's worked for me. She's given me no reason to doubt her honesty.''

"What about James and Charlie? I know Charlie's not on your team, but he works with all the fossils. Do you find them both reliable?''

Susannah stared at Alex indignantly. "Completely. You can't pin responsibility for stolen specimens on either of them.''

"I don't want to pin it on anyone. I'm just looking for an explanation. I've wondered about George. This morning he asked for a leave of absence. Is he so stressed out because of the baby, because he's had a bad summer? Or is something more going on? Does he need money? Is the strain of stealing from his friends getting to him?''

Susannah had started backing away from the whole idea. "What about Diane?'' she said angrily. "She travels a lot. She's probably a criminal mastermind with fossil-fencing contacts all over the world. Or Tim. He's always hanging around the museum, and preschoolers have expensive tastes these days.''

He smiled. ''Tim is probably the only person I haven't suspected.''

''That settles it, then. He's guilty for sure.''

''Have you noticed anyone behaving differently? Working odd hours, spending a lot of money, going out of town more often than usual?''

''I'm not going to start spying on people. It wouldn't be possible to work together after subjecting someone to that sort of intrusion.''

''That's exactly what Bruce was doing. It's what I've been doing since I arrived. I don't enjoy it. Being suspicious of everyone gets uncomfortable fast.''

He really did look unhappy. Susannah leaned forward, her wish to defend her friends expanding to include an urge to reassure Alex. ''You don't need to be suspicious of anyone on staff. There's another explanation. Kim could have been mistaken. A thief could have found the quarry. That's far more likely. You don't know the people here the way I do. We wouldn't hurt each other. We wouldn't damage each other's work.''

''And yet Bruce seemed to think otherwise.''

''I'll call him—'' She stopped, realizing she didn't know where to find him.

''I know this is difficult to accept.'' Alex stood up suddenly. ''Come with me. I have a surprise for you.''

Susannah wasn't sure she wanted a surprise from Alex.

''I want to show you something before we go to the windup.'' He opened the office door and waited for her to join him. ''Something nice. Have you noticed what's going on near the front entrance?''

Puzzled, Susannah shook her head. As she followed

Alex downstairs and into the lobby, she felt a stirring of anticipation, like a ten-year-old waiting for her birthday.

"In here." Alex pointed to a storage room around the corner from the lobby.

"What is it? New mops?" When she went closer, she smelled paint. "Oh! Alex. You've already started the activity room."

"Our staff artists got going my first day here. They're nearly done the walls."

It was the sort of place Susannah would have loved when she was a girl. Each mural represented one of the geological eras. The Precambrian wall was finished. Barren rock gradually gave way to oceans rich with oxygen-producing blooms of blue-green algae. The second wall introduced the Paleozoic era. Trilobites floated among seaweed in the shallow sea that had covered Alberta. Farther along the wall gaped the frightening jaws of the huge dunkleosteus…today's great white shark had nothing on that saber-toothed tank. The third wall took the children into more familiar territory—the world of the Mesozoic dinosaurs. Susannah could see faint sketches of Cenozoic animals on the fourth wall—early horses, North American camels, mammoths and saber-toothed tigers. Finally, looking small and defenseless, the first humans.

"I love it, Alex."

"We'll have sand tables in the middle, where kids can learn about erosion and water flow, and look for bones. We'll have a plaster table, where they can make casts of leaves and shells and footprints. And in the far corner—"

Susannah smiled. "Replica skeletons?"

Alex nodded. "I'm sure it can work."

"Of course it can."

"When we've got molds for replica bones we're making anyway, we'll make a second batch for the Discovery Room, just of smaller dinosaurs. I'm not imagining children could put a T-Rex together.''

"There are lots of three-meter dinosaurs.''

"Exactly. And a skeleton doesn't have to be finished by one group of children. It can take a week or a month or six months—we can take pictures and display a record of everyone who participates. They'll be part of something larger than themselves. That's good for kids.''

"I would have given anything for an experience like this twenty years ago.''

"So would I.'' Alex wandered closer to the Mesozoic wall. "Some days I wish I could roll up my sleeves and help with the painting, just lose myself here and forget about poachers. It's like a fairy tale, with dragons and mysterious lost kingdoms, but better, because it wasn't a fairy tale. It was real.''

"And even better than that, safely in the distant past.''

He turned from his study of the dinosaur wall, amusement on his face, eyes warm. "When I helped you out of the sinkhole, I thought I'd met a bold, adventurous woman.''

Never mind the emerald eyes and ivory complexion. She could be adventurous, couldn't she? What would it take? Fewer pots of tea, a reckless disregard for file management?

He came closer. "I don't think I was wrong. You did jump in after Matt.''

"With constant shaking and immense regret.''

"You're an intriguing mixture, Dr. Robb.''

She couldn't think with those observant eyes watching her so closely. She looked down, past the open neck of his shirt to his second button. A truly adventurous woman would undo it, slip her fingers underneath the cloth and slide the button out of the hole. How would he react, if she did?

"What are you smiling about, Susannah?" His voice was very quiet.

"Was I?"

"It was a faraway, dreamy smile."

"Oh. Well, no wonder. I was thinking about the wind-up—there'll be a huge bonfire and hot dogs and marsh-mallows." Susannah backed toward the door. "We should get to the camp, don't you think?"

"Absolutely. I don't want to keep you from anything that makes you smile like that."

EXCEPT FOR THE CLOUDS of hungry mosquitoes, mostly kept at bay by the campfire, it was a beautiful night. A row of tents, white in the moonlight, edged the winding riverbank. Behind them, hoodoos and hills threw bizarre shadows. Tall, thin monsignors in pointed hats seemed to walk through a disorderly hayfield.

"Your prime suspects are here," Susannah said. Diane and Tim had come to the windup. They were standing near the fire, threading marshmallows on willow sticks.

Tim hurried toward them. "Hi, Dr. Blake. Are you better yet, Auntie Sue?"

Susannah bent to give him a hug. "Much better. How about spending a couple of days digging with me soon, when your mom's away at Mount Field?"

"Can I, Mom?"

"If she doesn't work you too hard, or let you climb down sinkholes. Now let's go roast those marshmallows before they lose interest and jump on someone else's stick."

"That looks like a good idea," Alex said. "I'll grab us a handful of marshmallows before the kids get them all."

Susannah watched Alex make his way to the picnic table where James had piled all the makings of a bonfire feast. He was back in minutes, both hands full, his face free from the tension that had marked it since he'd arrived at the museum. The firelight made a dancing pattern of light and shadow on his face so that she could only sometimes see his eyes.

"Do you wear contacts?"

Puzzled, but ready to smile, he shook his head. "Why?"

"No reason." Darker blue ringed the outer edge of his iris. Maybe that accounted for the unusual depth of color.

He handed her a long willow stick. "I managed to wrestle five marshmallows away from Matt for you. He was trying to fill his entire stick, if you can believe it."

"I can." They found a spot beside the fire. Alex seemd inclined to go for the quick burn. Susannah held her stick well away from the flames, hoping for a crisp golden exterior and a melty inside. Under cover of the children's noise, she asked, "Did you know people think I'm frosty?"

"What people?"

"Around the museum."

"It can't be anyone who knows you well. Not Charlie or James or Diane. As far as the others go, I guess you've succeeded in fooling them."

"I haven't tried to convince anyone I'm a cold person. I'm not a cold person."

"I know you're not."

Susannah pulled her stick away from the fire to blow out flames consuming one of the marshmallows. A crackly black crust had formed. "You said I was like a stone, though."

He grimaced. "I'm such a sweet-talker. I think you do a really good impression of a stone, when it suits you."

"You do a really good impression of a pop paleontologist."

"Is that why you thought I'd be bad for the museum?"

"I may have been wrong about that."

Alex moved closer. "Some creep scared you off, right?"

Startled, Susannah stared at him. To her relief, some of the children called Alex to join them. He hesitated, looking from the just-roasted marshmallows to Susannah. "Do you mind if I spend a little time with the kids?"

"Go ahead. It's their last night."

As their stomachs filled, the children were calming down and beginning to talk to each other quietly. One boy, patiently turning a hot dog on a stick from side to side over a flame, said, "At last I'll have something interesting to write about my summer vacation. Instead of telling about all the car games I played while we drove for two weeks, and about all the museums my parents dragged me through."

"And stores," added Melissa. "Wherever we go for holidays, my mother wants to go shopping."

"Matt can write about the summer of the sinkhole," someone suggested.

"With all those dangerous snakes," Julia added quietly, in a tone that told Susannah she had learned the truth about Matt's claim.

The children were beginning to realize the end of camp could mean the end of new friendships. They had taken photographs, and exchanged street and e-mail addresses, but this time was over, and soon the wind and rain would stir the sand again, covering all traces of their visit.

THE STEALTH MOVED QUIETLY and smoothly through the night, headlights shining on the gravel road ahead. "You're very quiet."

"I was thinking about the kids, feeling sort of sad and satisfied at the same time. You really saved Matt's holiday with that contract. He's going home happy. He's learned a lot, and nobody is mad at him."

"And I'll eventually recover from this afternoon in the lab." Alex turned into the museum parking lot and stopped beside Susannah's car.

"Good night, Alex." Instead of getting out of the car, she found herself moving closer to him. She reached out, hesitantly at first, to trace the lines of his face. Slowly she trailed her fingers from the point where his hair swept back from his forehead, to the soft corner of his eye where laugh lines crinkled, to the roughness of his cheek and the line of his jaw. He brought his hand to her face, moving lightly from her cheek to her chin, lingering at the warm hollow of her throat, continuing to the notch between her collarbones, stopping at the first fastened button of her blouse.

"You're so beautiful. Do you even know that? It's not just your features. I mean, your eyes are distracting—that dark, warm gray, always changing expression. And your hair. I'd like to see it down sometime, no braids or elastics—"

"Alex..."

"But it's more than a physical quality. Maybe it's your intensity—"

"I'm not intense."

"You don't think so? We'll have to get the videotaping project going. Then you'll get a more objective look at yourself."

Susannah took a deep breath. "I've been trying so hard to ignore this feeling."

Alex nodded regretfully. "That's probably the best thing to do. It's what I keep telling myself. After all, I'm investigating everyone for fossil poaching. Then I'm leaving."

She felt a small tug of protest at the thought of him going. "You're not investigating me." It was half question, half statement.

Alex just looked at her.

"You're investigating me?"

He smiled at the incredulity in her voice. "Everyone." The smile vanished. "Why do you have fossils in your upstairs cupboard?"

At first, she didn't know what he meant. When she understood, she was angry. "You looked in my cupboard—"

"The day I took you home and made up the sofa bed for you."

"You went in my cupboard and you looked at my things and you used what you saw as evidence against me."

"Not as evidence. It's just a question, and you haven't answered it."

As she remembered bits of conversations they'd had from time to time, her anger mounted. "Those casual questions about my house, about whether I take fossils home to study—those conversations, when I thought we were getting to know each other better—those were part of your investigation? In the process of convincing me to trust you, you satisfied your suspicions by snooping in my home?"

"I didn't snoop." He sounded indignant. "I got a blanket for you. I just happened to see the fossils. Once I'd seen them, I had to look into it."

"I've had those fossils for years. My brother gave me the ammonite when I was still in high school. The— What else is in that drawer?"

"A piece of limestone imprinted with fish scales—"

"I found that along the riverbank on my property. I'm allowed to keep it. The coal with the leaf imprint I bought at Dorothy's. She has a permit to sell that kind of thing. My office shelves are full right now, otherwise I'd probably display them in full sight, along with my rock collection. Did you have any suspicions about that, by the way? I've got a piece of gold ore in there, you know. Maybe I'm stockpiling gold. When I get enough ounces of it, I can control the economy."

"I had to ask."

"No, you didn't."

"I couldn't assume innocence in anyone. But I have a different reason for asking you now. Since fossils have disappeared from your quarry, Henri has been interested in you."

"In me?"

"I need to be able to convince him you're not a good suspect. I can explain the fossils in your house now, and I can explain how you paid for your house. I did a land titles search—" At the look on her face he stopped. He took a deep breath, then pressed on. "I know how much you borrowed from your bank, and how much from your parents, and how much of a down payment you'd saved. It's clear you didn't get an unexplainable windfall to buy your house."

"Maybe I'll go see this Henri Beaubier tomorrow," she said. "If he has questions about me, he can ask."

"Don't do that. I'll deal with him."

Susannah stared out the window while she struggled with her anger. Slowly she was accepting the possibility that someone at the museum—not a convenient stranger—was stealing fossils. It could be a member of the board or a janitor—it didn't have to be a scientist or a technician—but someone was poaching, and apparently it was Alex's job to find out who it was.

She still wasn't sure how Alex and Sergeant Beaubier had ended up in the same town. More calmly, she asked, "Is what you're doing now part of the earlier investigation you mentioned?"

"No. Catching poachers is a full-time job for Henri, but it was just a temporary thing for me. The board heard about it, though, so when Bruce decided to leave, they approached me."

"You mean they didn't hire you because you were..." Susannah paused, uncertain how to phrase her question.

"A better paleontologist than you? No."

Weeks of tension left Susannah's body. She hadn't been passed over because of any professional weakness. The board had wanted an investigator. "Your interest in my quarry...is that mostly about fossil research or poachers?"

"I've been looking for anything that would suggest who might be stealing fossils, and how it's being done. It hasn't been easy to keep my attention on that goal. The excavation's exciting, the kids are fun...and I think about you all the time."

Susannah looked at her hands, folded neatly on her lap. He kept saying things like that, and it was beginning to seem less and less of a game.

"Thanks for the lift." She headed to her own car while she was still willing to go.

CHAPTER FIFTEEN

ALEX CALLED while Susannah was still half-asleep and lounging in her nightgown. "I had a great idea as soon as I woke up."

Susannah smiled, happy to hear his voice. "I'm still at the stage of wondering if I should get dressed."

"You should. The sooner, the better. I'm ready to go."

She peered at the clock. It was after ten, late enough to be energetic if you hadn't been up half the night replaying conversations about beauty and trusted friends being poachers. "You're going to the quarry with me again today?"

"I didn't know you were planning to work." He paused. When he continued, he sounded less sure of himself. "I'd like to take you to Calgary."

"To see Kim?"

"Her family isn't letting anyone through. There's no reason to go, except that we need some time together...at least, I think we do. A holiday." When Susannah didn't answer, he elaborated. "I want to get the sand out of my ears, see a movie, talk with you about something besides fossils. I thought on the way back you could show me where the serviceberries grow."

After a short silence, he said, "Susannah?"

"I'm thinking." Should she close her eyes and leap, or suggest something less intense? They could stay away from the sand and rent a video. They could do something less committed than spend a weekend together. What did a weekend together mean to him, anyway? "The overnight part…"

"Separate rooms," he said quickly.

Why was she hesitating? It sounded wonderful. Diane was right—if she succeeded in pushing Alex away, she would regret it. "What time should I be ready?"

"Can you make it in about an hour?"

"See you then."

Susannah stood beside the telephone. The fish would need a couple of blocks of dissolving weekend food. She would need to find a dress at the back of her closet. That meant she'd have to shave her legs. Maybe put on nail polish.

When the Stealth drew up to the front door, she was ready. She felt almost glamorous in a sleeveless light gray dress, with her hair pulled back and knotted loosely. Her nails were broken and uneven from work, so she'd forgotten about polish, but filed the edges smooth. She'd gone so far as to use a soft gray eyeliner.

Alex smiled when she got in the car. "I'm glad we're doing this."

"So am I." She threw an overnight bag into the back seat. For once Alex wasn't wearing jeans. His summerweight sport jacket was flecked with hues of sand and brown, just like the varied shades of his hair.

He turned the car and headed back to the municipal road. "I suppose we'll want to stop for lunch on the way."

"Lunch? I forgot breakfast. I just hurried."

"We'll pick up something at Dorothy's, then." He ignored the turnoff to the highway, continuing on the road to town instead.

At the sound of the door chimes, Dorothy looked up

from the lunch counter, where she was filling cream jugs and sugar bowls. "Well, good morning! You two are out and about early. All dressed up, too."

Alex reached for his wallet. "We'd like some breakfast to go. Juice and muffins, I suppose, something easy to eat in the car."

Dorothy shook her head in disapproval and wonder. "How you keep in such good shape the way you eat, I don't know. That's no way to start your day, Alex." She turned curious eyes to Susannah. "Now, don't you look nice? I don't think I've ever seen you in a dress." She glanced back and forth from Susannah to Alex, obviously longing to ask what was going on. "Tell me, how's young Miss Johnson doing? Better now?"

"Her parents took her to Calgary," Susannah said. "They wanted a specialist to take care of her. The last time I saw her, she was still very shaky and unsure of herself."

Dorothy's face had tightened. "I heard she was doing better."

"She is, slowly. It looks like she'll miss a term at university, though."

"The poor girl. The things some people will do." Dorothy turned to the icebox. She poured fresh-squeezed orange juice into two paper cups and popped lids on top. "I made these muffins myself," she muttered, slipping them into a paper bag with the cups. "Halved the sugar and used applesauce instead of so much fat. Oatmeal, raisins, apple chunks." She folded the bag shut, neatly creasing the paper once, twice, then a third time.

Her back still to them, she looked at the old photographs behind the grocery counter. "You know my dad was a fossil hunter." She touched the picture of the man with the ankylosaurus. "That's him. He dug up skeletons for museums out of the country—that ankylosaur ended up in Boston. I always thought I'd go see it in its new home, but I never got around to it. He made good money. Good for those days, anyway."

Alex moved restlessly. "I'm sure he did, Dorothy."

"There's still money in fossils. But you know that. Some folks look at those great bones sticking out of the ground and they just want one of their own. There's fossil markets around where nobody cares how you came by the pieces you're selling. I'm not saying I know anyone who would do such a thing—it's against the law now, after all—but I hear there's folks in Calgary who can help a person unload bones that aren't meant to leave the province."

"Is that so?" Alex asked. "But you don't know anyone like that."

"Heavens, how would I know that sort of person?" Dorothy put the paper bag on the counter. When Alex took a five-dollar bill from his wallet, she said, "No, dear. My treat. Have you been to Harry's Exchange in Calgary, that antique and pawn shop? It's an interesting place. My dad knew the original owner. I think his son runs it now." She looked as if she would say something more, then changed her mind. "Drive safely. The highway can be dangerous on the weekend." She walked slowly back to the lunch counter.

As the car pulled away from the grocery store, Alex said grimly, "Dorothy did everything but handcuff this guy at the antique shop. The question is, how involved is she?"

"Dorothy? She's not involved at all—"

"Susannah. You can't just declare your friends innocent because you feel like it."

"She's a sweet old lady—"

"She's not sweet."

"She's an old lady."

"Which proves what?"

"That she didn't hit Kim, and that nobody, including you or Sergeant Beaubier, is going to send her to jail."

"You'd protect her if she's guilty?"

Susannah stared at the road, smooth asphalt now. Would she protect a fossil poacher? "It would depend what she did. Dorothy's not behind the thefts from the museum and the quarries, I'm sure of that."

"Why are you sure?"

"She sells me groceries, she gives me advice about nutrition, she tells me to have kids whether I'm married or not…"

"Susannah."

"Dorothy isn't violent. She's upset that Kim's recovering so slowly. That's why she told us about the antique shop."

"She's obviously up to something."

"But something else, not the problem we're having. You saw her jars of fossils. Rock shops and hobby stores all over the continent sell that kind of thing. I wouldn't be surprised if she supplied small fossils like those, or if she sold the surface fossils that people around here like to pick up. Arthur talked about that, about how fossil hunting used to be like picking berries, about fossils being a resource like any other."

"So we protect her?"

"Absolutely."

"We shouldn't."

Susannah took a deep breath. She would expect someone who used to think of rules as speed bumps to understand why it was all right to bend this one. "I know we should protect the fossils and the information we can get from them. Of course we should. We should also protect an old lady who's lived here all her life. I'll talk to her about it, but I won't report her.''

Alex reached for the paper bag Dorothy had given them, and lifted out a cup of juice. He tore open the drinking flap, and took a long gulp of the thick, cool liquid. ''I'll think about it, Susannah.''

He'd think about it? He'd been in town for what, three weeks, and it was up to him to decide what happened to Dorothy?

They drove in silence, watching as the dry badlands became grassy, rolling, ranching and farming country. Grain elevators replaced oil wells. Clumps of deciduous and evergreen trees alternated with fields of barley and meadows full of grazing shorthorn cattle. Monday's heavy rain was still in evidence—the heavy heads of barley had been flattened, and mallard ducks were treating the full ditches like home.

THEY WATCHED the door of the antique shop from the car, the windows on both sides rolled all the way down to let in any passing breezes. Alex had folded his jacket on the back seat, and undone the top two buttons of his shirt. There was a relaxed, almost festive mood on the street. Vendors had set up under trees—there were hot dogs and miniature doughnuts, ice cream and pizza by the slice. To the delight of a few watching children, a clown tried to juggle helium balloons. A little way down from the antique store, a sweet-voiced girl strummed a guitar and sang about a boy who'd been careless with her heart.

''I'm sorry about this, Susannah. The whole idea of the trip was to get a break from fossils and poachers. It shouldn't be much longer. Henri said he'd arrange surveillance right away.''

''That's okay. This is fun. I've never been on a stakeout

before." Susannah reached into the bag on the seat between them and took another of the tiny cinnamon-sugar doughnuts. She finished it in two bites. "We'll be out of supplies soon, though. Maybe we should leave a bunch of money with the vendor and ask him to bring us bags at regular intervals, say every fifteen minutes."

Alex tried to keep his eyes on the store. "You wouldn't enjoy them as much if you couldn't see the circles of dough rolling along the belt into the fat and out again."

"That's true." She handed him a doughnut. "What will happen when the police get here? Will they search the store?"

"Henri said Dorothy's information doesn't give a judge a good enough reason to issue a search warrant. They'll need to find more convincing proof first."

"So we should catch someone going into the shop with a tyrannosaur bone over his shoulder?"

"That's the plan."

Alex's conversation with Henri had become tense at one point. The sergeant wasn't happy to hear that Alex and Susannah had discussed the investigation. After a long silence, Henri had said flatly, "You told her? Why?"

Because I wanted to. "I thought it would be useful to get some input from someone who knows the staff better than I do."

"And was it?"

"She's still thinking it over, getting used to the idea of poachers."

There was another silence. "I hope telling her wasn't a mistake, Alex."

"I've spent a lot of time with her. She's not involved. She's dedicated. Bruce Simpson trusted her." In an attempt to lighten the tension, he'd said, "Besides, she spends most of her time being mad at me. She doesn't have energy left to run a crime ring."

They'd left it at that, but Alex doubted he'd managed to get Susannah off the hook. Not that she'd stay there long. He was confident Henri wouldn't find any evidence against her.

"Just two left," Susannah said. "I guess that's one for you and one for me."

Alex looked away from the store, smiling. "Now who's the ten-year-old? Go ahead, have both."

"I shouldn't."

"There's cinnamon sugar down the front of your dress. And down the front of you, if I'm not mistaken." Sunlight glistened off the crystals on her skin.

"The store, Alex."

Reluctantly he turned his attention back to the antique shop, even though there was nothing to see.

THE RESTAURANT WAS IN a converted warehouse, with the original brick walls and scarred wood floor exposed. Alex and Susannah sat beside a large arched window with a view of the river. Outside, waterbirds swooped down, their feet touching the water with a splash, and away, holding nothing that Susannah could see. A swift, silent kayak glided by, then a meandering canoe.

Alex sat to Susannah's right, all the intensity he usually divided between fossils and poachers and campers now focused on her. She knew he was looking at her, and she was doing her level best not to look back. Since they'd arrived at the restaurant, all her doubts about the possibility of having a relationship with him had come flooding back.

"I guess it was too much to hope for, that a poacher would go to the antique shop the moment we were watching," she said. "Maybe Dorothy's wrong about the place. Just because the father had fossil marketing contacts, it doesn't mean the present owner is ready to break the law."

"It's worth a look, though. Without the right contacts, it can be difficult to unload fossils. Somebody—say, James, just as a meaningless example—could spirit away as many specimens as he wanted, but have to sit on them forever."

Susannah frowned. "It's not James."

They fell silent while a waiter exchanged their salad plates for wide, shallow bowls of Moules Provençale. Alex lifted the bottle of wine, ready to pour. "More for you?"

"Please."

"You look lovely tonight, Sue." His gaze slipped from her face to the low neckline of her dress and lingered there. "That's a very alluring dress—"

"Alluring?" Susannah sat back, making sure the neckline was as high as it could go. The dress had been pushed to the back of her closet for so long she'd forgotten the way the neckline draped. If she leaned forward, she was in trouble. "It's just practical. Wrinkle free. Perfect for traveling."

He smiled. "You struggle so hard to control your passionate side."

"Wrong on both counts. There's no struggle and no passionate side."

"No? You make so much effort to structure your life, but you lie naked in bubbles while stargazing. You feel pity for dinosaurs that were hunted seventy million years ago. You hold your body so stiffly, trying to hide how sensuous it really is. Don't you feel it crying out for attention? I do."

She took a deep breath and let it out slowly. "Is it because I'm here?"

"Is what because you're here?"

"Like Everest. Do you want to—climb me—because I'm here?"

His quick smile was followed by a frown. "I've never met a woman who asked so many questions about my reasons for wanting her."

Wanting. Susannah didn't like the word, not one bit. People wanted new cars, or fries with their burgers. "Maybe it's because there's a shortage of available women around the museum. Or is it just that you're challenged by someone you can't control?"

Quietly Alex said, "I don't want to control you. Life would be dull if people always did what I wanted. I like surprises."

Susannah's voice was stiff. "I'm afraid I can't offer you any surprises."

"You've offered me plenty already."

The waiter reappeared, expressing concern about Susannah's half-eaten dinner. Reassured that the problem was with her appetite and not with the chef's efforts, he carried the bowls away, promising to return with coffee.

"What about Carol?"

"Carol and I have a casual friendship."

"Casual sex?" It embarrassed her to say it, but she had to know.

"You seem to think I'm some kind of Lothario."

"Aren't you?"

He almost laughed. "When would I have time? I almost never take a day off. I dig for fossils for months on end. Covered in dirt, no showers for miles. Women don't like that."

"Women flocked around you in Australia."

Alex seemed to enjoy the memory.

"When you think back to those days now, do you see me?"

He nodded. "I see a quiet, shy girl who flustered easily."

"Not your type?"

"I didn't pursue women, Susannah."

The waiter glided by, setting two cups of coffee on the table. When he was gone, Susannah said, "I see. You were just being agreeable. All right then, what if I had pursued you?"

"I hope I would have suggested a game of cards or a walk, and made a date for about five years later."

"Do you really think that's all it was? I was too young?"

"Or I was too old and too wild."

"Have you ever had a serious relationship, I mean one where the availability of showers didn't matter?"

"I nearly got married once."

"What happened?"

"Heather thought I was the most fun she'd ever had. Then she came out to a quarry with me. She didn't like the long hours and the isolation. She didn't like how wrapped up I got in the work. She said I was just digging in the dirt with a bunch of unwashed men."

Susannah couldn't stop a small snort of indignation. "And you liked this shallow woman?"

"Not so much after that."

She smiled. "How wrapped up you get in your work is one of the things I like best about you." Feeling like she was jumping off the deep end, she added, "The surprising thing is, I like the way you are when you're not wrapped up in your work, too. Usually, that is."

Alex examined his coffee long enough that she wondered if she should have bitten her tongue. Finally he looked at her. "I have a strong urge to cancel one of the rooms I booked."

Susannah's heart gave a sudden thud, like a kick. "That seems…wasteful. We'd lose the deposit."

"All right. Should we just agree to move ahead slowly?"

Slowly seemed like a good idea. On the other hand, slowly took them into the future, after the poachers were caught and Alex was gone.

They walked back to their hotel and, just before Alex went to his own room, they kissed. He held her close, and she felt the warmth of his body through the cool fabric of his shirt. His arm curved around her, his hand on the small of her back. This time, Susannah made sure there was no room for discussion about whether it was really a kiss.

He was the first to pull away. "I suppose we should say good-night."

"I suppose we should."

They both heard her reluctance. He smiled, not the triumphant smile from the Gobi Desert photograph.

Susannah kept the drapes open so she could see the stars through the hotel window as she lay in bed. They had to compete with the starlike dots of light that shimmered from the city's tall office buildings, but they were the same stars she watched from her badlands home miles way. Her mind lingered on the thought of Alex lying in a matching bed on the other side of the wall. He hadn't mentioned deeper feelings, just desire. Maybe that was all he felt. Diane had claimed Alex liked her, though, and Diane was observant enough to find inch-long fossils in the mountains of British Columbia.

THEY TOOK THEIR TIME on Sunday, working their way home indirectly. Secondary roads took them through gently rolling hills and quiet valleys. They stopped at a market garden along Serviceberry Creek, where they picked strawberries and saskatoons, and bought biscuits and lemonade.

With the car windows rolled down to let in the summer air and the smells of wildflowers and ripening grain, they drove until they came to a cliff overlooking the Rosebud River. They pressed down wild hay to make a cushioned place where they could stretch out and enjoy a picnic of the berries they'd picked.

Alex produced a small package. "I went for a walk while you were sleeping this morning. I found a little something for you, just by chance."

The package was a square, maybe four inches wide. It was very light, probably too light to register anything on a scale. Susannah shook it. There was no sound. Curious, she untied the thin, curling gold ribbon and slowly unfolded the ends of the white, gold-flecked tissue paper. "Sponge toffee!"

"A candy store just down the road from the hotel makes it. Dorothy mentioned that you wanted some and that she was having trouble getting it, and incidentally, that she was worried about your teeth."

"Alex, thank you." She took a small bite and felt the candy melt against her tongue. That had always been her favorite thing about sponge toffee. "I think I'll save it. I'll have it in the bathtub tonight."

Rosebushes grew profusely all along the cliff. Alex stretched out on his side, his head propped up on one hand, popping berries into his mouth. "We'll have to come back in the spring so we can see the roses blooming."

Susannah wondered if he really thought they would still

be doing things together all those months from now. "I often come here in the spring. It's beautiful then. There's so much variety in the shades of the roses. Some are so pale they're almost white. Then there's a whole spectrum of pinks to a shade so rich and deep it's nearly red."

Alex seemed less interested in her description of the delicate five-petaled flower than in the news that she often came to the riverbank. "Who do you come with?"

"With various people. Sometimes by myself."

"With James?"

"James loves it here. Sometimes we go swimming." She glanced at Alex's profile. He looked tense.

"I've wondered what kind of relationship you have with James."

"A friendly one."

Alex pulled her down on the ground beside him. "Friendly? So no one's going to be mad if I kiss you again?"

"Not James, anyway." She wasn't really interested in a kiss right now, though. Her uncertainty about his plans was too distracting. "Won't you be gone by spring, Alex?"

"I've been thinking about staying. I wouldn't have to keep the job, if it's a problem."

"Of course you should keep it. You're wonderful at it."

"I'm sure the board would snatch me up in a second, in some other capacity," he said lightly. "After all, there's only one Indiana Blake."

Susannah gave a small groan. "You heard about that?"

He pulled her closer to him, so close she could feel his heart beating. Lightly he ran his lips along her throat, his fingers over the fabric of her blouse to her breast. Exhilarated shivers tingled through her, but her body involuntarily tensed. Alex noticed. "Is something wrong?"

"I should tell you…" She stopped. How could she say this? "I should warn you. I'm a dead loss at it. At sex." She tried to make it a joke. "I have no aptitude at all."

"Who says? The crumb-offering creep?"

She couldn't help smiling. "He wasn't a creep. Really. My…deficits just became obvious."

Alex released her and again lay with his head propped up on one hand. "That must have been convenient for him. Tell me about him. The jerk who wasn't a creep."

Laughing a little, Susannah sat up. "It's not a very interesting story."

"I'm not asking to be entertained."

"He was perfectly nice. He didn't turn me against romance, if that's what you're thinking…it's just a coincidence that I haven't had any more long-term relationships. I've been immersed in work."

"Where did you meet?"

"At a lab table. We shared a microscope." She raised her eyebrows, aiming for levity. "The rest is history."

Alex smiled faintly. "He's a paleontologist?"

"A paleobotanist." She paused, remembering. "He was very serious. I liked that. We studied together, and we talked about working together. After graduate school, he found a job in Montana and I found one here. Our relationship didn't survive the distance between us."

"He didn't have his priorities straight."

Susannah smiled, appreciative of the endorsement. "After a while I realized I'd misinterpreted his single-mindedness as passion…for me." She gave an embarrassed shrug. "I just moved into his line of vision and got swept up in his obsession with work. It wasn't like it is for you and me. We get excited about our work. For him, it was everything. I'm sure he hardly noticed when I wasn't there anymore.''

''I'm kind of sorry for the guy. He doesn't seem to have a clue what life is all about. Just floats through it, thinking about blooms of Precambrian algae the whole time.''

''That's him,'' Susannah said with a small laugh. ''We were going to get married, if you can imagine that. It's a good thing we didn't.''

''I'll say.'' He touched her arm. ''I get the feeling you're ready to test the waters again.'' The intent expression in his deep blue eyes distracted her. Gentian blue? ''There's so much I'd like us to do together. I want to travel with you and work with you, and share your enthusiasm for toffee and stars and fish—''

''You mean you want to go to fish club meetings with me?''

Alex hesitated. ''Sure. They must be very interesting. I suppose I'd learn all about the different species—''

''Don't worry. I don't go to fish club meetings.'' Susannah began brushing pieces of grass off her clothes. ''I wonder if there's any lemonade left.'' She looked around for the bags that had contained their snack. ''Oh, good, there is. Would you like some?''

Alex stared for a second, adjusting to the sudden change in mood. ''Thanks. And some berries, if there are any.''

They looked out over the river as they sipped lemonade and nibbled fruit. A wood duck floated by, every few moments going under for food, tipping its tail into the air.

''This reminds me of home,'' she said. ''There are saskatoons in my parents' woods, and we used to picnic by the water in the summer, just like this. They have a century farm right on a river.''

"What's a century farm? A hundred acres?"

He seemed to be serious. "You're such a city slicker, Alex, in spite of all the time you've spent in the wilds. A century farm is one that's been owned by the same family for a hundred years or more. One of my brothers is gradually taking over...the fourth generation to work the same land."

"I don't know how far back you'd have to go to find someone who knew how to grow things in my family. My dad has a store. My mother volunteers and worries about us, and my sister's a teacher. Nobody even has a garden. Potted plants maybe."

Susannah could believe it. "Somehow, I never thought of you as having a home base. It suggests you're not always off adventuring, that you just do ordinary things sometimes. Like watching TV and having the flu and being bored on a rainy day...except I can't imagine you ever being bored."

"I don't put up with it for long."

Even though Alex said it lightly, it turned Susannah cold. She had started to believe the fairy tale about long and wonderful days together, now and in the future. She would have to remember the reality—that Alex would always have one eye on the door.

CHAPTER SIXTEEN

THE QUARRY WAS DESERTED. The tents still stood—the dining shelter, the supply tent, the home away from home that Alex had erected beside the trackway—but Susannah's team hadn't arrived yet, and the science camp kids were gone for good. It was odd not to see them hard at work under the tarp. She would miss Matt's enthusiastic questions, Melissa's quiet competence, Julia's worried puzzling.

Susannah had come to the quarry alone, in a truck that suddenly and unexpectedly felt much too roomy. There'd been no sign of Alex at the museum. After the intimacy of the past two days, she'd half expected flowers on her desk, or at least a smiling Alex waiting outside her office. But there was nothing, not even a message.

When she reached the trackway, she stopped, stunned.

A huge rectangular chunk of rock was gone.

The ground was cut as neatly as if a piece of sod, rather than rock, had been removed. She stared at the wide cavity that was left, at its clean-cut right angles. A flattened trail led away from the hole in the ground, and tire tracks were visible nearby. It looked like the slab had been dragged to a waiting truck. With a sick, hollow feeling, Susannah hurried to check the rest of the site. The tangled pile of newly uncovered bones seemed to be undisturbed. The femur and pelvis Alex and the children had worked on the week before was gone.

"Hey, Sue!" It was James, rounding the last corner before the quarry. "Sorry I'm late. I've got the beer, as promised. Nobody else here yet? Where's Alex?"

"Alex? I don't know." James looked happy, no doubt relieved that he no longer had to do two jobs. She realized she should warn him. "Something awful has happened. Prepare yourself before you come any closer."

"What? You've got measles?" He grinned as he walked, swinging a cooler too small to carry more than a six-pack. "I actually slept on the weekend. Might be an odd thing for a guy in his prime to be happy about, but when you've been helping scared kids find the outhouse in the dark for weeks, sleep is an amazing— Oh, my God." He stopped, then let the cooler drop and hurried to the trackway. "What happened? How could this happen?" He looked around, saw the trail and the tire tracks, and the tears on Susannah's face.

"I didn't take any precautions. Isn't that ridiculous? I didn't know it was possible to steal something as heavy as this."

James still looked stunned. "I read about the same thing happening in Australia a few years ago…a trackway was stolen there, too. Stegosaurus prints, I think. If you have the right equipment…" He shook his head in disbelief.

"I'll go back to the museum and call the police, I guess. Can you—"

"I'll take care of things here," he assured her. "We'll keep digging. There'll be more trackway."

"But only one more femur. A not so complete skeleton."

James shrugged. "So he had a limp."

Being able to smile made things seem a little better. Susannah was about to thank James for managing to bring humor to the awful morning when she heard voices approaching. A moment later, the rest of the team appeared. All of the people she had trusted completely looked horrified. The new field technician seemed more interested in everyone's reactions than in the theft. When he saw her watching him, he started doing a better job of shaking his head in amazement. For all she knew, Alex had hired a thief.

CHARLIE STARED at Susannah, aghast. "Gone? How can a trackway disappear?"

"Can you imagine someone digging up and transporting a six-inch-deep slab of rock in the dark?"

"This is awful. You were so happy when you found it. Have you called the police?"

"Not yet."

Charlie looked like he was going to pick up the phone. "We don't publicize the locations of sites. Someone must have overheard a conversation about the trackway—everybody hears everything at Dorothy's eventually."

Susannah had forgotten that Charlie didn't know poachers were operating at the museum. She wished she could tell him. "It doesn't seem likely. Someone with the intention and capability of moving a chunk of rock that size just happened to hear gossip and got right at it?" She shook her head. "They were prepared for this, just waiting for an opportunity."

"What does Alex think?"

"He doesn't know. I can't find him."

There was a short, expressive silence. "I can't help but think wherever Alex goes, fossils disappear. He sweeps through my lab and I spend the next few weeks trying to trace specimens. He's with you when you find the trackway, and now it's gone."

Susannah frowned. Charlie was bending the truth, as he always did where Alex was concerned.

"Do you want to use my telephone?"

She should talk to Sergeant Beaubier, and she couldn't do that here. "Thanks, but I'll call from my office."

ALEX NODDED to the woman at the receptionist's desk and went right by to the interrogation room, as Henri had told him to do. The officers watching the antique store had spotted a black Chevy Silverado the previous night. The plates were so dirty they'd had to go right up to it to decipher the number. After tracing it through the DMV, they'd notified Henri. All the Mountie had told Alex was, "If you want to see who's been running the illegal Bearpaw quarry, come right over."

A video monitor suspended from the ceiling showed Alex what was going on inside the room. Small, and black and white, Paul Robbins sagged in a chair, looking sick. Henri looked as comfortable as he might in his own living room.

"Just tell me about your part in the thefts," he was saying.

Paul muttered something.

"Would you speak up for the recorder, please?"

Louder, Paul said, "There was an ad on my e-mail a few years ago. You can be a paleontologist and an entrepreneur, too! Bring prehistory alive! Call this number, e-mail another one and so on." He licked dry lips and swallowed nervously. "And I thought, why not check it out?"

"What happened when you contacted the sender?"

"Nothing much. They sent me pamphlets about fossil sales in Texas and Arizona and all over the place. These weren't black markets. Reputable scientists go to these fairs."

"They were establishing their credentials, reassuring you."

"I guess. All the pamphlets had forms to fill out if you wanted more information. So I sent one and got a letter back. It looked really official and aboveboard." He glanced at Henri almost appealingly, as if he wanted to be reassured he hadn't been a complete idiot. Henri said nothing.

"It explained how I could start making money without spending any. It reviewed the law. What things I was allowed to sell and where. There didn't seem to be anything wrong with that."

"So you collected fossils legally at first, things that can be sold or exported?"

"That's right." Paul seemed to be holding on to that idea, his proof that he hadn't strayed as far as people might think. "I didn't go into this with any intention of breaking the law."

"Did you apply to the province for ownership of the fossils you collected?"

Paul just looked at the sergeant.

"It's legal to collect specimens from the surface if it's your own property, or if you have permission from the property owner, but they still belong to the province. Before you can sell them, the province has to agree to transfer ownership to you, and that can only be done with a few kinds of fossils like ammonite and oyster shells."

"Oh."

"So, your collection and exportation was, in fact, illegal. What happened next?"

Paul cleared his throat. "I started exchanging e-mails with some guy, he called himself the Bone Man."

"What did this Bone Man want you to do?"

"Nothing. The next step was my idea. I thought if I

sold something from the quarry, I could finance my whole education. He said that was too risky.''

"Looking out for you, was he?''

"He said maybe I could get away with it if I just took one fossil a year.'' A look of shame crept across Paul's face. "I thought, one good fossil. There was a beautiful little alligator skull in the lab, no different from alligators today. I just tucked it under my shirt.'' After a moment, he added, "Ten thousand dollars.''

"That would go a long way toward financing the rest of your education. Or didn't you see much of the money?''

Paul seemed surprised the Mountie guessed that. "Well, there were costs. And he took the risk of selling it.''

"So you needed something bigger, more valuable.''

Paul nodded. "This year I got a message saying to push the envelope, to take as much as I could, then we'd be done. It was the first time he told me outright to break the law.'' He looked at the floor before continuing, "I found a nearly complete mosasaur skeleton.''

"Just what George Connery was looking for,'' Henri observed. "Instead of telling him, you told your contact.''

"Yeah. He arranged for a team to help me dig it up.''

"We saw the site.''

Paul rubbed his head as if it hurt. "There's another skeleton. A small plesiosaur.''

"Ms. Johnson's find, I believe. After she was out of the way, you directed Dr. Connery's attention away from it.''

Paul's eyes closed. He looked paler than before. "That's why I was at the store last night. Making arrangements for it to be moved.''

"Tell me about the attack on Kim Johnson.''

"Kim told me she was going to work late." His voice was tight. He exhaled shakily. "I guess she wanted to look around the supply tent. She came in one day when I was moving some pieces of shale into a cooler from a crate—that's how I've been transporting small things." Paul stopped. "The look on her face..."

"What happened then?"

"I told her I meant to put them in a crate. We joked about sunstroke, because it bothers her that I don't wear a hat out there. I thought she believed me."

Calmly Henri asked, "Did you hit her the evening she returned to the quarry?"

"No! I didn't. I wouldn't. I wasn't even there. I was worried about her." He had to fight to keep his face from crumpling. "The guys who excavated the mosasaur went to the supply tent and found her looking around." His voice shook. "They told me they would have just gone away, but she heard them. She saw them."

Henri asked, "Who is the Bone Man?"

Paul shook his head. "I don't know. I never met the guy. I don't even know that he *is* a guy. I want to help you find him. I felt bad enough when it was just the mosasaur. After they hurt Kim—"

"Who else at the museum is working with you?"

Paul looked at Henri, his face blank. "You think somebody else at the museum is doing this, too?"

As EVENING APPROACHED, Susannah rifled through supplies in her office, preparing for a night at the quarry. Although it seemed unlikely the poachers would risk coming back to the same site, especially during the week when there was more activity, she wasn't going to take any more chances. A sleeping bag, three flashlights, a package of sandwiches and a thermos of tea were piled on the desk.

"What's all this?"

Susannah turned sharply at the sound of Alex's voice. "Where have you been?"

"Why, what's wrong?"

"You haven't heard? The trackway's gone."

A couple of quick blinks showed Alex's surprise. Softly he swore. "Damn."

"Everything we saw that morning, Alex. The juvenile prints, the carnivore prints. The ground has this great hole in it…" Her voice wobbled.

Alex took a couple of quick steps to stand beside her. "I'm so sorry. I should have arranged more security. It didn't occur to me they'd take something so huge. What have you done about it so far?"

"I called the RCMP. Sergeant Beaubier wasn't available. They said they'd take casts of the tire tracks, that it might help them identify the truck used to cart the specimens away. I looked everywhere for you, Alex. Where were you?"

"Henri called me in to talk about the case. I'm sorry I wasn't here." He nodded toward the mound of supplies. "What's all this?"

"I'm going to tent at the quarry tonight. Every night, I suppose, until I know there's no danger of anything else being stolen."

"I don't think the poachers will be back, but I'll hire some security guards tomorrow." Alex shook his head. "I know. Barn door. We'll get to the bottom of it, Sue, and we'll put these people out of business."

"I think you hired a poacher," she said. "The new field technician reacted really strangely this morning—"

"He's an undercover cop. I should have told you."

Susannah hardly reacted to the news. Unusual events were beginning to seem normal. "That's okay. What about Sylvia Hall? She wanted to know where the quarry was and made a big deal of promising to keep it confidential."

"It's closer to home than that. Just like we knew it would be."

Susannah folded her arms across her chest, as if she were cold. "Who?"

"Paul was arrested, after visiting the antique store to arrange a sale."

Deep down, she had expected the police to see a stranger going into the shop, carrying a parcel wrapped in brown paper. Inside the parcel they'd find a hadrosaur vertebra, and that would be that.

Briefly Alex told her about the confession. "He's genuinely upset about Kim."

"Good for him." Her voice flat, Susannah said, "I would never have thought of checking the coolers. But they go in and out of the quarry more than anything else does, carrying fresh food and drinks every day. It's so simple."

"At first, he limited himself to taking very small things, and not too often. Recently there's been pressure to take more. He was told it would be over soon."

Susannah's arms were still tight against her chest. "A couple of weeks ago, the day I skipped your meeting, Amy insisted on putting some water bottles in the cooler for me. I mean, she really insisted. She had a good reason, but the whole thing looks different now."

"I had a similar experience with her, but I didn't think much of it at the time. She was handling coolers, but claimed to be ordering supplies." Alex shrugged. "It's not compelling evidence."

"Am I supposed to keep working with her?"

"If you can. Paul seemed eager to make up for what happened to Kim. If he does as he said he would, and goes about his business as usual, without saying anything to this Bone Man about his arrest, the others won't be alerted that we're on to them. We should try to keep it that way."

Susannah nodded unhappily. "I'm not cut out for this."

"You don't have to be. The town is crawling with cops now. Let them worry about the poachers."

She smiled shakily. "That sounds good."

"I was hoping to suggest something very different for us this evening. A romantic moonlit dinner by the river outside your house. Why don't we adapt the idea? The quarry's as good a place as any to watch the stars."

A moonlit dinner in the badlands. It would be more than that. Susannah placed her hands lightly on his chest and felt it rising and falling. She felt his heart beating, slowly and steadily. Only half joking she asked, "What if the poachers, or the police, are peeking from behind the hoodoos?"

"Is there some reason we're going to need privacy?"

"It's possible."

"We have a tent with a zipper."

"You were thinking ahead."

"If I'd been thinking ahead, I would have provided something more comfortable than one tiny camp cot."

The cot. That made everything seem real, and immediate. Susannah wasn't sure she could stick to the path they were following. A stolen trackway and sex, all in one day? She had been born in the wrong time. *This is so sudden, sir. I had sex ten years ago. I've hardly had time to catch my breath...*

"Let me take care of dinner," Alex said. "We'll need

more than sandwiches, and I have experience cooking over an open fire. I was a Boy Scout, you know.''

''That explains a lot. The bandaging skills, the urge to help old ladies into bed.''

He smiled. ''I do my best.'' He let go of her and checked his watch. ''I'll find some food. Can you get that other sleeping bag? We'll meet at the truck in twenty minutes.''

The sleeping bag Alex had used the night of the storm was in the closet of the staff room. She needed two trips to take the bags and other supplies to the truck. Did she have everything? Flashlights, food, tea…

She stared at her backpack with a sinking feeling. She was missing one important item. He'd take care of it, wouldn't he? Or would he assume she would?

She felt in her pockets and pulled out some change. Two nickels, a dime, a quarter. That certainly wasn't enough. She made her way back upstairs to her office and checked her desk drawers. Three more dimes. There was nothing in the pockets of the jacket hanging in her closet. Not bothering to lock her door, she hurried to the staff room, to the margarine tub that held contributions to a communal coffeepot.

She pried off the lid. There were quarters and loonies and toonies, a couple of handfuls, at least. She pocketed a couple of dollars' worth of each kind of coin, then wrote a quick IOU before heading back downstairs.

She checked the hall outside the women's washroom, then peered inside. No cleaning staff anywhere. On the wall was a large white metal vending machine. A dollar twenty-five. Not bad. Susannah hadn't expected to be given so many choices. She skimmed from left to right, then went back to the beginning and read more slowly. There were a lot of factors to consider, apparently, and it all sounded like advice on decorating—color, texture, contrast.

A loonie and a quarter in each slot, she decided. No, two loonies and two quarters, just to make sure. Press each button twice, and stuff the little packages into her pocket without even looking at them. Later, if the occasion arose, and it might not, she'd just throw them all on the ground, as if she'd broken a piñata, and he could choose to his heart's content.

At the designated time, she stood in the parking lot waiting. Alex must have been out once already—some split logs had been stashed in the back of the truck. The staff door swung open, and he emerged with a cooler under one arm. He wedged it beside the logs to keep it secure during the drive.

He touched the back of his hand to her cheek the way her mother used to do. "Are you all right? You're flushed."

"I'm fine. I've been rushing around."

When they reached the rough, winding path into the canyon, the sun was already low, throwing long shadows in front of the hoodoos and rill-wrinkled hills. Ahead, they could see a battered Plymouth Horizon in the parking area. "Friend or foe?"

"It's James's car."

"I'll assume friend." Alex looked away from Susannah's quick frown. "How was your walk into the quarry this morning?"

"Almost back to normal. I took the crutch, but I didn't need it. I should be able to help carry the supplies in."

"Maybe something light, like a sleeping bag. You still need to be careful." Alex jumped out of the truck. He grabbed the packages of logs by the ropes that fastened them and started into the canyon. "I'm being selfish."

Susannah lifted the sleeping bags and followed. "Selfish?"

"If a bad sprain doesn't heal properly, it can flare up months later. How will you manage the portage when we're white-water rafting next summer if your ankle flares up?"

"White-water rafting?" Next summer?

"My sister and I go every year, in the B.C. interior. Most of the runs involve a fairly rough portage."

He wanted her to meet his sister. "I don't think I go white-water rafting."

"No? It's one of the big thrills—fighting with the river for control."

"And if the river wins?"

"Then you might have one hell of a ride, or you might get dunked."

"And smashed on the rocks?"

"That hardly ever happens."

James was kneeling at the riverbank, chiseling and brushing. The rest of the team was gone.

"The gash in the ground will make you feel sick," Susannah warned, as Alex started forward.

Startled to hear a voice, James looked up from his work. "Oh good, it's you. I didn't feel like fighting off poachers. Great news, Sue. The trackway continues, just as we hoped."

She hurried to his side. A few depressions were visible where he'd been digging. She saw one huge, beautifully clear print, made by an adult.

Alex crouched beside her. "The juvenile and the carnivore will be there, too."

"That's right," James agreed. "We'll keep at it tomorrow, and we'll uncover enough to see the whole pattern again.'' He noticed the sleeping bags and logs. ''Staying the night?''

Susannah nodded. ''We're guarding the place. We've brought dinner. Want some?''

After a glance at Alex, James said, ''I don't think so. I've had enough campfire food to last me for—well, till next year's science camp, I suppose. My favorite microwave dinner's waiting in my freezer.''

ALEX MADE A BASE for the fire with two of the thicker logs, then layered a bed of tinder across them, leaving spaces between each piece of wood. With gradually thicker sticks, he arranged eight crisscrossing layers.

''I've never seen that kind of fire before.''

''It's good for cooking. It burns quickly and leaves hot coals.''

When Alex held a match to the tinder, it caught easily, and flames flared up through the dry structure. There was a rush of crackling heat, but as he'd said, it didn't take long for the fire to die down. Glowing embers collapsed onto the ground between the two base logs. Small flames flickered around the edges.

''Oven's ready.'' He reached into the cooler and began lifting out aluminum foil packages. ''I raided the cafeteria kitchen again. Baked potatoes. Chicken halves in barbecue sauce. Vegetables. Apples stuffed with raisins and brown sugar.''

''It sounds wonderful.''

''The potatoes and chicken take the longest to cook, so we'll have to remember to add the rest later.''

He spread out one of the sleeping bags near the fire and sat down. It looked like a comfortable spot, and there was lots of room for two, but Susannah moved to a boulder a few feet away. She sniffed the air. "The food already smells good."

Alex set out a bottle of red wine and two sturdy wine-glasses. "My sister and I cook over a fire after rafting," he said. "We camp within sound of the rapids and cook all those Boy Scout-Girl Guide treats—s'mores, apples wrapped in foil, cake in a soup tin."

Susannah accepted a glass of wine. "Next summer, I'll be the cook. I'll have dinner all ready for the two of you when you get to the camp."

"That's not how it's done." He tipped his head back, wineglass to his lips. Firelight flickered over his throat and glimmered through the red of the wine. "It's no fun unless you're wet from the spray and your clothes steam while the food cooks." His voice changed when he noticed her face. "You're really scared? You're not joking?"

"I try not to do things that could kill me."

His face softened. "Then we'll change our system. It'd be nice to have the food ready when we got to camp." He laid his hand on the sleeping bag. "Sit with me, Susannah."

Her heart started to thud. *Here we go.* This was no ordinary invitation to sit by the fire. It wasn't to warm her toes. It wasn't to evade mosquitoes, and it wasn't to sing Christmas carols.

He reached for her hand.

I'm coming. Hold your horses.

"Sue." He closed his fingers around hers and pulled her closer. "Don't you trust me yet? Nothing you don't want to happen will happen. If you want to sit here and tell ghost stories, that's what we'll do."

"That would be worse."

"Worse?"

She sank onto the sleeping bag, soft over the hard ground. Alex sat near her, not touching, and they watched the embers and the remaining flames. An occasional spark leapt skyward, tracing a fleeting line of light in the air. She sipped her wine, then set the glass down carefully on a flat rock.

Alex rested his head on the second sleeping bag, still rolled up. "This is the best part of campfire cooking, that we can lie back from the oven and look up at the stars."

"And no dishes."

"Join me?"

A mass of butterflies took flight in her stomach. She felt as nervous as she used to before an exam—more, because at least when she faced an exam she knew what she was doing. Carefully, as if the sleeping bag were breakable, Susannah lay down beside him, not thinking about stars at all. From head to toe her body touched his, sending flurried messages along nerve endings.

"This reminds me of the way we met a couple of weeks ago. We've never talked about the sinkhole. What was it like, Sue?"

"Dark and deep." She wasn't sure how honest she wanted to be. She could feel Alex watching, quietly intent. "I worried about everything. Maybe I had predators for company. Maybe Matt and Melissa would get lost. Maybe they wouldn't be able to tell anyone where to find me..."

"You had a long wait."

Laughing a little, she added, "It even crossed my mind, just for a second, that I might never get out, that I'd have to live in the sinkhole forever, catching rainwater in my hat and waiting for careless toads to drop in for dinner."

"Aren't toads poisonous?"

"I wasn't worried about the details." Susannah began to enjoy the story. "You can imagine the outcome. I would have done wonderful cave drawings of the toads, and archaeologists, eons later, would have been so excited to find them. You know, *Toads were of enormous importance, nutritionally and spiritually, to the reclusive sinkhole dwellers.* And think how happy they'd be to find my bones. *A complete skeleton! It must be the priestess responsible for the drawings.*''

''Aha!''

''Aha?''

''That's exactly the argument I was making the other day, but you weren't having any of it.''

''What are you talking about?''

''Look how much the archaeologists read into your drawings—and it's all wrong. I rest my case.''

''They wouldn't really do that.''

''They would. You're very perceptive.''

''Oh, now that you think I'm proving your argument, suddenly I'm perceptive.''

''That's right. You're coming to your senses at last.''

Susannah smiled. ''Surprisingly, you were a bit of a help after the lights went out.''

''I was? How did I help?''

''I'd just read your article about finding the Paleolithic cave in Spain. I wished I'd been there, crawling through the dark tunnels going who knows where, then opening up without warning into a painted chamber. When the flashlight went out and I was left in the dark on the edge of panic, I compared the experiences—unexpected, underground, underlit, and told myself it was close enough. If you could do it, I could do it, too.''

He touched her cheek, just once, and then his hand was gone. ''Glad to help,'' he said softly. ''You would have loved that cave, Sue. Sometimes I think of archaeologists spending years looking for something like that and never finding it, and then we stumbled on it. It doesn't seem fair. Not that I'd change the experience."

Susannah turned so her face was close to his. "I wouldn't change anything, either. Losing the job to you, the sinkhole fiasco, all the tension there's been between us…because all that brought us here, to this." She cleared her throat. "Um, just for your information…" She pulled the little packages out of her pocket and dropped them onto the sleeping bag. "Just in case," she said. "I don't know if you have a preference…"

Alex kissed her lightly. "Thank you. That couldn't have been fun."

"Maybe I can learn to make my own—from simple items I already have at home."

Firelight flickered across his shadowed face, and she saw tiny flames reflected in his eyes. Careful that it didn't catch on her hair, he unwound the elastic that held her braid in place, then pulled his fingers through the twisted strands until her hair was loose around her shoulders. "I've been wanting to do that for ages. And, if you knew how long I've wanted to kiss this dusting of freckles across your nose…"

His lips moved from one cheek across her nose to the other. He seemed to be trying to get every freckle. Susannah began to laugh, her body shaking under his, until he laughed, too. Softly, rhythmically, his lips touched her face. The repetition was mesmerizing. They stopped laughing, and Susannah felt her eyelids droop shut. "I think you got that one already," she whispered.

Slowly his fingers moved down the line of buttons on her blouse. One by one they were undone, until her blouse fell open. She shrugged it off, saw her own skin in the firelight and closed her eyes.

"My lovely Sue." He traced a lace-covered strap and

she shivered. The backs of his fingers brushed her shoulders as he slipped the straps down. Cooling night air touched her, and for a second, she wanted to go home.

"So beautiful," he whispered. He leaned close, pulled her hair to the side and touched his lips to the warm, soft places above her collarbone, behind her earlobe, along the back of her neck. She heard herself make a small sound of pleasure, and an aching warmth began to move through her.

"Alex…"

His fingers moved along her chin, her throat, then over the curve of her breast. Her nipples tingled. The feeling surged when he brushed his thumbs over their tips. Reticence gone, she tugged at his T-shirt. He raised his arms to help her pull it off, then discarded his jeans and boxers. She ran her hands over his chest, investigated the hard curve of his shoulder, stretched her arms to feel the long muscles of his back.

One hand slipped under her waistband. He slid off her khakis and underwear, following their course with his lips. She moaned quietly, lifted by a wave of warmth, and heard an answering sound from him. With hands and lips, he explored her body until she forgot they lay under the open sky, forgot dust and stone, forgot to doubt herself. She shifted impatiently, wrapping her long legs around him, caressing him, drawing him in.

He moved slowly at first, and she was still, almost not breathing, savoring the touch of their bodies. But then she was swept up by an unexpected intensity of feeling, waves of heat, a rippling release. Finally they lay together, reluctant to separate and feeling, at first, less than whole when they did. Limbs heavy, Susannah rested her head against his chest, listening to the thudding of his heart.

When their breathing returned to normal, he asked, "Was that marginally better than ghost stories?"

"By a wide margin," she said softly.

He made a low, pleased sound.

"Right up there with rafting, I'd say. The kind of experience a person wants to repeat every summer."

His chuckle rumbled under her ear.

It was a clear night, and so far from town the sky was bursting with stars. It was odd to lie under the Big Dipper with a man's arms wrapped around her. She had looked at it nearly every night of her life, but she had never made love under it before.

"Which constellation is that?"

She tried to follow Alex's pointing finger. "Give me a hint."

"It sort of looks like a sideways *W*."

"Cassiopeia."

"Cassiopeia," he murmured, drawing out the syllables. "Beautiful name. I wonder if we could get away with calling a daughter Cassiopeia."

Susannah pulled away from Alex's encircling arm, propped herself up on one elbow and peered into his face. "You can't call a child Cassiopeia. It would be bad luck. Cassiopeia was a very beautiful, vain queen who Poseidon punished by trying to feed her daughter Andromeda to a sea monster."

"Trying?"

He was such an optimist. "Perseus—a roving hero, like you—saved the daughter. He's up there, too. You see that bundle of stars south of Cassiopeia? And that smudge? Those are the lovers Perseus and Andromeda. I can't believe you don't know this stuff."

"I don't look up. I look at the ground. Dig in the dirt."

"Well, so do I."

"Yes, but you spend just as much time lying in the bathtub looking up at the sky through an uncovered window that anyone could walk by and see you naked."

"I told you, no one ever goes past that window. You're daydreaming. You wanted to pass by that window and look in."

Alex sniffed the air, then sniffed harder. He jumped up and rushed to the fire, trying to knock the charred foil packages of their dinner away from the hot embers. He swore under his breath. "I forgot all about our food. I'm sorry, Sue."

"I forgive you, under the circumstances. We still have the vegetables and apples." Susannah pulled the sleeping bag around her.

"I don't suppose you brought those sandwiches."

"I did, as a matter of fact. It wasn't that I doubted your cooking."

"You know, we forgot to take advantage of the zippered tent."

Susannah smiled. "We can correct that oversight."

CHAPTER SEVENTEEN

SHE WAS TURNED AWAY from him, curled up on her side with more than her share of the sleeping bag pulled around her, a person used to sleeping alone. He felt shut out, as if she had retreated into herself. He was afraid she would have regrets.

She opened her eyes, and he saw sleepy blankness, then surprise and watchfulness. Finally, a steady warming of remembered pleasure.

"Good morning," she whispered.

"Good morning." He wanted to kiss her, but he hesitated. There was still something closed and private about her. "How are you?"

"Wonderful. I had such a good sleep. No dreams and no waking and no aching joints." She stretched and made a contented sound. "We didn't bring breakfast, did we?"

"I didn't even think about breakfast. We didn't cook the apples last night. We could have those."

"Good. Later." She rubbed her leg along his shin.

"It might be better if we held off for now. They're here."

"Who's here?"

"The team."

She bolted upright, the sleeping bag clutched to her chest. "They're here?" she repeated in a panicked whisper that could probably be heard all the way to the road.

"How long have they been outside? What are they doing? Do they know we're in here?"

Alex leaned his head on one hand. "I think they're working, just like a normal morning."

"Okay," she said quickly. "Here's what we'll do. You go out first, holding a clipboard or something, just casual, as if you've been working for ages already. I'll wait awhile, fifteen minutes, half an hour, and then I'll go out with an ice pack on my shoulder as if I've been in here resting. That should work, shouldn't it?"

"They'll never guess."

"I wonder if I could slip out of the tent without them seeing me, and go out into the badlands a bit, then come back, as if I've been hiking—"

He shook his head. "They'd see you."

"They would, you're right. So, we'll do it the first way. And we'll just be cold to each other, businesslike."

"Okay." Alex stood, naked, and looked around for something to carry. The clipboard wasn't in the tent, but he saw a geological map on the table. He picked it up and got ready to go outside.

"Alex!"

He turned, questioning.

"What are you doing?"

"Exactly what you said."

She looked at him without expression for a few moments, and he wondered if his joke had misfired. Slowly she got to her feet, letting the sleeping bag drop to the ground. "Does the tent flap lock?"

He looked down at the zipper. "I could make a Keep Out sign."

She came to stand beside him. He was surprised how comfortable she was, after the short time they'd spent together, standing in the filtered daylight with no urge to cover herself. She was so close, breasts almost touching his arm, then retreating each time she exhaled.

"No one would come in," he said without conviction.

They both stared at the zipper. Then, Susannah smiled. "I've got it." She looked on the table, then on and under and behind the cot. She found what she was looking for lodged between the cot and the tent wall. "The shoulder sling. It's got a safety pin."

Alex took the pin and knelt by the tent's opening. He pushed his fingers underneath and outside to steady the fabric, then threaded the pin in and out of the zipper so it couldn't open even if someone pulled it.

"I hope no one saw your fingers," Susannah said. "It's like that cat-in-a-box quantum physics problem."

Alex's mind moved slowly from its urgent concern of the moment to the subject of physics. "You mean, the one where the cat could be dead or alive in the box but neither or both has happened until some evidence reaches the world outside?"

Susannah nodded. "Until someone actually sees us, or hears us, there's a universe where we're in here, and a universe where we aren't, but which one hasn't been decided."

"So we're alone, in a bubble, untouched by the world."

She came closer. He had to strain to hear her whisper. It was almost like lipreading. "But we have to be ver-r-r-y quiet. If the slightest evidence of our existence reaches the outside, we plunk solidly into that reality. Naked in a tent, surrounded by elbow-nudging co-workers." He wasn't sure what she enjoyed more—the secrecy, or the thought that the others might actually know what she was up to. She put her hand on his chest and backed him toward the waiting sleeping bag. "Lie down."

He did so, happily. He stared up at the long legs on

either side of his body and took a deep breath as she sank down.

"Shh," she said.

WORK STOPPED when Constable Sherwood and two officers in plainclothes arrived at the quarry. The team watched from a distance while they measured the trench left by the stolen trackway and made casts of the tire tracks the same way paleontologists made casts of footprints. They took pictures and talked to members of the team. The undercover cop gave no sign he knew them. Amy answered the questions with no apparent fear or guilt. Could they be wrong about her?

"Look at Amy," Susannah said. "She's the picture of innocence."

"We don't really have much evidence against her."

"I hope some proof one way or the other turns up— because even if she hasn't done anything wrong, I won't completely trust her after this. I mean, you can presume innocence in court, but you can't necessarily get suspicion out of your head."

Before leaving, the constable spoke to Susannah. "We'll do what we can, Dr. Robb. We've alerted Customs. Any vehicle big enough to move the trackway or the femur and pelvis will be stopped and searched. There's a chance the fossils will be recovered." His tone suggested it was a small chance.

"If they're going out of the country, that is."

He nodded. "Detachments along the TransCanada will be watching, too."

Alex walked partway out of the gully with the three officers. When he returned, he had some news. "Paul's had an e-mail from his contact. They're trying to trace the person now."

Concerned that someone might overhear their conversation, Susannah began walking along the dry riverbed, following the path Matt had taken the day he found the vertebra. "Will tracing him be difficult?"

"It sounds like it could be. Apparently he knows how to cover his tracks. They'll find him, though. Or her, I suppose."

"What will happen to the poachers once the police identify everyone?"

"It depends where they're operating. Laws and penalties vary around the world—in some jurisdictions, they could get off scot-free."

"You're joking."

"I'm afraid not. Henri said there'll be a fairly steep penalty for the ringleader if he's operating in Canada. A fine of up to twenty-five thousand dollars, or a jail sentence of up to five years. Maybe both. For the hired help, sentences would be milder. A year in jail, and a fine. Whoever attacked Kim could face an attempted murder charge."

"The ringleader could be anywhere, I suppose, if he just keeps in contact over the Internet. The States, Australia, Japan…"

Sympathy softened Alex's voice. "Far, far away from Susannah's friends."

"It would be nice."

One arm around her shoulders, he pulled her close. She pressed against him, glad of the renewed contact.

"What would you like to do when this is over?" he asked. "Work till snowfall, or put fossils out of your mind and take a holiday?"

"Work until snowfall, and then take a holiday, I suppose."

"All right. Where shall we go?"

She took a step back so she could see his face. "Liz and I are planning to visit our grandmother in the fall. Would you like to go with us?"

"I was thinking of Paris, or the Caribbean."

She smiled. "Three Creeks is better. You can drink tea from sunup to sundown. You can talk about wheat prices and sports scores for as long as you want, and no one will frown or change the subject. A dog will follow you adoringly wherever you go, and if it's winter, there'll be nonstop road hockey."

Alex looked interested. "Could I drive a tractor?"

"Sure."

"Then it's a date." They began strolling back to the quarry. "I don't think I told you what Henri said about Dorothy. I explained to him how people around here used to think about fossils."

"Did he understand?"

"I think so. What happens next depends on her. If she's connected with the poachers, she's sunk. Otherwise, Henri says we're saddled with her education."

Susannah brightened a little. "Really? Imagine that. After all these years listening to lectures on nutrition, it'll finally be my turn to lay down the law."

By the end of the day more prints had emerged, including a few made by a juvenile and the carnivore. When the surrounding hills began to throw shadows over the trackway, James approached Alex and Susannah. "You both look beat. Why don't you go home? I'll stay till the security guards arrive."

"That would be great." In as casual a voice as she could manage, Susannah asked Alex if he was ready to go, too. "I can drop you at the museum on my way." She glanced around and saw that everyone was smiling.

James held up one hand at shoulder level and waved his fingers. "See you tomorrow. Noon will do."

Blushing, she muttered to Alex, "Evidently, the cat-in-a-box theory is a crock."

SHE SLIPPED THE KEY into the lock and opened the door wide. It felt like an important moment, the first time she'd welcomed Alex into her house. He paused at the threshold and kissed her.

"What color are your eyes, Alex?"

"They're blue."

"Blue? The sky is blue. Irises are blue. Ink is blue. Your eyes are something else." She'd get it one day. It was beginning to look as if she'd have lots of time to figure it out.

"I might get into trouble if I tell you what your eyes make me think of," Alex said.

It was an odd remark. Susannah tried to smile. "You've taken too big a step into the abyss to avoid it now. You'll have to tell me. What horrible thing do my eyes make you think of?"

Before he could answer, she rushed on, gathering speed as she went, "And may I point out, while there's still time, that you're not yet in my house and that choosing this moment to alienate me suggests real ambivalence about being welcomed inside." She waited, clearly anxious.

Alex looked at her appealingly. "Could we just forget about this, and go in?"

"No."

He took the plunge. "Your eyes make me think of a gray flannel blanket."

Susannah thought it over. "Cozy, you mean?"

He nodded. "Warm and soft and welcoming."

"You're not talking about the itchy kind of wool that gives some people rashes?"

"No," he said quickly. "Absolutely not. The soft, comfortable kind."

"Comfortable." She frowned a little.

Alex took a deep breath. "Am I in trouble here?"

"I'm not sure." There was a pricking in her eyes. She blinked quickly, and it passed. "Do you want to be in trouble? You don't have to engineer an escape hatch, you know, because you're not committed to anything, if that's what's worrying you."

"It doesn't worry me at all."

"Are we going too fast?" she asked. "We meant to go slowly, and then we didn't. We can back up. We can forget about it altogether, if you'd prefer."

"Does it help if I tell you I love gray flannel blankets?"

"People love their old gray sweatshirts and their worn-out slippers and their smelly spaniels, too." She blinked again, with less success this time. "It's just not very exciting."

"Think about the past twenty-four hours. I'm not ambivalent."

Maybe not, but he'd made it clear he was holding something back. That shouldn't surprise her. He would probably always wonder what waited for him just out of sight.

"Do you want to come in?" She was prepared for him to say no, but he smiled with relief and stepped inside.

Susannah led the way through the kitchen. In the bathroom, she turned on the taps and squirted bubble bath into the jet of cool water filling the tub. She tugged at Alex's shirt. "These clothes have got to go."

"Since it's you who's asking," he said agreeably.

As she ran her hand over the shirt, she felt a small, uneven shape in one pocket. "What's this?"

He brought out the smooth, concave piece of ironstone he'd picked up the first time they'd walked into the quarry together.

"You keep this with you?"

"All the time."

"Have you been that worried?"

"You've worried me to distraction."

She traced her finger from the notch between his collarbones into the sandy curling hair on his chest. "I always wanted to see further than your shirt would let me." Slowly she undid his buttons, letting her finger trail a few inches lower each time. She reached the waistband of his jeans and stroked her finger back and forth across tight muscles before flicking open the button. Obligingly, he let the jeans drop to the ground and kicked them away.

"Come with me," she whispered. "Come into the tub. It's time for another astronomy lesson."

THE NEXT MORNING, Susannah turned her gaze from the scenery outside her screened porch to the profile of the man sitting next to her. Alex looked as contentedly languorous as she felt, not at all like an adventurer hungry for his next challenge.

"I could get used to this. Tea on the porch, a game of fetch with the fish…"

"You're still thinking of staying?"

"Stay part of the year, travel the rest, maybe."

Susannah looked back at the river. Once he traveled, would he come back? Maybe a part-time relationship would be the best thing for both of them. They weren't used to sharing their lives so intimately.

"Would you go with me sometimes, Sue? I have another chance to work in the Gobi Desert in a few months. Your quarry would be closed for the winter. James could oversee the lab work for a while.''

She tried to hide her relief. ''Work with all those unwashed men? I'd love it. At least, I'd love to work with one particular unwashed man.''

Alex's attention shifted away from her. He put down his mug and went to fiddle with the loose board where Susannah hid her key.

''What are you doing?'' she asked lazily, still lounging.

''The board won't go in all the way. There's cloth or something sticking out. What did you put in there?''

''Just the key.''

Alex eased the board away from the wall. Silently he removed something from the cavity. He unwrapped a piece of cloth and held up a rock for her to see. No, not a rock. A flat piece of shale. Even from her chair, she knew what it was. One of Diane's missing specimens.

''The Opabinia,'' he said softly. ''Are you sure no one else knows about the hiding place?''

''Only you and me.''

They stared at each other, disbelieving suspicion carving an chasm between them.

''I would have stopped you from looking.''

''Of course you would have. I didn't really think—''

''Yes, you did. You'd better go.'' The harsh words hurt her throat.

''Sue. Obviously, someone is trying to make you look guilty.''

''You believed I'd rob my friend.''

''I know you're not a thief. You wouldn't steal your own trackway—''

''You believe in my innocence because it wouldn't make sense for me to steal? Don't you believe in *me?*''

Somehow she found the self-control he had so recently persuaded her to let go. "I want you to leave. Now."

She meant it. There wasn't anything he could do to change her mind. Still, she nearly called him back when he went.

"YOU OVERREACTED, SUE."

Susannah shook her head, trying not to cry. She had told Diane everything—about the relationship that had unfolded since the weekend in Calgary, and about the police investigation that, aided by Alex, had targeted everyone who worked at the museum.

"Doesn't he get to make mistakes?" Diane asked. "You insisted from the beginning that he wasn't perfect. And he isn't. For a second, he wondered if you were the poacher."

"Which second was it, that's the question." Susannah's voice was tight. "This brief moment of believing I was capable of that kind of deception came after he spent the night in my house! You know how hard it was for me to trust him."

"And you can't forgive him?"

"No! This proves it was all a sham, the whole relationship. He should have realized right away that someone was trying to frame me. *Frame me.* I hate this whole business. We're all talking like TV crooks. How did any of this become part of my life?"

"Someone has made it part of all our lives, and it wasn't Alex."

The telephone rang, interrupting their conversation. Susannah picked up the receiver. A small eager voice greeted her.

"Dr. Robb? Hi. It's Matt."

Susannah tried to speak lightly. "What a surprise, Matt! Missing us already?"

"No. I mean, sure. Actually, I'm glad to be home. I just called to tell you about something."

"What's up?"

"I keep thinking about something that happened in the lab, Dr. Robb. I think it's important. Anyway, my mom said to let you know about it, since it's your quarry I worked at, and you can decide if it matters."

Mildly she asked, "What happened?"

"That day in the lab, I had a good look around. I wanted to see all the fossils."

"Dr. Blake told me."

"Yeah, he was pretty mad. Anyway, I was just looking at all these long shelves with big bones and big slabs of rock with fossils inside. And I know I wasn't supposed to touch anything, but I couldn't help it. I didn't think about it then, but after I got home, I started thinking about it—"

This was going nowhere. "Just tell me what you're worried about, Matt."

"They were light, Dr. Robb."

"I'm sorry, Matt. I don't get your point."

"Fossils are heavy. These bones were light."

Susannah blinked quickly as her attention finally sharpened. "You picked up fossils—labeled specimens, not replicas—and they were light?"

"Yeah. But Dr. Blake was so mad at me, I just forgot all about it for a while."

"You're sure they were stored with the real fossils? You weren't looking at replicas the technicians were making?"

"I'm sure. It's important, right?" The excitement in the boy's voice went up a notch. "Is there something crooked going on? Like in those stories Dr. Blake told us about the Gobi Desert?''

"What did he tell you?''

"You know. About the time he was in the Gobi Desert and poachers attacked them and stole their fossils and two of the guys were knocked out and Dr. Blake tracked them across the desert and caught them and found the fossils and they went to jail. But they were only the thieves, not the guys who arrange things. Those guys are still out there and now they're at your museum, right? And Dr. Blake will catch them.''

If she ever spoke to Indiana Blake again, she would have to tell him he'd retained his hero status with Matt after all. "I don't know. Maybe they're here, and maybe he'll catch them. Or maybe somebody just put the replicas you saw in the wrong place. In any case, thanks. I'll let you know what happens.''

She replaced the receiver. Was it possible that no one else had noticed replicas labeled as authentic specimens? Charlie, Carol, Marie, Alex last Friday when he had chased Matt around the lab—had none of them been aware of something a curious child had found out in one afternoon?

Briefly she explained Matt's call to Diane.

"If the poachers have been replacing fossils with fakes, they've taken far more than we realized,'' Diane said. "I wonder how long they thought they could get away with it?''

"Long enough to finish the job and get away, I suppose.''

"Do you want me to put off my trip to Mount Field till next week?'' Diane was supposed to leave later that afternoon.

"Thanks, Di, but I'll be fine. I can't keep crying on

your shoulder about Alex, and the police will handle the thieves. I'll pass Matt's information along to them, and then get back to work before James thinks I've lost interest in the trackway."

It would be impossible to work at the quarry without thinking about Alex. About shadows from moonlit hoodoos, about firelight on his skin. Three weeks ago, he'd hardly been a memory. How long would it take to feel that distance again?

ALEX LEANED BACK in his chair, feet on his desk, and wondered who had tried to frame Susannah. That was the question right now. There was no point wasting time regretting his momentary suspicion. If there was anything real between them, she would forgive him in time.

It had to be someone close to her. When it came right down to it, almost anyone at the museum could have taken the Opabinia, but few people would know where Susannah hid her key. Diane and James were the most likely to have noticed. If one of them had betrayed her, he could hardly imagine the hurt and self-doubt she would feel.

There was another question. *Why* had someone tried to frame Susannah? Even if his suspicions had lasted longer than a minute, an investigation would have proved she hadn't stolen the fossil. At best, it was a brief distraction...

Something was about to happen, then. Whoever had planted the fossil wanted time...time to move more fossils? To disappear? The cost to Susannah—a little heartbreak, a tarnished reputation—was a small price for the poacher to pay. A wave of anger flashed through him. He reached for the telephone, but before he could call Henri, it rang. He lifted the receiver and a voice said urgently, "Alex, Susannah's in trouble. She needs help, quickly."

CHAPTER EIGHTEEN

TWO POLICE CRUISERS passed Susannah, going the other way, when she drove to the museum the next morning. Three more were parked near the staff entrance. A security guard stood just inside the door.

"Morning, Dr. Robb."

"What's going on?"

"I'm not supposed to say. I'm just supposed to watch who goes in and out. Kind of late for that, if you ask me. They've closed the museum, too, just for the day, though."

"And you can't tell me what's happened?"

"Sorry."

They must have caught the poachers. Why else would there be police cars all over the place? Up to now, Beaubier's team had made a point of staying out of sight.

She looked into the prep lab. A police officer stood at the open door to the storage room, checking the security camera. Along with Marie and a guard, another officer examined fossils on the shelves in the main room. Constable Sherwood loomed over Charlie, his notebook and pen in hand. Almost as pale as her lab coat, Carol leaned against a worktable. When she saw Susannah, she slipped into the hall.

"Everything's crazy this morning. We're all being

questioned. Alex is gone, and a bunch of fossils are gone, too.''

Susannah felt her face go stiff. ''What are you talking about?''

''He certainly had us all fooled. Except you and Charlie. I know neither of you trusted him from the beginning.''

Susannah didn't wait to hear any more. She hurried upstairs. Police officers, some in uniform and some in plainclothes, were clustered near Alex's office. ''Is he all right?''

One of the officers stepped away from the group. ''Dr. Robb, I think?''

''Yes. Has something happened to Alex?''

''I'm Sergeant Beaubier. Could you come into Dr. Blake's office, please?'' Inside the room, empty of Alex's sand table, his dinosaur models, his books and papers, the sergeant said, ''This computer was left on, and a file open. The file is a note to you. I want to ask you to read it, and tell me what you think.''

''Of course.'' Susannah touched the mouse. The screen saver disappeared, and a few short lines were displayed.

Sorry, Sue. I hope all this doesn't hurt you too much. We had fun, right? You made the job more interesting than usual. You'll forgive me about the trackway, won't you? Alex.

Susannah's eyes closed. The words bored into her, deep and sharp.

''Dr. Robb?''

She opened her eyes. ''It's not difficult to type a message on someone else's keyboard. You don't need a password to use our word-processing program.''

"You don't believe Dr. Blake left that message for you?''

"Absolutely not.'' It would explain some things: his anger when Matt touched fossils in the lab, the trip to Calgary at the same time someone stole the trackway, the stolen fossil planted for him to find. Trying to keep her voice from shaking, she added, "That isn't the way Alex expresses himself. He makes statements—he doesn't ask questions.''

"Thank you for your help. That's all for now.''

Susannah didn't budge. How could that be all? They hadn't told her what had happened to Alex. "May I speak to you privately, Sergeant Beaubier?''

At first, she thought he would refuse. Then he said, "In your office?''

She led the way, standing aside to let him go in, then closing the door behind them. Beaubier was tall and imposing in his uniform. Susannah went to stand behind her desk.

"Alex told me he's been working with you to catch fossil poachers. I understand there may be things you can't tell me. Has he disappeared intentionally, to trick them somehow?''

"That's a colorful idea.''

Susannah didn't know what to make of his response. "If it's part of a complicated plan, I don't want to stumble around upsetting it. If it's not part of a plan, then I'm worried. You must be, too. What if the poachers attacked him the way they attacked Kim Johnson a couple of weeks ago?''

"Why would they attack him if he's one of them?''

She was quiet for a minute, fighting growing fear. If Sergeant Beaubier didn't believe in him, who would help him? "Did you know we found one of the missing specimens at my house?"

Beaubier's eyes changed, like binoculars refocusing.

"Someone left an Opabinia there, to make me look guilty. Didn't Alex tell you?"

"He doesn't tell me much that involves you."

"What if the same people are trying to frame him?"

"And they went to the trouble of emptying his office and his apartment? That's more than you need to do to throw suspicion on a person. Why would they bother?"

"Apparently, to get every cop in southern Alberta paying attention to him." She had spoken too sharply. More calmly, she said, "You can't believe he's a thief."

"He's gone, and a significant number of fossils are gone from the lab." The detective shrugged. "People can be unpredictable."

"If Alex could hear you now, he'd certainly agree."

That wounded him, just a little. "Dr. Robb, my first reaction was exactly like yours. Certain evidence has swayed me, but I can tell you that I'm keeping an open mind." He thanked her for her comments, and then he was gone.

Susannah sank into her chair. Of all the questions tumbling in her mind, only one mattered. Where was Alex?

As soon as the last police cruiser drew out of the parking lot, Susannah headed down to the prep lab. Matt's information about replicas suggested it was the most likely place to look for clues. She could justify taking a good look around by claiming to be reviewing the inventory of her specimens. Even the most suspicious person wouldn't think twice about seeing her there.

Although she'd spent some time in the lab nearly every day for years, she went in with a dry mouth and thudding heart. The room was a mess. It seemed deserted. Maybe everyone had gone for coffee, too upset to work. With a clipboard and pencil for props, she began to browse through the tagged and shelved specimens, lifting bones to test their weight.

"Sue?"

She jumped guiltily. "Charlie, hi. I'm just checking my stuff." The remark sounded defensive. "If there's anything left, that is."

"Between Blake's efforts and the so-called investigations of the police, I have no idea what condition your specimens are in." His voice was a bit sharp. Maybe that was understandable. "We have bones, fake bones, messed-up bones and missing bones. But if you hope to find any of your bones, you should look at the next row of shelves. Labeled Hadrosaur Quarry."

"Of course." She decided to stay as close to the truth as possible. "I can't seem to do anything right today. I'm too distracted about Alex to think straight."

"His guilt was staring us in the face from day one, when he left the fossils disorganized. It must have been a cover for his thefts, even then."

Susannah nodded. "I guess you haven't heard the whole miserable story. I sort of fell for him—"

"Don't feel too bad about that. It's not the first time a man like that has deceived a woman. After a while you won't mind anymore. Remember, you didn't even want him here at first."

Said in another tone, the words might have seemed supportive. As it was, their coldness startled Susannah. She had resisted the idea that her longtime friend could be responsible for the specimen losses even by accident. But it was time, past time, to face facts: Charlie had too much contact with the specimens to be unaware they were being substituted with fakes. Either he was involved with the poachers, or he was completely incompetent.

She knew he wasn't incompetent.

"You look so sad, Susannah. Look at it this way. You're a shoo-in for the job he's just vacated."

After all these years, she didn't know Charlie at all. "I guess that's the best way to look at it. I'll get back to work, keep myself busy. See you later."

She tried not to hurry out of the lab, although her instinct was to run. Why hadn't she ever sensed danger from Charlie before?

She walked quickly past the galleries, checking once to be sure he hadn't followed. Halfway to the security office, she stopped. If you wanted to get fossils out of a museum, who better to have on your side than the guards? The lobby then. There was a row of phones near the door. One call to Beaubier, and it would be out of her hands.

The RCMP receptionist answered promptly. "I'm sorry, ma'am, but Sergeant Beaubier is out indefinitely."

"Can I talk to someone else?"

"I'm afraid all the officers are out on assignment."

"Then I need to get a message to the sergeant."

"I can take a message and relay it if he calls."

"This is important," Susannah stressed. "He'll want to know as soon as possible. Will you tell him Charlie Morgan, the head conservator at the museum, is one of the poachers and that I think he's done something to Alexander Blake?" She might be jumping to a conclusion or two, but this was no time for carefully weighed statements.

"Charlie Morgan," the receptionist repeated calmly. "I'll let the sergeant know what you've said."

Susannah hung up the phone and closed her eyes, trying to think. What did she know? Not much, not nearly enough.

Matt's news about replicas suggested the poachers had stepped up their collection of fossils. They'd started by taking a few small specimens; now they were taking complete skeletons and trackways. That meant they didn't care about keeping a low profile anymore. The ringleaders must be getting ready to move on, the way they had in the story Alex had told Matt. They didn't care if low-level people like Paul and Amy were implicated. Did that mean Charlie, calm as could be surrounded by fakes, was one of the ringleaders?

"Are you all right, Dr. Robb?"

Susannah opened her eyes and saw the concerned face of one of the artists who was painting the Discovery Room murals.

"It's an upsetting day for everybody," he said sympathetically. "I never would have thought Dr. Blake was a crook. The funny thing is I saw him with Charlie yesterday, on the East Coulee road. I don't know how he spent the day around East Coulee and managed to clear out all those fossils, too. Must have had help, I guess." He leaned closer, and added quietly, "Kind of makes you wonder about Charlie, doesn't it?"

"Did you tell the police all this?"

The man looked surprised. "The police?"

Already heading to the door, Susannah said, "I think you should. Right away."

Keeping one eye out for Charlie and the security guards, she hurried around the back of the building to the staff parking lot. She pushed aside remnants of respect for his personal property and opened the driver's-side door of Charlie's truck.

It was dustier inside than she would have expected, dusty enough to have been driven miles down a gravel road, or even through the badlands. Odds and ends filled the glove compartment: a flashlight, some antacids and bandages, some granola bars and licorice, a map of Alberta. She reached under the seat. A tool kit. A rope. She pulled, then pulled some more. A really long rope, with dirt embedded in it.

A voice came from behind her. "This is a real disappointment."

Slowly Susannah turned to face Charlie.

He grasped her arm, not gently. "I wish you'd stayed out of this." He pushed her toward the truck. "Get in."

She wouldn't get in. That was the worst thing she could do. No one could help her if she got into the truck and Charlie drove off. She stomped at his foot as hard as she could and heard a sharp intake of breath, but his grip tightened and she couldn't pull away. She filled her lungs, ready to yell loud enough to be heard inside the museum. His hand clamped over her mouth. Twisting her arm, he forced her into the truck.

"Be your usual nice self, Susannah, and get in before someone sees us." He kept pushing until she had no choice but to climb over the stick shift to the passenger seat. He followed her into the truck and pressed the automatic door locks. "You know, you wouldn't make a very good spy, Sue. I could see every stage of realization as it hit you." His voice became softer, slightly feminine.

"I don't think these are real fossils. Oh dear, I think my friend Charlie is a bad guy. I'm scared of my friend Charlie. I better go for help." His voice returned to normal. "Did you? Go for help?"

They stared at each other, calm eyes into furious, frightened ones.

"Of course I did. I called the police."

"And then you came to look at my truck all by yourself. I guess they weren't very useful. Never there when you need them."

"Is Alex all right?"

"For now."

"I don't care about the fossils, Charlie. You can steal fossils till the cows come home. I just want to know where Alex is."

"I need more time."

"How much time?"

"A couple of days."

Days. "Wherever you've got Alex, will he be all right for that long?"

"Probably."

"I'll give you as much time as you need. Just let me go to him."

"And then what? He'll give me all the time I need, too?"

"If I ask him."

Charlie smiled tightly. "I suspect you overestimate your influence."

"Hurting Alex isn't going to get you anywhere," she said desperately. "He's not the only one breathing down your neck. Do you think this charade today will distract the police for long?"

"Long enough." Charlie turned the key in the ignition.

"What are you going to do?" She was annoyed to hear her voice wobble.

"That's a good question. It's been on my mind ever since I saw those lovely long legs beside my truck. I've worked too hard to let you ruin this, Sue."

The expression in his eyes changed abruptly as he focused on something behind her. An RCMP cruiser had pulled into the parking lot. It stopped by the staff entrance and Henri Beaubier got out. Susannah started to raise her hand, but Charlie gripped it and forced her down, out of sight. The fabric of his trousers, full of chemical smells from the lab, was tight against her nostrils.

Finally his hands let go. Susannah sat up and took a few deep breaths of fresh air. "We're all right," Charlie said. "He's gone inside." He backed out of his parking space. "I guess your call to the police wasn't as useless as I thought."

He pulled onto the access road. Once he was out of sight of the museum, Charlie gave the truck more gas, and it roared ahead. Steering one-handed, he took a cell phone from his pocket, pressed a button and waited.

"Hey, it's me. An old friend of mine is causing some trouble. One of the people who's provided so generously for my future. Looks like it's time to cut our losses.... Really? They must have picked somebody up, then. Or turned somebody—Paul's been edgy since those idiots lost their cool out at the Bearpaw. Oh well, we knew it wouldn't last much longer. Meet me with the chopper. Ten minutes? Good."

Susannah had tried to hear the voice on the other end. It couldn't be anyone she knew, or Charlie would have referred to her by name. "Who were you talking to?"

Charlie gave a little laugh. "Sure, I'll tell you all my

secrets. That wouldn't be very smart, would it?'' It was the first suggestion that he might let her go. ''Of course, you paleontologists always think you've got a corner on brains.''

''Could you just tell me if it's somebody I know?''

''It's my e-mail pal.'' He slowed down to meet the speed limit as they passed the town, accelerating again as soon as he saw the turnoff in the rearview mirror.

''Not Bruce?'' That fear had been crouching at the back of her mind for a while.

''That's enough, Susannah. We're not going to play Famous People.''

''Did he hook you with some kind of e-mail offer?''

''So they did turn somebody,'' Charlie observed.

''Nope. I hooked him.''

Did that mean he'd recruited the other poachers, too? Charlie, who had always refused to adjust to new technology, was the Bone Man?

''Did you put the Opabinia in my house?''

''That was kind of underhanded, wasn't it? I didn't feel good about it. Blake was always snooping around, though. I heard the scuttlebutt, so I sneaked in the other night and hid the fossil, with a nice little tail of cloth hanging out, hoping that one of you would notice it while Alex was there. It was a long shot, but it worked. You'd be well-advised to lock that porch door, Sue.''

He turned south off the main road, skidding on loose gravel. A siren sounded not far behind them. Charlie checked the rearview mirror. ''Close, but not close enough, Sergeant.'' Dust filled the air when he turned too fast into a dry field. Far from the road, a helicopter waited, blades rotating.

Charlie raised his voice to be heard above the sound.

"I think this is going to work out for both of us." He smiled at Susannah, almost friendly. "I've never been able to say no to you. Did you know that? You've always been my favorite."

Keeping one eye on the cruiser's approach, he continued, "Your sweetheart's in a sinkhole. Thanks for the neat idea. Three kilometers down the East Coulee road, turn in, a kilometer east, another kilometer south."

He braked suddenly and Susannah slid forward, nearly hitting the dash. The door was open and he was out of the truck. "Take care of yourself, Sue." He ran a few steps, then turned and called out something she could barely hear. Something about Bruce. And he shook his head.

Not Bruce. The moment of kindness made Susannah's heart ache.

Bending low, Charlie ran to the helicopter and disappeared inside. It lifted off the ground moments before Henri Beaubier arrived.

"Are you all right?"

She nodded. "Charlie trapped Alex in a sinkhole—"

The sergeant looked from Susannah to the rising helicopter. "I can't stop now." He spoke into his car radio and headed back to the road.

SHE DROVE QUICKLY, following Charlie's directions. Aware that she might be destroying fossils just under the surface, she drove off the road and onto the ancient plain.

A kilometer east and a kilometer south. That was a long way from the road. No one would have chanced by to find Alex.

She slowed as she neared a large sinkhole. About a meter away, she parked and got out for a closer look. The hole was deep. Much deeper than the one Matt had found. She couldn't see the bottom when she shone Charlie's flashlight down, and when she called, she couldn't hear any answering shout. Maybe it wasn't the right place. Maybe Alex couldn't answer.

If he was down there, he'd be hungry. She stuffed the granola bars and licorice in her pockets. Charlie's gloves were on the seat. She pulled them on. To keep the truck from rolling backward into the hole, she engaged the parking brake and wedged two rocks behind the rear tires.

She tied one end of the long rope to the hitch at the back of the vehicle and made a simple lever by looping the rope through the axle. After clipping the flashlight to her belt, she sat on the edge of the sinkhole, her foot hooked through the loop. She wriggled closer, until she thought the ground might give way, then gradually let the loose end of the rope go, easing herself down into the darkness.

The makeshift lever took the strain off her shoulder, still tender after her last sinkhole descent, and this time she had gloves. Even so, her shoulder soon began to hurt. When she had gone as far as the rope would allow and had no idea how much farther it was to the bottom, a voice, strong and unafraid, cut through the darkness.

"Hello? Who's that?"

"Alex?"

"Susannah?" The incredulity in his voice made her laugh.

His hands were on her legs. They felt their way up to her waist. "I've got you." He lifted her to the ground and held her tightly. "Indiana Sue. My hero."

"I'm glad you realize that," she said breathlessly. It had been a tough climb. "You're not hurt?" She could see him in the flashlight's glow. He seemed all right. Cold, though.

"I'm fine. Just be careful where you move. This is more of a ledge than a floor. Did Charlie have second thoughts?"

Unsure how big the ledge was, or where it ended, Susannah pressed close to Alex. "Not exactly. He told me where to find you just before he got on the helicopter. Sergeant Beaubier was close behind, although how close you can be when you're on the ground and the other person is in the air, I don't know."

"I can see I've missed a lot. We'd better get out of here before you fill me in, though. The ledge is narrow. It shouldn't be too long a drop, but you never know. Can you climb back out?"

"There's no way I can do it."

"Maybe if I went first, I could pull you up."

She shook her head. "I'm sorry. My shoulder's not working very well after coming down. I don't think I could hang on long enough." Trying not to sound scared, she added, "No one knows where we are, though, not unless the police catch Charlie and he tells them."

Alex stroked her hair. "They'll catch him. Even if they don't, we'll be okay. I've been exploring. There's a network of tunnels leading away from here. One is bound to come out at the surface. I think we can get past the rattlers safely—"

"Rattlers?"

"Mmm-hmm. And I could hear running water lower down, so theoretically we could follow the underground stream to its exit point."

"Theoretically." Susannah could feel his eagerness. He wanted to try it.

"It'll work. We've got two flashlights now. You don't need brighter light than that. It'll be like the Paleolithic cave. You'll love it."

Susannah laughed. Rattlers and darkness—of course she'd love it. "I'll give it a try."

"Good. Let's get going, then." His voice was calm, but he communicated an urgency that frightened her. "Keep the wall at your left side. The ledge ends to your right."

The ground was slippery, so they went slowly. Susannah tried not to think about the distance down. She kept one hand on the cold, damp stone of the wall. "It's like a really deep, really awful basement." She laughed shakily. That was what you called positive thinking.

"We're going to turn left now."

"Away from the ledge," she said, with satisfaction.

"That's right. We'll be going into a tunnel."

When they left the ledge, they moved into deeper darkness. Alex shone his light at the ground. "See here, Sue? It's uneven, so watch your step."

Her feet slipped on the soggy ground. He put out a hand, and she held it gratefully. "I think I hear water. Are we getting close to the stream we can follow?"

"Not yet. There's a drop to the next level just ahead. I'll go first, and catch you."

"A drop?"

"Only about seven feet. I'll catch you," he repeated.

Her flashlight showed him disappearing down a hole. Then his hands reached up, and Susannah let herself down into his waiting arms. The air felt heavier to breathe.

"It's still a tunnel," Alex said, "but a smaller one. You'll need to bend over a bit as we go."

A bit? Soon they were on all fours, sinking into wet clay.

"Are we going down?"

His voice worked its way back to her. "There's a gradual slope." Gradual soon became steep, and they sat and slid down. Alex braked by putting one hand against the ceiling. "The next part is tricky."

Susannah had begun to shiver with cold. "The snakes?"

"They're not right at our entry point, and they won't like our lights. The thing to remember about rattlesnakes is that they'd really prefer to ignore you, as long as you leave them alone. Do you hear how much louder the water is?"

She nodded. "Not too much farther, I'll bet."

"I stopped at the snakes before, so I don't know. But I think you're right." He shone the flashlight on all four sides of the chute they'd be sliding down. "All right, no legless occupants. Start down as soon as I'm in."

Susannah got ready, and when there was room for her legs, she held her arms to her sides and let herself go. She came out of the chute fast, taking small stones and dirt with her, and slid into Alex. The snakes were about eight feet away, damp bodies glistening in the flashlight's beam.

"I'll keep my light on them. You check that there aren't any stragglers where we're going."

She examined the floor, walls and ceiling. "I don't see any. I don't see an exit, either."

He pointed at a spot on the cave wall. "There."

She stared, then finally saw. "That? It's a gopher hole."

Alex grinned. "Just about." Still keeping a light on the

rattlers, he started sidestepping toward the small opening. "Now, check in the gopher hole for snakes."

"I can only see in a few feet. It's fine that far."

"Here goes nothing," Alex said. He propelled himself headfirst into the hole.

Susannah followed, only because it was better than staying where she was. Inside it was barely wide enough for her shoulders. She could see Alex's feet ahead of her, inching forward.

"Okay, Sue?"

"I'm reconsidering climbing back up the rope." She thought she heard him laugh.

She couldn't tell how long they stayed in the tunnel, heads down to keep dirt they knocked off the ceiling from falling in their eyes, shoulders folded in so they wouldn't get stuck against the sides. She could see only the soles of Alex's shoes, and the unchanging ground moving inch by inch under her. Finally she noticed the sound of water again, louder by the minute, and the air felt fresher. Alex's feet disappeared, and faint light reached her.

She wriggled and pushed with her feet, and her head emerged from the tunnel. She took a huge breath, filling her lungs with good air. Alex put his hands under her arms and helped her the rest of the way out.

"How's the shoulder?"

"Happy to be out of that wormhole."

They were in a chamber just a little higher than Alex's head. It opened to a dimly lit tunnel, high enough for them to nearly walk upright. They waded through shallow, cool water, out to the badlands and the bright, bright sun.

"That was so easy!" Susannah nearly shouted, buoyed by relief. "We weren't even very long getting through. Charlie's truck can't be far away."

Alex sat on a rock and lifted his face to the sun, eyes closed. Susannah leaned against him, her face pressed against his neck. His skin was so cold. She moved closer, helping the sun warm him. "Do you want me to bring you up-to-date about Charlie?"

"I want you to kiss me."

"You don't want to hear that Charlie's the Bone Man?"

Alex opened his eyes. "Charlie?"

"I think so. He admitted using the Internet to recruit his partner. This all might be over soon, Alex. All the Mounties were out of the office today. Maybe they were picking up the poachers they've identified." She decided not to tell him that Beaubier had been ready to believe the worst of him. "You're really all right?"

"Completely. A bit hungry."

"I've got some food, sort of, from Charlie's glove compartment." Susannah pulled the granola bars and licorice out of her pockets.

"Great." Alex wiped the worst of the mud from his hands, then ripped a wrapper off a granola bar. Between bites he explained how he had ended up in the cold and dark of an East Coulee sinkhole. "Charlie called me yesterday afternoon. He told me a tourist had reported seeing hadrosaur eggs eroding from the side of a hill in the East Coulee area and that you'd rushed off to check it out."

"I'd be out here in a flash if I heard a rumor like that."

"That's what I thought, too. He said, knowing how dangerous the area could be, he'd gone with you, but you'd fallen into a sinkhole anyway. You were unconscious and your leg looked broken—"

"You believed I'd fall down a sinkhole again so soon?"

"It seemed unlikely, but strange things happen." Alex sounded embarrassed. "Charlie claimed he'd called James to come after us when he could, so off we went, with me believing help was close behind. He watched the rope while I climbed down, and while I was looking for you, he pulled it back up…leaving me to think about you and your arms around me, and to wonder if I could do anything to prevent myself from becoming a mysterious pile of bones."

"Alex," she murmured. She reached up to touch his cheek. "I'm so sorry…that I took offense and told you to go away."

"I'm sorry, too. You know I never really thought you were a poacher."

"Sure you did."

"Maybe for a second." He smiled. "Maybe for the first week. No more than that. I was certain it wasn't you almost from the beginning."

"That's all right. I wondered about you for a moment or two, as well."

"I think Charlie was counting on it being a lot longer than a moment. He needed everyone's attention on me, so he could get away with as many fossils as he and his friends could carry."

Alex lifted one of Susannah's hands and kissed its palm. "I don't know what I was doing the other night outside your house when I said that about your eyes…"

"You were afraid of being tied down, getting bored."

"Something like that. I didn't want to have to pretend to be more respectable than I am. I didn't ever want to say I couldn't go on a dig because the roof needed reshingling."

"I never want you to say that, either."

Alex shook his head. "I'm not being clear enough." He spoke slowly, figuring it out as he went along. "I've always worked for something that I never seemed able to achieve. I had a sense that this goal, whatever it was, was there, but I couldn't reach it. The other night at the quarry, watching you with the moonlight on your face, I realized that nothing else is enough without you...and it seemed like I'd been reaching for you all along."

Susannah whispered, "I love you, too."

"Do you think we should get married before or after the Gobi Desert quarry?"

"Before."

"Today or tomorrow?"

She smiled. "Many days after tomorrow. I want fingernails for my wedding."

"You know what I want? I want to find Charlie's truck. Then we'll drive to your house, and after we feed the fish, we'll climb up to the loft. We'll fall asleep together tonight and wake up together tomorrow."

"Sounds good."

They started walking in the direction the truck should be, keeping an eye out for sinkholes and the glint of emerging bones.

She would have to tell Liz about this, Susannah thought, about the two scientists who got the fairy-tale ending, the one with the long and wonderful days together, now and always.

PETITE AND PRETTY, the woman stood near the cluster of hoodoos, pleased that her close-fitting coffee-colored business suit complemented the shades in the rock so well. "Start with a wide shot," she told the cameraman, "then zoom in on my face."

When she heard the go-ahead in her earpiece, she spoke into her microphone. "This is Sylvia Hall, live from Hoo-doo Rock. In a major move today the RCMP closed in on a fossil poaching ring operating right here in the middle of the Alberta badlands. With help from local paleontologists, police charged eight men and a woman with offenses under the Cultural Property Act, and an undisclosed number of fossils were recovered from an antique shop in Calgary. Sources say more serious charges relating to an assault earlier this month are pending. The alleged ringleader of the group, museum employee Charles Morgan, was apprehended when a police helicopter forced the one he was traveling in to land near the Canada-U.S. border. Local storekeeper Dorothy MacDonald told reporters she's not surprised to hear of Morgan's arrest—a change in his spending habits over the past year had aroused her suspicions. According to Ms. MacDonald, Morgan had started buying an unusual number of magazines, 'four or five of the seven dollar ones at once,' she said, and tins of red salmon instead of pink. Alexander Blake, head of dinosaur research at the museum, could not be reached for comment."

Coming in May 2002

**Three Bravo men marry for convenience—
but will they love in leisure? Find out in
Christine Rimmer's *Bravo Family Ties!***

Cash—for stealing a young woman's innocence, and to
give their baby a name, in *The Nine-Month Marriage*

Nate—for the sake of a codicil in his beloved
grandfather's will, in *Marriage by Necessity*

Zach—for the unlucky-in-love rancher's chance to
have a marriage—even of convenience—
with the woman he *really* loves!

BRAVO
FAMILY TIES

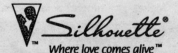

Where love comes alive™

EMERGENCY!

The Family Doctor
by Bobby Hutchinson

**The next Superromance novel in this dramatic
series—set in and around St. Joseph's Hospital
in Vancouver, British Colombia.**

Chief of staff Antony O'Connor has family problems.
His mother is furious at his father for leaving her many
years ago, and now he's coming to visit—with the
woman he loves. Tony's family is taking sides. Patient
care advocate Kate Lewis is an expert at defusing
anger, so she might be able to help him out With this
problem, at least. Sorting out her feelings for Tony—
and his feelings for her—is about to get trickier!

*Heartwarming stories with a sense of humor,
genuine charm and emotion and lots of family!*

On sale starting April 2002

Available wherever Harlequin books are sold.

HARLEQUIN®
Makes any time special®